About the a

I am a mother, dog-lover, teacher, writer and traveller. I spent my twenties enjoying long summer holidays, backpacking round Asia and Africa, and was inspired by countless adventures and near-death experiences. I would stumble my way through term times in London, longing for my next adventure, until I met and married the woman I love and had two beautiful twins and three disobedient, semi-feral dogs, and am always hoping to get one more rescue to add to our home.

AN UNUSUAL YEAR

MIA KAZI

AN UNUSUAL YEAR

Vanguard Press

A CIP catalogue record for this title is
available from the British Library.

ISBN 978 1 80016 361 4

Vanguard Press is an imprint of
Pegasus Elliot MacKenzie Publishers Ltd.
www.pegasuspublishers.com

First Published in 2022

Vanguard Press
Sheraton House Castle Park
Cambridge England

Printed & Bound in Great Britain

Dedication

To my family, who put up with my eccentric sleep habits fuelling my desire to get up early and write. And to my friends who supported me, my mother who encouraged me to write and my colleague who forced me to write better.

Part One

THE START OF IT ALL

Something Changed

Normally it is hard to pick out the moment something started, but I can even tell you the approximate time. It was about two p.m. on a damp and overcast Wednesday in February a year before my ill-fated trip to Laos. I had known Izzy for six months before I saw her properly for the first time. It wasn't that I hadn't seen her — it was that I had never really looked.

She was talking to Fay Quimby by the door to the Common Room. I was going to walk past and nod a quick greeting as usual, when something made me stop and take a second look. There were no orchestras playing in the background and the scene did not suddenly become black and white or start moving in slow-motion, but my perceptions all seemed subtly intensified, as if accompanied by a magic mushroom-induced shimmer. How could I not have noticed her cat-like green eyes? I was fascinated by her small, pale and perfectly formed nose and the way her hair framed her face. She was laughing about something with Fay and her whole face seemed to radiate energy and joy. Why was my friend laughing with someone else? Sure, Fay was Izzy's closest friend at Brown's School, where we worked. I never understood why.

Fay was in her forties and there was nothing young or fun about her that I could see. She always wore dark or muted colours, though rarely black itself. Today she was wearing dusty brown suit trousers, a beige blouse with a floral-style pattern and a bagging grey cardigan on top. Fay was one of those teachers who had no interest in change and no interest in promotion. She was Head of Classics, a department that consisted of herself and two other teachers. One of her department, Alistair Cross, looked as though he should have been retired years ago. He was striking in his hawk-like appearance, with implausibly thick, bushy white eyebrows and hair and a personality that was a cross between Mr Chips and Ms Trunchbull. He was always either instantly feared or loved by students and staff alike. The other Classics teacher, Alice James, was fresh out of college and qualifying whilst working at Brown's. She was perhaps the smallest person I had ever known and, although one of the kindest, was struggling hugely with controlling her classes, and Fay was, thankfully, being kept busy helping her manage her classes and her fear of Alistair. Fay was far too prim and prissy for my taste, and although I often ended up having to talk to her when we both sat with Izzy, we would never have sought each other out otherwise. I don't remember her ever saying something funny or laughing at one of my jokes. Izzy caught my eye behind Fay's head and smiled, and a surge of emotions seemed to course through me like electricity.

"Hi, Iz, Fay. How are you?"

Fay knew that my question was intended for Izzy and waited for her to answer.

"Oh, you know, typical Wednesday. Just had bottom set Year 9 and it dragged. None of them seemed awake yet and Sean Benson was so focussed on clock-watching for his next game of football in the rain that I swear he almost set himself on fire twice with his Bunsen burner. I nearly started walking round the room with a fire extinguisher."

Even Fay laughed; everyone except the sports staff who taught Sean was exasperated by his total lack of desire to learn anything in lessons and complete inertia at all times except on a sports pitch. Then he transformed in a way that made most boys admire him and girls start to giggle and blush if he so much as looked at them. Which meant that he could disrupt an academic lesson even when apparently asleep.

"I'd have been tempted to let him. A mild burn might have focussed his mind a little," said Fay in a completely level tone of voice which conveyed no sense that she was joking. It should have been funny and I laughed politely, but the way she said it did have me wondering, not for the first time, whether she was actually a sociopath.

"Anyway, do you fancy taking your mind off the perpetual rain and drudgery by going for a drink after work with me tonight, Iz? Just the Sun. Seven-ish?" I blurted out without even having had the idea internally first.

"Wow. Okay. Nice idea. Why not? Shall I meet you there or pick you up at yours?" she replied.

"I'll pick you up."

"Fine! See you later."

I was not sure exactly what I was asking her, but I was excited that she had agreed to it. Did I fancy her? I had never liked women in that way before. I had only been out with men and I liked being with them, touching them, being touched by them. I don't know what came over me, but I am an impulsive kind of person. I want to live and to experience everything — a 'not going to die wondering' type. When I asked her out for a drink, I was acting purely in the moment. She looked so beautiful in the basically furnished, bland, white common room, standing framed in the little patch of sun that was allowed through the high windows which protected this sacred space from the prying eyes of students. I barely had the thought before I acted upon it. I felt a surge of inexplicable anger that she was laughing with Fay instead of me. It made no sense, but I just had to interrupt. I did not even know why I wanted to have a drink with her.

Suddenly, sixteen years rushed backwards and I felt like I was thirteen years old and blushing whenever anyone whispered Tommy Jones's name or if I managed to catch a glimpse of him in the corridor. I felt more like one of my students than a teacher. And what if something happened tonight? I found myself imagining us kissing, possibly tonight. Well, when I actually thought about it and pictured the idea of leaning in for the kiss, I decided that it would be stomach-churningly vile to actually kiss a girl! It would be a story to tell. I felt excited and slightly drunk and I decided that it was ridiculous to have gone through university and almost all of my twenties without ever having a lesbian experience. I was not sure how I felt about kissing someone with breasts, but I knew I had to find out.

That afternoon, I gave one class a surprise test and decided to randomly give another a revision sheet to work on in silence or in quiet pairs. I needed some peace while I spent the day veering between almost hysterical excitement and panic. It was not too late to back out and just go for a friendly date, and I kept wondering whether I had misread the signs I thought I was getting from Izzy since we first started working together. I was sure that she fancied me, and when she told me she used to play hockey, it only confirmed my suspicions that she might be a lesbian. I was always a little butch, so she was not the first woman to flirt

13

with me; but after feeling nothing but friendship, suddenly I found myself wanting to reciprocate.

And what did this say about me? Was I a lesbian now? Bisexual? Why had I never fancied any other woman? Bi-curious, perhaps? And what does a perhaps-straight, perhaps-gay woman wear to go for a drink/date with a colleague and friend who she perhaps wants to snog but isn't sure and does not want the rest of the staffroom to find out? And why do these bloody children keep asking me questions about my worksheet when I am trying to think?

An Innocent Drink

She looked beautiful that night. Tight, dark blue jeans to accentuate the incline of her hips, and although she was wearing yet another loose-fitting V-neck top, for once it was small enough to highlight her impressive cleavage. Curvaceous rather than thin, I envied her figure. She tended to wear baggy cover-up clothing because she was embarrassed by the top-heavy abundance of her breasts and was fearful of the inevitable male attention that followed them everywhere. I could tell she was sporty at first glance, because she was toned and compact. I had tried to reassure her and encourage her to emphasise her size 12 body rather than conceal it, but she was weighed down by the constant scrutiny of her mother's unforgiving gaze coupled with some past girlfriends who resented the male attention her curves attracted. Being a happy 14 to 16 myself, I could never understand this, and now I found myself casting an admiring glance across her figure as I followed her to the car.

I hardly spoke on the way to the pub. That was unusual for me, but she can talk for both of us, so she did not notice. When we got to The Sun, I checked that she wanted her usual white wine spritzer and went to the bar to get drinks and nibbles. Izzy had chosen a corner seat at the forgotten back of the bar with large, comfortable leather chairs. It was dark but cosy and gave us plenty of privacy. I was not sure whether I was pleased or intimidated by this, so I drank my wine quickly and Izzy ordered us another round about fifteen minutes later. While she was at the bar, a group of women sat down at the table next to ours. One of the women smiled at me and I feigned recognition and racked my brains to try and remember where we had met. I am terrible with faces — too self-absorbed to really notice others. People tend to remember me. I am the cocky one who speaks a little too loudly just as the room seems to go quiet. Or who turns up in jeans and a shirt when everyone else is dressed smartly because I forgot to check the dress code. I like talking to new people, but seem completely oblivious to their appearance. She was probably the mother of someone in my class, I decided, and then became self-conscious about being in the pub with Izzy. Relax, I told myself, we were just two women enjoying a drink, like this woman and her friends.

When Izzy came back from the bar, she complimented me on my outfit and told me that she thought I had lost weight. I had deliberately worn my favourite jeans and shirt — they were not particularly dressy, but they were flattering enough to imply curves rather than bulges.

"I feel embarrassed that I am just wearing an old V-neck which is too small for me now," she said.

"You look lovely! It's not too small. It shows off your beautiful figure. I like you in it."

I could feel the colour rushing to my cheeks and I was grateful for my Indian complexion, which has helped keep my emotions largely unfathomable to others. Izzy seemed to blush, too. She smiled self-consciously and her head dipped as it always did when anyone gave her a compliment these days. Was my comment too obvious? Would I have said that before ten o'clock this morning? I did not know what was happening to me and where I thought this drink and friendship were going. Izzy was my friend and it was madness to jeopardise a good friendship for a bit of mad experimentation. Anyway, I enjoyed sex with men, so what was I doing flirting with a woman?

My brain searched for a change of topic.

"It's good to be out of school. Hope your lessons went more smoothly this afternoon?"

Izzy seemed as grateful as I was for the opportunity to end the silence that was becoming awkward after my very uncharacteristic comment.

"Yes. I had my lovely L6th and a free. I thought about going home, but you know how it is at the moment. Someone always seems to be watching and you have to stay a bit longer or take a bag full of books home."

"Of course, the relentless drive for 'raised standards'."

"I know, Jo. Honestly, I work so hard. I think I am doing a good job and then whenever my class do a test, I feel anxious when I check the database in case they have not done as well as the others."

"I bet they have, though. Everyone knows you're a great teacher."

16

"Thanks, Jo. That's really nice of you to say so. And yes, they always do pretty well. And so much better than Tyrannosaurus Bex."

Bex McAvoy was not even old enough to act like the dinosaur she was. She was in her forties, perpetually single, and the only thing she enjoyed or would talk about was hockey. The children had coined her nickname because she could be unpredictably savage in her discipline and criticism of their work and because someone had overheard her correct a new and nervous young teacher who referred to her as 'Rebecca' with an unduly firm "Bex, not Rebecca; I hate being called Rebecca", as though it was obvious. Once the staff had got wind of it, the name had spread. Staff who had been teaching longer than her were accused of being reactionary and younger staff, PC because they kept up to date and tried new things. Her steadfast cynicism in every staff meeting was now tired and people discreetly kept their distance, fearing to openly upset her.

"Iz, if Tyrannosaurus Bex hasn't been fired, none of us will. I don't think anyone likes her. And everyone likes you. The kids think you are great. The staff think you are great. I think you are great."

She looked at me oddly. It was another blunder. I am not usually rude, except for comic effect. But I tend not to compliment freely and had probably never given Izzy so many compliments in a day before. She knew something was up.

"Are you okay, Jo? Was there something you wanted to talk to me about? Is that why you invited me?"

"No! No, of course not."

"Sorry I asked."

"I didn't mean it like that. I just wanted to have a drink with you this evening. You know. I thought we were friends. I was just being normal, going for a drink with a friend."

"O… Kay… Glad we got that sorted!"

Although she was still staring at me a little, she seemed amused more than suspicious. I felt like kicking myself under the table. I was acting like a complete fool. I just needed to compose myself, so I gulped down the rest of my drink and offered to get another round. She looked angry and as though debating whether telling me off. I realised what she was worried about.

"I'm getting a tea. Some relaxing blend. I know I am driving."

She relaxed. She was glad I had not made her say it out loud.

"Oh, I fancy a tea, too. Thanks. Lovely idea."

We both needed an excuse to compose ourselves and I had to force myself to walk away as naturally as possible.

The bar was in the middle of two rooms and the barman was on the other side, serving a group of customers at the front. I considered sitting down again and waiting till it was quiet, but I needed to think. My heart and my head were both pounding with emotions and I was grateful for a few minutes by myself to calm down.

"I guess we'll be waiting here for a while; he seems busy," said the woman who had smiled at me earlier.

"Yeah, they're usually quick here, though."

"I'm Fiona. I come in here often, but I don't think I have seen you before."

I felt the tension pass out of me and smiled with relief that she was not some parent about to drag me into a long discussion; I don't usually mind, but this evening was tense and confusing enough. I was too preoccupied with deciding whether to be hetero or homo to discuss Johnny or Sarah's lack of concentration or lost book. Fortunately, this woman had no such agendas. When she smiled back at me, I realised she was just being friendly. She had endearing brown eyes that looked gentle and trustworthy. Her small but kindly face was framed by soft brown hair cut to a short bob that was greying slightly at her ears but still looked shiny and well-conditioned, showing off eyes that radiated good-humoured curiosity. She was well-dressed in dark, understated colours that made her almost invisible in the dimness of The Sun's back room, but the narrow circle of full light surrounding the bar revealed well-cut clothes with small attentions to detail, like her gold necklace with a red stone to match her shirt and petite diamond earrings which drew the eye as she played with them while she spoke.

"I'm Jo. I come here often, too, but I normally sit in the other bar," I replied.

"I prefer this one; it's a little dark, but that just makes it more intimate, don't you think?"

I nodded and could feel myself blushing, so I smiled like an idiot to hide my embarrassment. Suddenly, I felt like the whole world knew about my feeling for Izzy. She continued to talk and I nodded and smiled at what I hoped were the right places, whilst thoughts rushed through my head. Eventually, the barman came and I pushed through the embarrassment of having to ask about the herbal teas and then order some at nine p.m. The burning sensation in my cheeks only intensified. I hardly remember what Fiona said; indeed, I would have forgotten her name if it was not for the fact that she handed me her card as I moved to leave the bar. She was a Deputy Head of a local school and she told me to call her if I was looking for a job or any advice on my career. I thanked her and felt a surge of confidence that she had recognised my teaching talents even when I was off-guard and embarrassed in a quick conversation between strangers. Hopefully, Izzy saw the same thing.

As soon as I reached the table, before I had even sat down, Izzy asked me who I was talking to at the bar. I passed her the card and told her about the offer to contact her. Izzy's eyes narrowed and darkened and deep lines appeared across her forehead, which were quickly replaced with a smile that was not matched by any change in her gaze. She complimented me on getting the card with a clipped edge to her tone. I could not understand her sudden change of mood. I apologised for taking so long at the bar and explained that the barman seemed to be on a go-slow. She nodded and muttered for me not to worry. It seemed colder in the bar and I wondered if someone had left the door open, but it was shut now. We drank our drinks in near silence. I tried to cast a few lines of discussion, but Izzy would not bite. It was clear she did not like me having the card. Was she jealous?

I couldn't remember the last time there was silence when we were together. My mind went back to the card. Was it a come-on? Perhaps. I wondered whether the woman had seen me trying to chat up Izzy — was I sending out some kind of signal? I retreated into a private maelstrom of thoughts and emotions about my sexuality. I was now sure that she had made a pass at me and I wondered whether this was because I was now giving out different pheromones or signals or something. Normally, I inhabit a peaceful world protected by my own indifference and inattention. I doubted I would have suspected anything, were it not for

Izzy's reaction. I picked up my glass, relying on yet another steadying gulp, and was left thwarted by an empty glass. As was Izzy. Having sat in near-silence as we raced through our drinks, we decided that we may as well go home. I was cross with myself; instead of charming her with my witty anecdotes and killer pulling pants, we had sat in silence and I had lost my moment. Both our eyes flicked to the card on the table and I pocketed it quickly, just catching a frown flash across her forehead as I did so. I tried to steel myself for another try in the car on the way home, but the barriers were up and I was thrown into confusion. I was not sure why I had picked the card up, but I was sure that it had not helped my chances with Izzy. I drove quickly and when we got to Izzy's flat, she did not offer me a coffee and I did not ask for one.

Trawling the Net

I did not sleep properly for the rest of the week and I just got through my days at school. Luckily, I did not see Izzy the next day, but on Friday I saw her whilst sneaking in ten minutes before break for a coffee before everyone else came. She must also have been free. She was already in the staffroom pouring herself a synthetic latte and I had walked in, head down, looking at some homework that had been left in my pigeon, trying to guess whose unnamed work it was by the oversized scrawl and terrible opening paragraph. She was standing in a patch of sun by the window, wearing a lime green jumper and patterned blue skirt. By the time I saw her I was halfway across the room and she had her back to me and I instinctively turned to run away. As I turned to my left instead of my right, I stubbed my toe on a chair, only half-stifling an "ow" of pain as I dropped my pile of essays and grabbed my foot.

"Jo, are you okay?"

Izzy had put down her mug and rushed over, placing her arm round me as she arrived. As she did, I gave another start and nearly toppled over. The pain in my toe was fading to a dull ache and I put my foot down to steady myself and start to muster some dignity.

"Yes. Just being a clumsy oaf. I don't know what hurts more, my toe or the thought of marking these."

She bent down with me and we picked up the essays together. She had slight bags under her eyes, too, and I wondered whether she was also not sleeping. The idea of her in bed nearly caused me to stagger over as we stood up.

"Are you sure you are okay? You look tired, Jo. Is anything wrong?"

"No, no, fine. At least it's Friday. Long week."

I knew I sounded a bit abrupt and rude, so I added, "I enjoyed our drink, though. I hope you did."

Izzy blinked and stared back at me as she spoke. "Yes. I thought it was a nice idea."

"Well, maybe we could do it again some time. Or a coffee, and perhaps you could come to mine for dinner."

This time her eyes narrowed as she spoke, but there was a smile, too.

"Yes. I'd like that. Are you sure you are okay, Jo?"

"Fine. Thanks. I have to go, busy day. But we'll arrange a time."

I could almost feel her trying to interpret my expressions as she looked at me, so I made my excuses and walked away as quickly as I could, whilst trying not to obviously look as though I was running away. My toe was still throbbing, which ensured a semi-wobble anyway as I walked. But perhaps I had earned a second chance, and now I just had to figure out whether I wanted to take it.

My love life so far was a series of brief but engaging exceptionally short stories. They generally had some plot twists and sub-stories and mandatory sex scenes of varying quality, but generally ended (by me) after a big finale but before the boring setting up house part. Having descended from a long line of commitment-phobes, I was never a girl who longed for marriage and stability. I was not prepared to sit and squabble about whose turn it was to put the bins out, and nor was I willing to have a lover walk in on me in the bathroom.

By the time I had got home, made myself a cup of tea and sat down with a lonely bowl of soup and some bread to start my weekend, I had concluded that I was attracted to Izzy. I needed to be alone. I had ducked out of Friday work drinks by saying I had softball drinks and told softball I had works drinks. I had the whole weekend to think this through, but I needed to sort myself out. The indecision was starting to be part of everything I did. Yes, I was attracted to her. I could not deny it, but was it just a crush or an experiment? Was I becoming a fully-fledged lezza? I was straight; she was a friend and a colleague; I had no actual proof that she was even a lesbian, let alone that she fancied me — I just sensed some chemistry which I thought had come from her but may have come from me. I had known Izzy for six months and we were friends and she had not told me that she was gay, so I should not just assume she was. It was not that she looked dyky — it was more a general impression that she was trying to flirt with me. It was not the first time that I had been convinced that a woman liked me. If anything, I looked more obviously gay than her. I certainly had shorter hair! No. I was sure she liked me. I

22

was not being vain — it's just that for me to even suspect she might be flirting, some massive signals must have been sent!

Believing that the attraction was mutual made things even more confusing. Did I want to be a lesbian? What a horrible word. There are hundreds of euphemisms for homosexual men, but I could only think of the unpleasant sounding 'dyke' for women and a vague recollection that Queen Victoria did not believe any women would do it. Gay men always seem to be the funniest, best-looking and coolest men, but if I took the plunge with Izzy, suddenly I wouldn't belong to a class which few people even bothered to deride or joke about. Aside from Ellen, I could not name any lesbian role models; I could only picture the obvious butch, tattooed, stereotypical lesbians with more body hair than head hair and, more worryingly, I was not even sure what to do with another woman's body, assuming I got there. The only sensible and productive thing left for me to do was to spend some time Googling 'lesbian' to see what I came up with.

My search proved both rewarding and terrifying. There were the boring factual hits with definitions and a host of support groups which were terribly over-supportive and emotional; not my kind of thing at all. Next, I tried the joke sites, which were far more entertaining: endless cat jokes and one liners, about bringing furniture to second dates with more risqué comments about lesbians with long nails being single and countless references to carpet-munching. I had started to enjoy myself; the wealth of internet sites made me feel like part of a community.

Emboldened, I decided to click on the advert sites at the bottom for real-life sites. Just a tip for any novices out there — they are a real eye-opener. Forget seedy old sex shops; these were an open education. Ann Summers may be regarded disdainfully by my more adventurous friends, and I have giggled my way round some high-end sex shops on Tottenham Court Road on hen nights and after drunken nights with girlfriends in the past, but having looked at the websites I started to feel terrified about whether Izzy was a regular patron of these shops and what exactly two women did together.

I was feeling less comfortable now and my mouse pad finger hovered between directing me back to the joke sites and leading me onto the sites promising images and chat lines. I could feel my stomach temperature drop, as it always seems to when it is nervous. It has to be said, inputting 'lesbian' into Google is perhaps the best case for staying heterosexual I could imagine. The fact that the top hits include sites like 'lesbian porn sites featuring naked lesbo pussy in hot lesbian sex' and 'lesbian sex movies at wank page' is no easy introduction to a faltering hetero-waverer. Eventually, my persistence paid off and I found some sites for women about 'first-time sex', including one which gave a ten-stage guide to sex that did not sound too off-putting. I left the tribadism link for later and chose not to speculate too deeply on the advice to 'leave the toys in the drawer first time round'. I started searching for pages for women thinking about being lesbian and found them much less intimidating, and even found some of the descriptions mildly erotic and arousing.

Then I looked at a site saying that straight women can be more aroused by lesbian porn than heterosexual porn, and was back to worrying whether my weird and sudden crush on Izzy was actually an indication of anything other than boredom and a desire to experiment. Suddenly, I was aware that I had just been researching lots of hardcore porn on my home computer and I was terrified that the police vice squads were already locating me on their satellite dishes. In my mind I could see an airbrushed picture of a bikini-clad body scanned under a picture of my head, with the headline: 'pervy porno professor at posh private school and her lesbian love life of internet porn', accompanied by allegations and innuendos about my conduct with female students.

I realised that I could almost hear my heart pounding and I felt my body temperature drop. I was alone and safe in my flat, but I suddenly felt watched. People could see browser histories, and I wondered if any of these sites were trigger sites. I imagined someone remotely watching my screen, maybe even using my laptop camera to stare back at me. And what would they make of me? A bland woman?

My pulse was racing as quickly as my imagination. I instructed my computer to delete any temporary internet files so that no trace would be left of the sites I had just been surfing. Quickly, I shut it down, placed it on a dining room chair, tucked under the table on the other side of the room so that it was completely out of sight and I would not bump into it accidentally. This seemed better, but I was sure I could still feel it watching me and daring me to have another look. I was acutely aware of my intestines gleefully churning a reminder of their warnings not to look at such sites. Clearly, it could only be explained as a desperate search for alternatives so that I could finally settle down and please my mother. Though this would certainly not placate her in terms of grandchildren. Best not to think about my mother. I needed Lexi. When I called her, she was out in a noisy bar somewhere. She called me back a few minutes later, having stepped outside for a cigarette, and told me to join her. She was with some of her journalist mates who I had met up with before, but I was in no mood to drag myself out to Canary Wharf, so I arranged to meet her for a late brunch the next day and I tried to distract myself by watching mindless TV, eventually settling on *Notting Hill* yet again.

Check for Courgettes!

Unusually for the start of the weekend, I looked out of my window on Saturday morning and saw a bright blue and almost cloudless sky. I decided to cycle to meet Lexi at The Anchor in Chiswick. The sun was gently warming but it was a windy day, so I appreciated the shelter I got from the trees on the towpath, cycling slowly along the river's edge, watching the rowers and trying to avoid hazards such as oncoming joggers and dogs at ground height suddenly swerving directly into my path. Lexi was already there when I chained up my bike, sitting outside smoking, taking in the view and people-watching with obvious and unashamed interest. She was wearing jeans and a slightly stripey top with a couple of holes in, though it still looked expensive, underneath a Harris Tweed sports coat. I was in jeans and a Joules quilted jacket and had made an effort, but always briefly felt under-dressed when I met her. She did not care. We had been friends too long.

We were both in the mood to talk, so we ordered a pitcher of Pimm's and picked up some menus to take to our usual table, which offered slight shelter from the wind and a bit of sun to keep us from freezing. Even as we sat down, Lexi was telling me about her exploits of the night before, with brief interruptions for us to chase after the paper menus, vainly attempting to pin them down with ashtrays. Inevitably, when the waiter came to take our order, without looking at them we simply handed them back and ordered our usual dishes.

Lexi's adventures took us through the first half of the pitcher and started the main course, including breaks for her to simulate diving onto a waterbed and feigning seasickness. I was happy to be entertained, because I did not know how to begin my news, but finally she asked me what 'goss' I had, so I forced myself to talk. Lexi had met Izzy before for some supposedly friendly tennis matches last summer, which always ended up fiercely competitive singles or doubles, with balls being aimed at female players' assets or bums by opponents and partners for banter, skill or laziness. Izzy had injected a previously absent level of skill of concentration that helped our team to victory over Lexi and her brother, Tim. Initially, this had sharpened Lexi's acerbic comments when buying the post-match drinks for the winners, but there had been a general thawing as the Sunday matches progressed.

"Well, I went out for a drink with Izzy last week."

"Hardly goss, darling. You must have had a dull week."

"Play nice, Lexi. I haven't had a chance to tell you the gossip part!"

"Go on, then. Amaze me."

The sarcasm in her tone almost made me tell her straight out, so to speak. But it was clearly mocking Izzy, and suddenly I wished I had rehearsed the words I would need.

"Well, we, erm, I mean we went to The Sun and, you know."

Lexi was staring intently at me. I stared back and could feel a gentle warmth in my cheeks which I hoped would not be red enough for Lexi to see. She took a drink before she spoke.

"Look, I know she is your friend. And she has grown on me. Tim and I would be happy to play you both again when tennis season comes around. Sorry if I was rude. Just habit. I didn't know you minded."

"It's not that. Things have changed. I think. It's what I want to talk about. But can you listen and be nice?"

"Now you have my attention. You know I love you, darling. Talk away."

She rolled another smoke and let me speak.

"Well, the thing is, I asked her to go for a drink as a kind of date."

Lexi's eyes bulged and her hand paused on the way to the ashtray with her roll-up.

"A date, date?"

"Yes. I don't know. I just keep thinking about her and just sort of acted on impulse; but now I can't stop."

"Blimey. Are you a lezza now or just testing the water, so to speak?"

"I don't know."

"Well, unless you've been holding out on me, you haven't shagged anyone in ages. It's been weeks. Months really. Are you sure you're not just scratching an itch, darling?"

27

"No. But, to be honest, I'm not massively sure about anything. It's not about her being a woman. I think it's about her. But if not her, right now, maybe another woman. Someone gave me her card in The Sun, and it kind of ruined things with Izzy, but I kept the card."

"This gets better and better. I kind of suspected it for years. Tell all, and right from the start. I want to know everything about the whole evening."

I can't even remember what we had for lunch, except for the delicious sticky toffee pudding at the end. We talked all the way through and it got easier and Lexi held back on her usual innuendos and mockery, knowing I was a bit fragile. It was good to be able to speak so honestly to a friend. She said that although she found Izzy a little dull, she was happy for me and liked her now and could see us together. Then, as she picked up her engraved silver tobacco tin, forcing her to lower her eyes away from my gaze, and commenced rolling her next cigarette, she told me to "go for it and make sure I reported back fully".

"Easier said than done, Lexi. To be honest, I don't know what to do!"

I told her about my internet research and that if I did act, I would be the equivalent of a twenty-nine-year-old virgin, who would have to go slow, probably taking weeks to even steel myself for a kiss. Lexi was having none of it.

"Oh, for goodness' sake, Jo, you're nearly thirty years old! There's no third date rule or need to prove that you don't put out for anyone. If you like her, shag her. Simple as that."

She took a drag on her roll-up, pondering her words, and then added, almost as an after-thought, "But check for courgettes!"

I laughed, more out of nerves than humour. Do lesbians actually use courgettes? I could not remember if they were smooth or prickly and started to picture myself chopping one, trying to recall whether the sensation was smooth or coarse. I shuddered at the very idea, as my memory took me back to my school days and silly jokes about cucumbers always staying hard, being easy to pick up at supermarkets and never running off with other women. Perhaps courgettes were the new cucumbers, brought to the lesbian community as part of the influx of the Mediterranean diet. Lexi certainly knew more about sex than me, though

I did not even want to speculate about whether the comment was based on fact, imagination or mischief. Needing some space for my own thoughts, I changed the subject and asked how her work was going. Then I settled back to be entertained by her stories about her stressed editor frantically chasing deadlines, exclusive lunches accompanied by freebies and promotional tickets, and tried, for the umpteenth time, not to feel jealous about her lifestyle. School holidays were always my trump card in any such debate.

All things considered, our lunch-date helped settle my nerves and prepare me for the uncertainty and risks ahead. I was calm as we said our goodbyes and headed home. Then I got the text from Izzy inviting me for supper on Saturday. Saturday is date night. Perhaps my flirting had only just worked its way through her subconscious and she was now trying to ask me out? She knew I was straight — she wouldn't dare try to ask me out and possibly ruin a friendship. Well, I might as well go, if only out of curiosity.

Dinner for Two

My favourite outfit had worked on Izzy, so I went round for dinner on a Saturday night in a pair of jeans and a T-shirt Izzy had once complimented. It was certainly not dressy, but I figured that if I was going to be a lesbian, I might as well start dressing down now! Fortunately, she was similarly dressed and still liked the top. Izzy chatted away as I tried to muster up the courage to tell her how I felt. She gave me various little jobs to help with dinner, and whilst preparing the salad, I could not help but notice a large, almost marrow-sized courgette sitting boldly on the worktop. Izzy followed my gaze and picked it up and handed it to me and asked, "Do you think it is too soft? I do, but possibly we can still use it."

I forced myself not to look shocked and to think of the courgette only as part of the ingredients. Surely Izzy was too gentle and caring to want to start using vegetables as sex toys; but my mind kept racing back to the more hardcore pictures I had recently been perusing. I needed to distract myself from conjuring up wholly unwanted images and wondering whether there was some kind of sign or rule about who got to put the courgette where. I had to force myself to stay, but replied with some obvious intensity, "Definitely too soft, best get rid of it."

"Okay, then. I am sure the sauce will be fine without it. I just wanted you to taste it at its best."

When she clarified that she only wanted us to eat it, I wanted to tell her it would be fine, but how could I explain what I was expecting. I tried to wipe the perspiration from my forehead and poured myself a cool glass of water from the fridge. Relax, I told myself.

"It's lovely. I always enjoy eating your food — it's one of the things I like about you."

"Okay, thanks, Jo. Didn't know you liked food so much!"

I imagined myself being chatted up by a man like this and decided that by now I would probably be texting a friend and asking them to call me and create a reason for me to have to leave, or tipping extra chilli into the food.

"It's not just the food. It's nice to spend time together. I'd like to do it more often."

"Yeah, it's nice. Would you mind grating some parmesan for me?"

I made myself busy so I could not make any more stupid comments, grating the cheese and then laying the table. I dithered over whether to put the plates next to each other, but we always sat opposite each other and it would be weird to change that. Izzy had finished cooking and I returned to the kitchen, only to be handed more bowls as we made our way back.

"Enjoy," said Izzy.

"It's lovely."

"Glad you like it."

We ate in silence for a minute, then both spoke at once. I gestured for Izzy to continue.

"It will soon be tennis season again. We could play after school one day if the nets are up. Or with your friend Lexi and her brother."

"Great idea. I'd love that. Though the nets don't go up till next term. We could book one at the Barnes club."

"Maybe. Happy to wait, though."

"I love playing tennis with you, Iz. It will be good to get back into it."

"Are you okay, Jo? You don't normally say things like that. I had no idea you loved my cooking and normally you just take the piss out of my tennis. Have you had an appraisal or something where you've been told to be less sarcastic to the students?"

"Do you think I'm too sarcastic?"

"No — it's funny. It's one of the things I like about you, as you would say. The kids love it, too. Most of them find you hilarious. You just seem unusually nice this evening. It's a little unsettling from you."

"Sorry. I just wanted, well, I don't know. Never mind."

"Jo, what's wrong? I like your sense of humour. It can be so sharp and it sometimes makes it hard to have a proper conversation, but it's part of you and if I didn't like it I wouldn't be friends with you. But you clearly have something on your mind — just tell me."

"Thanks. I am trying. I value our friendship. I don't want to damage it."

"Oh, for heaven's sake, Jo. I can take a joke. Don't worry about offending me if you make rude comments about my cooking. Has someone said something to you at work? I wondered why you kept asking me out for drinks and for supper. Do you think you've upset me?"

"No. No one has said anything. Forget it. I am fine."

Izzy had stopped eating and leaned across the table and placed her hand on top of mine and stared directly into my eyes as she spoke.

"Jo, I have never seen you like this. So flustered and uncomfortable. I do care about you. I am not just a colleague. Tell me and let me help."

I took a deep breath. When she had placed her hand on mine, I had almost yanked it away automatically, but I left it on the table and felt her hand warm and soft on top of mine. Her touch felt electric and I was so conscious of its presence that it felt simultaneously like a feather and a lead weight. I realised I was staring at it and she noticed and took it away.

"Sorry, Jo. I didn't mean to offend you."

"You haven't, Izzy. I'm making a mess of this. Forgive me."

"Making a mess of what, Jo? Have I done something? Just tell me."

"You haven't done anything. The opposite. I don't know what to say. Since last Wednesday I just, just…"

I was ruining things, and every word I said just seemed to make things worse. There was no way I was going to glibly steer the conversation round. Suddenly, I realised that for most of my dating life, men had always had the lines and the moves. But I had gone too far to back out now, so I just said what had been in my head all evening.

"Iz, I find you very attractive. I don't know why, but I just haven't been able to stop thinking about you all week."

Silence. Then Izzy nervously chewed her lip and stared directly at me.

"Please, say something. Iz?"

"I'll just clear up the plates."

I got up to help her, but she pushed me down and then pulled her hand away quickly. I knew I had made a mistake and wished I could take back the words, but I guess I had to know. I wanted to follow her to the kitchen, but realised she needed space. She had never told me she was a

32

lesbian and I was left feverishly questioning my assumption both that she was and that she had been flirting with me. Her reaction just now showed no indication that she either expected or wanted my clumsy seduction. My mind recoiled in horror at the idea of me making a lesbian pass at her and her telling our colleagues all about it. I imagined how I would have felt a week ago if she had done the same to me, and I wanted to run. I got up to leave and was just heading to the kitchen to apologise to her and beg her to forget my comments, when she came back in and asked me to sit down, motioning to her sofa.

She sat beside me and asked me to explain what I meant. I started to apologise for offending her and she stopped me. She told me that she had fancied me for ages, but had decided that since I had only talked about men, I was not a lesbian, and she had settled for friendship only. She asked me whether I had gone out with a woman before, and when I replied that I had not, she said, "I really do like you, Jo, so I don't just want to be someone you experiment with. I don't want to ruin a good friendship for the sake of your curiosity at my expense."

I assured her that I was serious, but how could I be sure? Anyway, my words could never be unsaid, so the friendship was compromised anyway. In a mix of fear and excitement, I told her I was genuine. She asked if she could kiss me.

My heart was exploding inside me. I could feel the blood racing around my body and rushing to colour my cheeks. If I didn't say yes now, my embarrassment would have been for nothing, and I doubted I would ever feel bold enough to take this step again. At least I would know quickly whether I liked it or felt revolted by actually kissing someone of the same sex. Murmuring an inaudible "yes", I leaned in to her, my body rigid as our lips met. It was surprisingly good, and we went back for more. This time our feet followed and we embraced. My body started to relax, but tensed again as her hands started to wander. They paused, and she asked me if she should stop. I answered her with a kiss and held her tighter. She explored further, pushing her hand underneath my T-shirt. As my mind struggled between fear and desire, my body took over and I found myself lifting Izzy's T-shirt over her head. It was as though I was in a dream or a film and suddenly it felt very right. She got up and suggested we would be more comfortable in the bedroom, putting me back on my guard. I wanted to, but I had no idea what to do with another woman.

"Jo, I understand, and we don't need to do anything. Just stay the night with me and we'll hold each other. I don't want you to go home now. I just want to be with you."

It was as if she had read my mind, and I felt the same.

"I have got a spare toothbrush," she added to clinch the deal.

I headed for the bedroom, but she headed for the bathroom, handed me a toothbrush and said, "I won't be a moment; the machine's just finished, so I've got to hang the washing or it will smell in the morning."

This was new. Certainly, I had never been to bed with a man who expected me to wait while he attended to laundry. This was my first night with a woman, a momentous occasion — and she was worrying about fresh-smelling knickers! I was so appalled I almost left, but at least it gave me think time. We had moved so fast and in the space of an hour I was rushing from declaring my attraction to going to bed with a woman. It even felt right, if a little surreal. There was no frenzied tearing away of clothing whilst I desperately sucked in my stomach and aimed for dark corners and to be under the covers quickly. This would be a night of good dental hygiene and folded clothes before climbing into bed like a proper couple. At least it meant I was able to watch Izzy undress whilst safely shielded by the duvet. It all felt strangely natural, so, of course, we did not just sleep that night.

When Izzy got into bed, I forced myself to relax, though part of me wanted to jump out the other side, put my clothes back on and run. The other part wanted to climb on top of her and do something, though I was not sure exactly what I wanted or what I was supposed to do. Izzy asked me if she could come closer and put her arm round me and kissed my forehead gently.

"No pressure, Jo, we don't have to do anything. Tell me what you want or to stop and I am genuinely happy to just sleep with you, or sleep holding you if that is all you want."

I was still nervous, but Izzy's words made me relax and I cuddled closer to her and we both stroked each other's backs. I wanted to move my arm further down and I forced myself to move slowly and only gently cup her firm but slightly curvy buttocks. She moved closer, gently pushing her leg between mine as she did, looking into my eyes for consent, and I kissed her on the lips as my reply. This was starting to feel natural and I could feel myself becoming more aroused, and for the first time I found myself thrilled to touch and explore her curved sensuous body. It did not matter at all that she was another woman; the more we kissed and held each other, the more I got lost in the moment and forgot that I had only ever touched male bodies this way before.

I had never given my own breasts much thought before. They were just things which looked good but were a bit of a nuisance that made me spend time choosing the right bra and check whether my blouse buttons left a gap too big to teach in. Suddenly, I wanted to caress, hold and kiss Izzy's breasts all over and feel the curve of her thighs and the softness of her belly. When she responded, I almost moaned with pleasure. We could have lain like this all night, but when she put her hand between my thighs I was suddenly scared again. I wanted her to touch me and I wanted her to touch me there, but I didn't know what sex with a woman involved.

She sensed my anxiety and took her hand away, retreating a little from me at the same time.

"It's okay, Jo, I understand. Not tonight. Next time."

I liked the idea of there being a next time, but also felt a bit frustrated at stopping, and part of me wanted to continue.

"I want to, Izzy. I just haven't done this before. I mean — do we need something? A dildo or something."

I felt myself redden as I blurted out the word 'dildo' and looked away from her. She also looked down, but I could see her force herself to look up. She paused and seemed to collect herself before answering.

"Jo, sex with a woman is different. I've never slept with a man before — I always knew I liked women. But you can do what you want. Be imaginative. It doesn't have to be about going inside or dildos. We can just use our hands, or our tongues, or something else. But in our own time and at a pace that we both want."

Suddenly, she seemed a lot more than five years older than me and certainly more experienced. She blushed as she spoke, but she was clearly determined to at least appear in control, and I felt reassured. I moved towards her and wanted to go further, but she gently told me to turn round and part-turned me with her hands.

"Relax. Let me hold you and we can sleep together. I don't want to scare you and I don't want a one-night stand. Next time, or when it feels right and we are both relaxed and able to enjoy it."

I didn't think I would be able to sleep and her arm around me felt irresistibly sensuous and yet gently reassuring, and I fell asleep almost immediately, feeling relaxed and more at peace than I can remember. That was how it had started and when it had been perfect. All too briefly.

Part Two

LAOS

Tired (C6)

I lay in bed listening to her rhythmless snoring. It would start quietly with a series of gentle rising snuffles, punctuated by occasional wheezes and deep throaty snorts. The whole ensemble reminded me of trying to start my motorbike on a cold winter morning back in London, with gentle attempts by ignition to wake the system up, eventually leading to a faltering beat kept alive by the rolling of the accelerator to get a satisfying roar from the engine. I wondered how she could sleep through her own noise; how she could sleep at all, come to that. I was covered in sweat, cursing Julia's insistence on saving the couple of dollars required to gain some precious air-conditioning for the night. My mosquito bites, now too numerous to count, begged to be itched, and I was in a constant state of turmoil, forcing myself not to scratch and listening for the terrifying buzz of another tormentor whirring past my ear.

At least it was nearly morning and the frustration of failing to sleep would soon be over as I faced another day feeling hung-over and irritable, feigning enthusiasm and wishing I was back at home. As the sun's rays gradually leaked in through the broken, dusty window at the top of the wall opposite the bed, I could just make out a line of ants making their purposeful journey from the left-hand corner of the door to the opposite side of the room and out through a hole in the plaster to whatever lay beyond. After a month travelling, I was immune to commonplace insect horrors, having worked through such traumas, as listening to cockroaches scuttle under the bed in the dark, when I needed to go to the toilet, or finding them in the bathroom. I was now so used to seeing spiders dangling from webs above my head as I lay in bed, that the thought of them abseiling down to land on me no longer ruined the prospect of an orgasm. The ants provided a welcome distraction as I watched their orderly progress as they formed an almost perfect, moving straight line across the room. I wondered if ant discipline would lead to ostracism or a sound thrashing from the queen if any of them broke ranks or swerved left or right as they hurried along. I even managed to feel envious of their obvious unity, wondering what I would need to do to achieve it, having clearly failed to 'find myself' on this supposed adventure with Julia.

She had picked me up a few months ago in a coffee shop, whilst deciding whether or not to forgo her pastry. Stuck behind her indecision, she had deflected my impatience by seeking my advice, and when I decided that we should both indulge, she treated us to almond croissants and asked me to join her. She was not naturally beautiful, but she had a striking blend of unkempt, greying brown hair and casual, tastefully expensive, un-ironed clothes. Her face was soft and engaging and the traces of wrinkles beginning to creep across it only added an attractive sense of wisdom and experience. It was her confidence and the absolute certainty of her own correctness, though, which sucked me in, leading me to follow in her wake.

We had only slept together a few times when she told me about her trip to Asia. At the time I found everything about her exciting, even the chaotic piles of books scattered randomly around her Wimbledon house. The fact that they were too dirty to touch infused their obscure and intelligent-sounding titles with extra glamour. She was vague about her age, but she must have been about twenty years older than me. I liked the idea of an older woman and allowed her to take the initiative, including in the bedroom, so she was surprised when I suddenly introduced the idea of me going with her. She was initially hostile and keen to assert her independence.

"I like you, Jo," she stated emphatically, "but I'm not about to change my ways for someone I've only just met. You're good in bed, but not that good."

Surprised that she even rated me as 'good', I took the whole thing as a compliment (though I would have rated her as 'excellent'). I only just stopped myself from thanking her, before replying that I was just after some fun and that her dates coincided with my summer holiday. I love the perks of teaching, and never tire of making my friends envious; but, if I am honest, sometimes the summer can be boring. I explained to Julia that by agreeing to take me with her, she would be saving me from the inevitable prospect of supplementing the viewing figures of the *Jeremy*

Kyle Show, possibly leading to yet another re-commissioned series. She laughed and then became serious, agreeing to go travelling with me, but making it clear that it would be on her terms. She warned me that we were not in a serious relationship and that travelling together would probably kill any ideas I might have, about starting one.

As I lay sleepless, unable to even toss and turn for fear of waking her, I pondered how right she was. Any hopes I might have had of a relationship had disappeared. The sex had been great at the start — a whirl of new experiences and sensations — but now I was bored of sex, bored of travelling and bored of cheap, dirty hotels, where we haggled for the cheapest room in whatever village or town we happened upon, regardless of whether it had a proper toilet or a hole in the ground. At thirty, I was too old for this level of dirt and discomfort. Even as a teacher I earned enough to pay for a decent room, and whilst Julia's money came from a vague source of family money, supplemented by part-time work as a life coach, I was sure that she was being tight-fisted rather than reasonable as she constantly sought her idea of the 'authentic' Asia. Vang Vieng seemed more like a dirty backwater than the peaceful haven described in the guidebook. I was now counting down the days till we were back in Bangkok and I would be able to fly home to a hot shower and my own bed. The only thing interesting enough to warrant the discomfort of the last few days was meeting Jonno at the Sunset Restaurant last night. Of course, Julia had disapproved and gone back to the room abruptly rather than talk to him. We had spent a pleasant evening, flirting gently, without him guessing that Julia and I were lovers and that men had long since ceased to attract my attention. Julia was asleep when I finally returned, and slipping under the threadbare sheet, deliberately avoiding contact with a blanket that I suspected of harbouring both bacteria and bed lice, I reflected back on how simple life had been a couple of years ago before I met Izzy.

Exploring Vang Vieng

Julia rolled over, trapping me with her arm. I suppose it was meant tenderly, but it felt oppressive, weighing me down, creating a layer of sweat where our skin touched. There was no chance of sleep now, just more discomfort as she continued to snuffle, sleeping well into the morning, blissfully unaware of my restlessness. I remembered how Izzy and I had fitted together so perfectly when we were finally so exhausted, we had to sleep. There was no awkwardness or embarrassment. She did not feel the need to sleep in a sort of star-formation, hogging as much bed as possible, as some of my lovers had done. We snuggled, her stomach and breasts warming my back and even our legs managing to nestle comfortably together. Julia's charming eccentricities and unpredictability now seemed crazy rather than exciting. I wanted London and either my bed or Izzy. She would not have me back now. I had hurt her too much. The sex and adventure had been good and, at times, great, but so what? The mundane routine of Izzy's nesting and nurturing finally seemed alluring, now that I had traded it for new experiences and a friendship broken by an almost claustrophobic intimacy.

The old cliché — the grass is always greener. My restless heart had always believed that contentment would be round the next corner. I still hoped it was right. I hoped I had not lost it a few turns back. I now knew it was not here. I would not tell Julia that, of course. There was no need. We would travel back together, touching each other on the rare occasions that we stayed in places which were not too dirty to kill my libido and cool enough so that we had the energy. Then I would not call her when we were back in England and she would probably not call me back, and the break would be clean and uncomplicated. She would go back to her books and her life coaching and move on with someone else. What would I do? I could carry on as before, drifting from bed to bed, only now I found myself wanting to be held tenderly. Suddenly, I yearned to go to bed just to read in companionable silence. Or just sleep alone in clean sheets.

She stirred and displayed her yellowing teeth in a huge yawn, breathing her morning breath all over me. With feigned tenderness, I went through the motions, kissing her and making needless chit-chat, before escaping to the shower. Even Julia understood that I became grumpy when hungry; so, claiming starvation, I rushed her through her rituals and we were quickly heading out to Saybaydee restaurant, where most of the foreigners hung out. Jonno was there, eating on his own, and asked us to join him. Julia tried to walk on, but I agreed, happy to have the distraction of a third party to carry the conversation. He was staying at the hotel where we had eaten the night before, which was the most luxurious in the area. We were staying in the cheapest. I envied him his clean, pressed clothes, making our Millets' traveller cut-offs and faded T-shirts seem more crumpled and scruffier than ever.

He was funny and confident and had one story after another of exotic travels, his ex-wife, business partner and restaurants. Even his stubble was immaculate — the product of careful grooming rather than a failure to shave. His brown hair was greying at the temples, giving him a distinguished, even sexy look. I was suddenly acutely aware that my hair, normally soft and shiny, had become dried out by cold showers and humidity. It was a long time since I had felt any attraction for a man, but I could feel myself either wanting him or wanting something. I was not sure whether it was his talk of London, the fact that he was relaxed and cheerful, rather than strained and intense, or whether it was simply his clean, fresh-looking linens that attracted me.

I could feel Julia's irritation and realised that I was probably laughing too much at his jokes. I doubt she would care if we went our separate ways, but she would care that I had gone with a man. That would be unforgivable to her. She would never believe that my journey of self-discovery could lead to the realisation that men were right for me after all. Perhaps my tastes were simply Izzy or men. No! That was naïve. The last year had certainly been full of fun.

His hand brushed mine and again as he reached for the sugar or to check the menu. It was surely not an accident, because he hardly looked at the menu after his hand had run the length of mine to get it. He simply ordered more drinks and brushed aside Julia's objections with a casual, "My treat." Jonno was leaning back in his chair, laughing, sipping his drink, with the morning sun like a spotlight on him. Julia was on the other side, squinting into the light, hand flicking up irritably to shield her eyes, hair wild but tied tightly back, and sitting bolt upright, radiating tenseness. I could feel the last of my attraction eaten away as we breakfasted together. I suddenly found myself desperate to prolong breakfast or spend the day with Jonno. I doubted there would be ants, spiders or even mosquitoes in his hotel room. I wanted him just for the thought of clean linen and the glimpse of his hairy chest through a pale blue shirt, outlining a taut but cuddly frame. It had been a while since I had experienced a man against me, inside me, but my memories were certainly more pleasant than my recent ones of Julia.

"I am not feeling very well, Jo. I think I need to head back to the hotel. Now."

"Oh, sorry to hear that. I hope you're okay. I'll check on you when I get back."

"Aren't you coming with me?"

"Why — do you need help getting back to the room?"

"Never mind. Why don't you two just stay here together?"

"Oh — thanks. See you later. I'll let you have a nap."

When I looked back at Jonno, he appeared relaxed and had a smile on his face. He offered to take me to the nearby caves on his motorbike, and, of course, I agreed. I rushed back to our hotel to get changed into my least-soiled clothes.

Julia was lying on the bed, reading and looking perfectly well.

"Feeling better?"

"Yes, I just needed to get away from that place."

I talked whilst I selected my least-soiled linen shorts and a red T-shirt that hid some of the stains and had been at the top of my rucksack and was less crumpled than the rest.

"You're dressing quickly today."

"Just heading out for a bit with Jonno. Give you a chance to lie down and relax. Hope you feel better soon, love."

"Where are you going? I'll come with you."

"The caves. But we're going on his bike, so he can't take both of us. If you were feeling ill, it's best you rest. I'll probably be back by lunch. Have a nap."

Julia had got off the bed and I could physically see her indecision as she partly moved to block me, but her pride pulled her back. I knew I was being a cow, but I needed a break from her. It was just a day out, maybe only a morning — how much harm could it do?

Trapped

Riding pillion to the caves got my heart ticking almost as loudly as the ancient engine powering his rusty and unidentifiable bike. The scenery was a colourful blend of rivers, paddy fields and rustic bamboo bridges. The roads themselves had been churned into ruts and craters by the heavy rains and tourist buses. This, combined with the insanely reckless driving of the locals, created a journey of jolts, swerves and nausea-inducing moments. I had not been close to a man, for some time, so there was some comfort in the unfamiliar feel of my arms tightly encircling Jonno and my thighs gripping around his with all my strength, but the hormones coursing through were generating adrenaline rather than lust. Jonno stopped at a petrol station along the way and whilst he arranged to fill the bike I strolled along the fields on the other side. I was impressed by his knowledge — he was even able to speak a few words of Lao, or whatever they called the local language. I realised guiltily that I did not even know the name of it, let alone any useful phrases from the guidebook. I would not even have recognised it as a petrol station: it just looked like a rusty shack with some barrels. Jonno, on the other hand, seemed to be on familiar terms with the owners, shaking hands, talking in dialect, and he even picked up a parcel to take with him. As we mounted the bike, he asked me to put the package in his rucksack, explaining that he had left it there last time he rode past because he had nowhere to put it. Julia would never have had the confidence to do that, for all her claimed understanding of the natives. I grabbed hold of Jonno as he started the bike, trusting him fully, but wanting to be near him.

As usual, there were lots of tourists crowding the entrances, cameras snapping the pictures even before their owners had bothered to look without a lens. Jonno had not even brought his camera and appeared to know the place, so I was embarrassed to take out mine. I could feel him studying me as I went into my bag and he turned away when I produced a camera. I furtively trained the lens in what I hoped appeared an arty way, but as I twisted it to zoom in, I was amazed to find I was focusing on Julia, standing at the entrance, looking our way. I nearly dropped the camera in confusion and my sudden movements attracted her attention and she started to walk our way. Jonno grinned at her and told her he was pleased she felt better. He did not seem at all annoyed and even seemed to be amused by her appearance. She told me that she had improved quickly after leaving the restaurant and had decided she also wanted to see the sights and had taken the first bus after I left.

Julia never liked to lose at anything, especially not to a man, and I had no illusions about why she slipped between us and grabbed my hand as we walked. There was no point trying to fight against it; she was far more thick-skinned than me and would have liked nothing more than an embarrassing scene for Jonno to watch. One of the touts picked us out and headed straight for us, offering to be our guide. Julia started to tell him firmly that we did not need him, but Jonno spoke to him in Lao, then introduced him as Mai and told her that he had shown him round before and was really good. Jonno seemed wholly unfazed by Julia's intense stare and we walked behind him as he animatedly chatted to Mai.

It was impossible to even attempt small talk with Julia — her face was too rigid, her lips pursed in determination. My limp hand was compressed by hers and I was sure it was no accident that her nails were digging into my palm slightly if I lagged behind her side for a moment. I dared not suggest she loosen her grip. I considered lessening the awkwardness by coming up with some story such as a burning ambition to ride pillion on a motorbike. I had given up all thoughts of a prospective fling with Jonno. He was good looking and distinctly cool, but I realised that I just felt no real desire to be with a man any more. I was running away from what Julia and I had at the moment. There was nothing in the way of romance left. I was becoming a sulky teenager and she was becoming an angry mother-figure.

I could feel her leading me towards a stall by the roadside, and I broke the silence by telling her I had brought some water with me. Rather than take my rucksack off, she stepped behind me and looked inside, pulling out Jonno's parcel.

"What's this?"

"Just a parcel. Jonno picked it up at a petrol station."

"Why are you carrying it?"

"Can't you see? He hasn't got a bag and he could hardly hold it whilst riding his bike."

"Why didn't he bring a bag if he knew he was picking up a parcel? And did you ask what was in it?"

"No — some of us can just do a simple favour for someone without questioning everything."

"I don't like him. He is too slick and there is something dodgy about him. He is not driving now — he can hold it himself."

She grabbed the parcel from my bag.

"You're just jealous!"

I turned round and spoke louder than I intended and people near us looked. Jonno and Mai looked agitated and started to walk over.

"Jealous of what? If you like him, you are welcome to him. I knew I shouldn't have let you come with me. This was my solo trip of a lifetime and when you act like this you ruin it for me."

Jonno had reached us and Mai was hanging back. Julia had kept her voice low and although some people were still furtively looking, Jonno had stared at them as he arrived and they had turned away and carried on walking.

"Calm down, you two."

As Jonno spoke, he tried to grab the parcel from Julia, but she was holding it too tightly and it ripped apart in the brief struggle.

"What the hell is this, Jonno?"

Julia was brandishing his opened package and there was no mistaking the powdery substance inside. Mai and Jonno started to argue in Lao, attracting more glances and open curiosity from tourists around us. Julia interrupted them with her attempt at a whisper which was clearly audible to at least the neighbouring groups.

"You know it's the death penalty here? That woman in the news last year got pregnant rather than face it. What the hell do you think you're doing? You're a fool, Jo. How did you not suspect he was using you?"

It was all becoming horribly clear and I realised what a fool I had been. Mai was the first to react, trying and failing to grab the pack and then running away, shouting something incomprehensible. Jonno's pallor confirmed his guilt and he ran for his motorbike, muttering "You fool" as he left.

People were staring and two policemen started to run after Mai. Julia reacted quickly by pushing the package back into my rucksack and me inside the cave, urging me to act normally. We joined the throng looking round the caves and hiding in the dimness of the half-lit caverns. When we had walked for a minute or two, with no following footsteps, we retreated to a dark corner, pretending to need some water and a sit down. Julia was about to speak, but the tears brimming in my eyes and my quivering mouth told her that I did not need to be scolded by her. She was more generous and forgiving than I would have been, hugging me. She defaulted back to her role as my protector — the older, wiser woman. I needed to be held.

She let me go a moment later, telling me that we should not attract any more stares by being two women hugging and caressing in the dark. I had a package of drugs large enough to clearly be a dealer's stash in a country where even private drug use could mean decades in prison. Jonno and Mai running away would have attracted even more attention. If they were caught, they would definitely try and blame us. And we were the ones who were going to be caught in possession. For all we knew, this quantity of drugs would probably mean the death penalty here, too, so neither of us were willing to walk up to the police and hand them the drugs and hope they would believe us. I had no idea whether Laos's police were corrupt, but I was not willing to trust them when the stakes were so high. Our only hope was to get rid of the drugs as quickly as possible and hope that Jonno and Mai were not captured and did not betray us.

Although we were both so terrified that we were white with fear and the scene caused by Mai running off and Jonno had caused a bit of excitement amongst the tourists next to us, there were so many people it would be easy to blend in if we tried to act normally. We went through the touristy rituals, taking pictures when others did and pausing at the right moments, but neither of us had any interest. We simply wanted the time to pass and our heart rates to slow so that we could find a bin or somewhere hidden to get rid of the parcel. There were no bins in the cave, but lots of dead ends where some litter lay in the crags of the cave walls and we found a ledge about shoulder height in the cave, dumped the parcel and forced ourselves to walk as slowly as we could away from the area. I almost wet myself with the relief of getting rid of the drugs and my rucksack felt as though I had emptied it of boulders as Julia and I, in the standard Western uniform of dirty clothes and battered rucksacks, calmed down and faded into the tourist throng and beyond the suspicion of any police officers. When we re-emerged into the daylight, our squinted glances could not detect anything. There were clearly more police than when we arrived and they were either looking round or talking animatedly, rather than strolling along, bantering with the stallholders. Julia let go of my hand and prodded me firmly in the direction of the bus stop. There was no sign of Jonno or the guide, so there was no one to point us out. Relieved, we climbed onto the bus and sank into the torn and grimy leather seats. We dared not look at one another, fearing that the shared joy of our escape would betray us still.

LEAVING LAOS

We knew we had to leave as quickly as possible. As we packed frantically, we discussed our options — there were very few tourist buses a day, and it would be easy for Jonno to track us if we took one. He might be expecting us to still have the drugs. We decided to try and ask the hotel to hire us a taxi. I finished packing first and went downstairs to check out and arrange something, whilst Julia did a last room check and finished.

I scanned the lobby and kept looking round, and was sweating even in the air-conditioned reception area. The manager looked at me strangely and asked whether I was okay. Without thinking, I formed a plan.

"No. My aunt's died. I have to return to England. My mum's booking a flight, but we need to leave now. I can't wait for a bus. We need a taxi."

"I'm very sorry, madam. It is terrible to lose an auntie. I will help you. Wait there."

Julia had come downstairs and was glancing round the lobby and at the door like I was, and I explained my plan.

"Good idea, Jo."

The manager came back quickly with a man in an old faded white shirt and red trousers and brown sandals.

"This is Havi, he does odd jobs here but has a car. He will drive you for $50."

"Hello, madams. I am sorry for your loss and will drive you. We leave now. Two to three hours to the border and then I will help you negotiate the rest of the way in Thailand."

"Thank you, thank you! You are so kind."

Julia and I could not quite believe our luck. As we were gathering our bags, we saw Jonno on the road outside. He was pacing up and down, looking agitated. Clearly waiting for us. Fortunately, Havi was parked at the back and we followed him through the hotel via the staff door to an ancient blue Daihatsu vehicle that looked like a van with most of the back cut off. He had tools and old bits of wood and metal in the back and we pushed our rucksacks in with them. Our bags were battered and mucky already, but we had no time to think or worry about them getting ripped and even filthier. Over the past few weeks, we had travelled in many mini-buses of varying ages, but the front of the truck was the messiest yet, and even the seats had missing chunks held together with tape. We did not have time to be choosy and climbed in. He turned the key and the van barely shuddered into life and we held hands instinctively, before letting go before Havi saw us.

We drove past Jonno, who was definitely casing the hotel. His linens were a lot less fresh looking and he looked hassled and angry, but he was concentrating too much on the door to think to look inside a workman's van. We had escaped for now!

Havi was in good spirits. He was quiet as we left the town, but then became more and more chatty as we drove. We were tense and quiet and wanted to talk to each other, but his constant questions about our lives in England and stories about his family helped us calm down. It was less calming to have him pass photos across whilst driving, but he drove more carefully than most tourist bus drivers and the journey passed quickly. When we got to the border, he would not take our money until he had found a driver who would take us to Bangkok, and he negotiated us a good price because it had already been paid for by the other passengers, but had two spare seats and the drivers would get to keep the cash for themselves.

The other tourists on the bus were friendly but clearly mildly irritated to lose a couple of spare seats in a cramped bus. The bus was ancient but smoother than many we had been on and the driver put the air conditioning on, for a change. The journey took the rest of the day and we dared not talk about what had happened in front of the others. We sat separately on rest breaks and managed to make plans. We were so happy to be in Thailand and relieved to have escaped that all the tension that had been building between us disappeared.

"I'm so sorry about everything. I was an idiot, Julia. I don't know what I was thinking."

I had not apologised yet. Julia had been taking things well, but I wondered whether apologising would open the floodgates.

"Jo, we both know exactly what you were thinking. You can't just enjoy what we had — there always has to be something else for you. You always want more. I knew we should not have done this together."

"Julia, I... I... I'm just sorry. Please..."

"It's okay, Jo. I've had a long time to think about it as we've been driving. I'm not angry. Not even about this mess — it's been quite exciting in a way. Only an idiot would have taken a parcel from a man they barely knew, but we're in Thailand now and it's all over. I'd have liked to go on to Luang Prabang. You know, one of the wonders of the world. And we've missed that. But I'm sure you'll make that up to me somehow."

"I didn't just mean the holiday, Julia. And you know it."

"I do, Jo. But I think we've both known for a while that this has become just a holiday. We don't need a dramatic break-up scene. Let's try and be grown-ups. We could even stay friends. At least for the rest of the holiday."

I looked at her. Was she just being proud and keeping her dignity? Suddenly, I felt rejected. How did she care so little? I knew I was being ridiculous.

"Thanks. Sorry, if I have been shit."

"No problem, Jo. You have been shit, particularly this last week. But you have been fun. We weren't ready for this. We have had fun. If we stop trying to pretend it is a great romance, we might even be able to enjoy the rest of the holiday."

It was time to get back on the bus for another few hours of driving. We filled the rest of the journey choosing hotels from the guidebook and making plans. We were due to fly home soon anyway, so we would spend our last few days relaxing in Bangkok and getting some clothes made. We considered going somewhere else, thinking Bangkok too obvious a destination. We doubted that Jonno would follow us, but if he did, he would expect us to stay in Banglamphu, where everyone else hung out, so we decided to book a hotel away from the centre and travel in. This had the added attraction of entailing a better-quality hotel. Drug trafficking was also punishable by life imprisonment or death in

Thailand, but we had disposed of the drugs, left Laos and escaped. We should be fine.

The last few days of our holiday went quickly. Julia found us the cheapest hotel she could off the main strip. We were exhausted. Although the hotel was grimier than anything I would stay in back in England, it was palatial compared to the last few weeks. It was targeted at Thai travellers, so standards were higher than for English backpackers, and air conditioning and our own bathroom were automatically included. The room had a double bed and we both paused, wondering whether we should go back downstairs and ask for two single beds. But we were too tired and we had shared a bed for so long we could just continue. I let Julia shower first, whilst I unpacked; and when it was my turn, I took my time, washing away my dirt and nerves. Julia was still in her towel when I came out in mine. She was standing by the window, brushing her freshly-washed hair. The relief of our escape both from Jonno and the rut of relationship had taken away all my sense of irritation and resentment towards her. She looked elegant again. She smiled at me.

"I know that look. Okay. But no strings. No pressure. Just two lesbians forced to share a bed!"

She pulled my towel away from me and pushed me down onto the bed. I offered no resistance. She parted my legs and inserted her fingers into me without tenderness or preamble, more an act of marking her territory than of love-making. But she was gentle and, once more, I was grateful for her taking control and making me feel I could depend on her. Afterwards, we held each other tightly and fell asleep almost immediately.

I woke up first the next day. Julia was lying on the far side of the bed facing me. The morning sun was illuminating her and warming us through the thin curtains that were much more suited to trapping dust than sun. I studied her. She looked old but undeniably elegant and still attractive, but I no longer felt anything but companionship for her. I was grateful to her for sharing this adventure with me and for being so forgiving about the mess I had got us into. We had had to change our plans and miss a major part of our trip, but we had escaped and managed to deal with the end of our relationship as well as could possibly be expected. I was grateful for that, but still felt my heart pounding as I remembered the panic in the cave and the terror of our hasty flight from Laos.

Julia woke up and smiled at me.

"Penny for your thoughts!"

"Thank you!"

I did not need to elaborate. She stroked my cheek gently, almost maternally.

"It's okay, Jo. When we look back at this, we can remember the sites — that beautiful beach when we were so happy to be together, the food, the beautiful places, and that we have laughed and had fun together."

"Yes. We have. I'm sorry for the drugs thing and, you know, everything else."

"Jo. It's okay. We were both getting on each other's nerves. No need to assign blame. Let's forget the impatience and sullenness between us, along with the dirty rooms, the hole-in-the-ground loos, the mosquito bites, and just remember all the good. When we are safely back at home, the business with Jonno will simply be an amazing story to tell all our friends."

"Thank you. Again."

"Nothing more to say, Jo. We have a few extra days here before we go home — let's be friends. And maybe a bit of fun like last night. Now what shall we do today?"

I wanted to suggest going out and exploring, but was worried that Jonno might find us. It was Saturday and we would not fly till Tuesday. We could not simply hide in our room till then. Jan, another teacher at school, had been wearing some lovely outfits she had bought cheaply here, but she warned me to allow as much time as possible for tailoring or we would get badly-made clothes and pay a high premium. I suggested a trip out to the tailors first and then breakfast, and we would take it from there. Julia agreed and took our guidebooks with us to plan whilst we ate.

We went to a tailor recommended by the hotel, figuring that if Jonno was following us, he would look in the ones in Bangalampoo. It was nearby and most of the next few days were spent visiting the sites in between visits to the tailor for fittings. We ate on the strip, always on the look-out, and though we both occasionally thought we could see Jonno, we could never be sure and dismissed it as our imagination. The rest of the time was spent exploring the parks, finding the best cafés, drinking as much fresh coconut juice as possible. Julia and I did not have sex again until the last night, knowing it was the last night together. I kept thinking of Izzy. Occasionally, I nipped out to an internet café to catch up on my email and to spend time composing emails to Izzy that I always ended up saving to drafts or deleting. What are the right words to say 'sorry I used you and then shagged around whilst you had to see me every day at work'? I could try honesty.

"I knew you loved me and I loved you, too."

I wanted to ask Julia's advice, but although we were getting on better than we ever had as lovers, we were not there yet. For the first time in my life, I was starting to realise that I was in love. I had been on what was probably the trip of a lifetime, but all it taught me was to value what I had back home. Or what I had lost back home. I was exhausted and relieved to be safely away from danger. I knew now that I wanted to be with Izzy and hoped that she had not spent her summer finding someone else. I had no idea what it would take to get her back, but I had to try. I doubted I would have given her a second chance if she had done to me what I did to her, but she was gentler and more forgiving than I was.

For a couple of weeks our relationship had been amazing. After the initial fear and uncertainty, the sex had got better and better. I had imagined a world of courgettes and strap-ons, but Izzy was patient, loving and undemanding. For the first time in my life, I experienced a relationship where the sex was fully about both our needs and not just primarily about him satisfying himself whilst keeping me happy enough to agree to more. Her gentle, loving caresses made me feel comfortable with my inexperience and confident enough to tell her what I wanted and explore myself. Briefly, I felt at peace. As I felt her falling more in love with me and found myself wanting to reciprocate, I told myself that it was sex, not love. I was convinced that the sex was so good and so easy, not because I was in love, but because I was with a woman for the first time. I was certain that if the sex was this good with the first woman I slept with, it would be amazing with the next one and would get better and better if I slept with more and more women.

I remember Izzy's face when I broke up with her. I tried to keep my options open and suggested we stay friends, telling her simply that I needed time and space to explore my new sexuality. To me it seemed perfectly reasonable that she should grant me this, but not to her. Her face screwed up and contorted with tears. She reminded me that she told me that she did not want to just be someone for me to experiment with and kept asking me how I could be so callous as to now force her to go to work each morning only to see me there. I remember that she took several days off sick in the weeks that followed and the comments from other teachers about her attendance. Other teachers who were angry about covering or simply gossip, who, knowing we were friends but didn't know we had been lovers, had started asking me questions about her. Her pale face and her obvious unhappiness lasted long enough to even attract gossip from her students. Her attendance and appearance did not improve until after the holiday, but even when she became more like her old self, all my attempts at recapturing our friendship were met with anger. I was a long, long way from any kind of reconciliation, but at least I knew what I wanted now.

Part Three

HOME

Back in London

It was a long flight back to London. Julia and I had become relaxed in each other's company again. We were much better friends than lovers, so the transition had been easy. We reminisced about the high points of our journey, edited our separate travel diaries together, and as we put the miles between us and the incident in the caves, we speculated about what could have happened. We were safe now and were already starting to embellish the details in our diaries to develop the most exciting version to tell our friends.

Of course, Julia did not let us take a taxi home from the airport. We were both exhausted, smelly and thoroughly un-ironed, but she insisted that the amount of time and convenience gained would not justify the cost of an unbooked taxi. I disagreed, but was too tired to argue. I hoped she would decide to take the Heathrow Express, but, of course, she opted for the Piccadilly and Circle lines. We took no offence that even on a crowded tube line, other passengers decided that they would rather stand than sit next to us. We had not done any washing for weeks — my red T-shirt was a faded and dusty version of its former self, and there were stains all over my cargo pants. Julia's white T-shirt was now brown-grey and her shorts were only marginally better than mine. We smelt enough that we could even smell each other, and though we were used to standing out a little as the oldest backpackers in the area, at least we all dressed the same there. Here, we were surrounded by businessmen and other travellers in pressed linens with matching luggage. But we were beyond embarrassment and happy to have a little room to spread out.

My journey finished at Putney and she had to continue to Wimbledon. We did not kiss goodbye and I shouldered my rucksack and other bags and walked the short distance from the tube to my flat as quickly as I could. I charged up the stairs to my flat with my bags banging into my legs and the wall as I ran. Inevitably, the noise caused Doris to poke her head out from the door opposite mine. I cursed myself for not remembering to tip-toe past. My neighbour was old, but despite the self-professed deafness which caused her to shout most words and demand I do the same, she seemed to hear absolutely everything. Over time, I had learnt to dread her firm tap on the door, followed by the manifestation of her in faded flannel pyjamas and shapeless brown dressing gown, leading up to a cascade of dishevelled grey hair, asking me with apparently endless patience and politeness to turn down the music/TV/volume of my guests' voices, regardless of whether it be morning, afternoon or evening. Nevertheless, she had promised to keep an eye on the flat for me, and I knew no burglar would get past her constant vigil, so I answered her questions as briefly as I could, praying my body odour would be enough to force her back to her lair. I was grateful when after only a couple of minutes of questions, accompanied by frowns and grimaces as her eyes scanned my outfit and my bags, she said, "Well, I must let you get on. I am sure you'll be wanting a bath and to do some washing after your travels."

Finally, I was inside my own sanctuary. I felt almost like a stranger and did not know what to do next. There was no milk, so there could be no tea, and I had not thought to even leave myself a packet of biscuits. I dreaded going back past Doris, but there was no choice. I chucked the entire contents of my rucksack on the floor, then put the better half in the machine and the beyond-redemption half in the bin, cursing myself for not throwing it away in Thailand instead of flying it half-way round the world before realising I could never wear it again. There was no need to separate, as nothing was still white inside. I started running myself a bath slowly before sprinting across the road for some milk, a Pot Noodle, crisps and, just to be healthy, organic chocolate. My diet and complexion could wait. I took them all to the bathroom with me, whilst I scrubbed myself clean and pondered how I was going to spend the remaining eleven days of the summer holiday winning back Izzy.

It was nearly lunchtime and I emerged from the bath much cleaner, still ravenous and with a plan. After a quick trip to the supermarket and with some home-cooked food inside me, I called Izzy. My plan was to pretend I needed information about the INSET day and could not access any of the examination results because I had forgotten my password. I could barely breathe as I hoped she would answer. She did, and I felt a surge of tenderness at the sound of her voice, but as soon as I spoke her voice went cold and brusque.

"Why are you calling me, Jo? Got tired of Julia?"

"No — I am sorry. I just needed your help because I forgot my password. I miss you. Can't we at least try to be friends?"

"Friends don't promise they are not just experimenting with you, use you for sex, then rub your nose in it at work every day. So no, we can't just be friends. Email me what you want from your Yahoo account and I will forward the mails. I don't want to be an arse, but I will not let you hurt me again."

There was nothing I could say to that. It was the first time I realised how immature and callous I had been. Her feelings had simply not registered with me and she had only told me she loved me when I broke up with her. At the time, I assumed it was just said out of shock. Never having been in a relationship where love was even an issue, I had assumed she felt as little as I did. Only now was I starting to realise that I was probably in love with her all along. I gave up men to be with her! Of course she was special. I had to win her back, but had no idea how to make her trust me again.

I would show her that I was different now. We worked together, so she would have to forgive me. And then I would make her like me again and take me back. No matter how long it took, eventually she would see that I had grown up and was ready for a proper long-term relationship. I could feel myself starting to cry and I was not ready for Doris to knock on the door to ask me to sob less loudly. I needed a distraction. I reminded myself that I was currently single and scrolled through my mobile numbers. Pru. Perfect. I texted her:

'Pru — Just back from backpacking trip to Asia. Had to end it with Julia and back in London. You in town and up for some fun?'

It took her under five minutes to text back that she was free tomorrow afternoon and could come over. Clear, unambiguous Pru. She wanted carefree sex with no strings. Why couldn't all girls be like that? Now that I had something to look forward to, I could sort out the flat, check in with my parents and actually look through my students' GCSE results and catch up with my school mail. I could even try drafting a reply to Izzy that would be step one of a very long journey to get her to want me again.

Prudence

Pru was great. I often found myself wishing I was her or trying to act like she would act if I found myself in an awkward situation. Her family had generations of wealth and privilege behind them and Pru had grown up oblivious to barriers and the kind of worries most people have. She never consciously flaunted her advantages and she managed to be charming, likeable and always fun to be around. The stricter her parents were, the wilder she became. If they tried to cut her allowance, she managed to find any number of ways to secure money which she was conspicuously vague about and always ensured that, in the end, her parents ended up reinstating it. She was tall, thin and blonde, and much more the archetypal rich girl all men lust after than someone whom I would ever have picked up on with my gaydar. When I first saw her in the Candy Bar, I assumed she was a straight girl having a laugh and only let her pick me up out of curiosity. She was wild and wholly uninhibited in bed. She made love with the confidence and skill of someone who had slept around but with the intensity and desperation of a virgin. And she was insatiable, as all bisexuals are. One afternoon with her and either I would be over Izzy or at least have a better perspective on what to do.

She rang the doorbell and when I opened it, she was standing there in denim hotpants with so many designer rips that left almost nothing to the imagination and a baggy T-shirt slipping almost completely off both shoulders. Her hair was tied back in no discernible pattern, but the overall impression of her having made no effort whatsoever made her even more desirable and I had to restrain myself from dragging her straight to my bed.

"Pru, great to see you. Coffee?"

"No, darling, it's boiling outside — no need. Let's go straight to the bedroom and make ourselves thirsty first."

She knew I loved her arrogance and that I had texted her hoping for sex. A tiny inner voice was telling me to show a bit of pride and restraint and at least feign indignation, but I was too busy watching the sway of her bum to have any qualms about following her.

When I finally got us both some drinks — Camparis with tonics — I really was thirsty and certainly needed some ice to cool down. We lay naked in bed, sipping our drinks, and Pru was sprawled between my legs as I told her my Izzy dilemma. Her advice was as expected: disinterested, disdainful, but uncannily perceptive. She told me that I was wasting my time and youth falling for someone so high maintenance. In her world view, monogamy was only for ugly, boring or religious people. She also told me that I was now starting to qualify for the boring category because every time she saw me, I talked about Izzy and clearly, I was hooked. Her final advice, before going off to shower, was that, if I must hook up with Izzy again, I should let her fall in love with me first and then suggest an open relationship. I decided that next time Pru's allowance got cut, I would not suggest that she supplement her money with a career as a relationship guru.

After she left, whilst still feeling comfortingly sexed out, I picked up my iPad and began drafting an epic email to Izzy. I was rather pleased with the end result of two hours' labour:

'Dear Izzy,

Thanks for forwarding these. Results not great, but pleased with some of mine. Thanks for always being so great and helping me once again. I was too stupid to realise how hurtful my behaviour was at the time and I regret hurting you more than anything I have ever done.

Please let me apologise to you in person. You don't even have to forgive me. Meet me at Café Nero — it's public and where we have shared so many coffees. I won't try anything except apologising and hoping we can become friends again.

Sorry

Jo'

All that remained was to keep checking the iPad for the rest of the evening to see whether she replied, and just a few days later, when I had given up hope of a reply and was planning my next move, she emailed back agreeing to meet for a 'quick' coffee a few days later. Result!

Just Good Friends

Izzy and I reached Café Nero simultaneously. She was dressed casually and although she looked great, she had clearly not made any special effort to impress. Nevertheless, I had to make a conscious effort not to look wistfully at her beautiful physique. She had lost weight and I hoped that that was not my fault. Having said that, she was thinner in all the right places and her hips and breasts curved tantalisingly. My wandering eyes were snapped into place when I inadvertently glanced into her eyes. She was well aware of my attempt to surreptitiously check her out and her expression was neither cordial nor forgiving.

"Can I get you a coffee, Iz?"

"An iced latte."

Izzy's obvious frostiness made me get a warm drink and I automatically bought Izzy her favourite almond croissant. She was in no mood for small talk, so when we sat down, I immediately tried to apologise and start repairing the damage I had done.

She was not aggressive to me or even unpleasant, but the blank and unresponsive way she listened to my apology was, if anything, even worse. She pointed out that I had promised her at the start that I was not just using her, but then I did just that. She also said that she knew from the start that I was too young and too immature to be ready for a proper relationship and that she should have avoided me in the first place. I tried to tell her that I had grown up and would not act so rashly now, but she said that she had heard it before. Then she said that contact with me was just too painful and she was not sure that she would ever trust me again and so it was unlikely we could ever be friends.

Her final killer line was to say, "Jo, if you really are sorry and you really do care and have realised how much pain you caused me and want to make amends, then you should have the decency to just leave me alone."

And then, her coffee half-drunk, her croissant untouched, without a raised word or any sudden movement, she quietly stood up, turned around and left.

It would have been better if she had slapped my face and thrown her coffee all over me. Now, if I tried to text or call her it just made me more of a villain. There was no way of gradually proving myself to her — the only thing I could do for her was not contact her. I could try to tell myself that absence would make her heart grow fonder again, but that was clearly rubbish. If I did as she asked, all that would happen would be that I could watch her from a distance in the staffroom as she gradually got over me and moved on. How could I call her now?

I should have given her more time. I should have approached things gently and not always tried to rush and grab what I wanted. I should have been more patient and careful. Once again, I had failed to consider how she might react and how she might be feeling.

I had to show Izzy that I would respect her wishes, but in a way that would still get her to fall in love with me. As I stayed in the café eating her croissant and finishing her latte, suddenly I was inspired. I knew what to do. I would wait till we were back at school and make friends with Fay — Izzy's closest friend at work. It was a good plan with only one small problem. Fay hated me. She always had done and had warned Izzy away from even being my friend, and when she heard we were dating, she had pleaded with Izzy to stay away from me. Izzy had asked me to try and make friends with Fay and although I had promised her I would try, I had made no real effort whatsoever.

When we broke up, Fay was always by Izzy's side at work and would bring her cover work in and take books home if she was off. If I bumped into her in the staffroom or even the corridor, she took every opportunity to show her dislike, but stopped short of obviously outing Izzy and I to the whole staff. Well, I was up for a challenge and willing to play the long game. My only route back to Izzy would be via Fay, so I had to try so that I could at least believe I had a chance.

I could feel my phone vibrating in my pocket and hoped it was Izzy calling to say she was coming back; but when I looked at the number, it was Julia. I let it vibrate and shoved it back in my pocket, before finishing my drink and leaving. As I walked home, she called twice more. The third time she left a message and I was intrigued. The Julia I knew would have been too proud to call me more than once, so I listened to the message. She sounded frantic — she didn't make much sense, but kept saying something about Jonno and Vietnam. I called her back and she picked up immediately and half-begged, half-ordered me to come round.

"Don't flatter yourself that this is about trying to get you back. Far from it — this is about me clearing up one last mess of yours. I swear Jonno is stalking me. You started this, so you owe it to me. You have to come."

I had no idea why Jonno would be stalking her or how he would even know where she lived or who she was, but the fear in her voice was genuine and intense enough to force her to be vulnerable. I was trying to be responsible, and if she was right about Jonno, then I had got her into this. I was not going to leave another ex, hurting and hating. If I could sort Julia out, then Izzy would follow.

She told me not to meet her at home and set up a rendezvous in Hyde Park by the Reformers' Tree Memorial so that she could scan the area. It was bizarre. Julia was eccentric, but had never seemed this odd before. She was a life coach, for God's sake! Surely, she should be counselling herself to calm down. Physician heal thyself and all. Still, if I started doing good deeds and making amends, maybe the Karma would help me get back with Izzy.

Feeling Watched

It took me over an hour to get to Hyde Park — it would have taken fifteen minutes to get to her flat. I was not amused, and after standing around for five minutes I was just about to text her and leave when my phone vibrated. It was Julia texting to say that she was on the bench opposite me. When I walked over to her, she looked harried and twitchy. She had a scarf over her hair on a hot day and she kept glancing round. She looked sweaty and hotter and more dishevelled than she had looked backpacking in Asia. All my anger evaporated and I sat down to listen.

She told me that she kept seeing or imagining that she could see Jonno. The first time it happened was a couple of days after we got back to England. She thought she saw a man who looked like him hanging around when she looked out of her window, but he walked off quickly. She thought it was because he had seen her, but she dismissed it because it was too ridiculous. The next day she saw him again, and the day after that. That time, she was sure he wanted to be seen, because instead of moving away when she came to the window, he smiled and then sauntered off slowly and deliberately. She had a good look and despite a beard and a different haircut, she was sure it was him. When she went out later, the man appeared again and seemed to be following her and happy for her to know it. He kept his distance and after a while turned a different way.

This morning he had been there again, and when she came to the window, he tipped the rim of his baseball cap at her and nodded. Then he just stared until she moved away. She had taken three different taxis to get to Hyde Park instead of her car, just to ensure that he could not follow. What on earth could he want with Julia? How would he even know where she lived, and why was he stalking her? We had not taken his drugs and I had not found anything else in my rucksack, so there was no reason for this man to be him. Either way, if any man was following her, it was worrying. Julia told me that she knew how crazy it sounded, but she was sure it was him. She was an instinctive people-watcher and analyser and she said that the beard did not detract from his identical build, gait and even style of dress. She even thought he was wearing the same pair of trainers.

Two things were clear — Julia believed what she was telling me and she was a wreck. I told her that I would help and she suggested coming to stay with me for a bit. I dismissed the idea quickly — if he was following Julia, he would not be able to track her at mine so we could not confirm her suspicions and then she might just end up staying indefinitely, and that would just be awkward. My new, responsible inner voice forced me to offer to stay at her place. I told her I would need to get some stuff but then would come back to her place afterwards. If he showed up again, we would photograph him and call the police. She begged me to hurry and I have to admit, it felt empowering to be needed by someone like Julia. Mystifying and scary as her story was, it was also thrilling and exciting, and it made me wonder what the sleeping arrangements would be that night. I might even be allowed to relax and take the lead if I were invited into her bed. Izzy had rejected me, so I could sleep with whomever I wanted. Especially if I was comforting a damsel in distress at the same time.

When I got back to my flat and started to pack, I suddenly began to worry — at the very least I should tell someone where I was going. I could not tell my mum because she would tell me not to go. I called Lexi. She was in a rush and off to interview some lawyer about some small print which made some company's takeover bids illegal, and even she was bored by the details and told me again how she would love to switch from her daily to a fashion column. I interrupted her to give her a quick summary of my meeting with Julia and even she went silent.

"Fuck me! But no courgettes. And you're not really my thing, darling. How exciting and terrifying! I need all the gossip — when shall we meet?"

I told her that I had to go — just wanted her to know where I was and that I would call when I could as I had lots to tell and needed her opinion on everything. As I left the flat, I suddenly remembered the ridiculous heavy workman torch my dad had given me in case of power cuts and decided to take that, too. If Julia had really been going through this on her own, no wonder she looked a state and had let her guard down. If it was Jonno, it had to be my fault.

We Meet Again

Julia was obviously glad to see me when I arrived about an hour after her. She said that she had checked everywhere on her way home and kept looking out of the window, but there had been no sign of Jonno. She had made us risotto for supper, which was one of her specialties and which she knew I loved. If it was a ploy to get me back, it was a bit extreme, but I did wonder what the sleeping arrangements would be.

"Don't read too much into it, Jo. I know you love this, but I made it to say thanks for coming. I didn't know whether you believed me or whether you would come, think I had gone mad and run away. So I am cooking for you. To say thanks. But that is all the thanks you get. You can sleep on the sofa if you prefer or in my bed with me as a friend because it is more comfortable. Sleeping is all that is on offer. And if you can handle that, I think we would both get a better night's sleep in the circumstances if you opt for my bed."

Julia was never one to mince words, and it was a relief to have things clarified. Nevertheless, despite the inevitable tension of waiting to check for stalkers, we had an incredibly pleasant and relaxed evening. Julia was an excellent cook and I always over-indulged when she cooked. I worried that a long stay here would do irreversible damage to my waistline. We had such a pleasant evening that that seemed to be the only possible danger on the horizon. Although Julia and I had a few glances outside the window, there was nothing suspicious and it was hard not to believe that Julia was imagining things.

When we had finished the second bottle of wine, we decided it was time to retire and I accepted her offer of a shared bed, though I had not thought to bring pyjamas. Julia's response to my admission, along with a raised eyebrow and a grin, was, "I can lend you a pair of mine, but I have seen it all before and I am sure I can control myself. That is, so long as you are sure you can keep your libido under control and not try to blame anything on this rather fine Viognier."

I assured her I could and we ended up in bed together — her in her Cath Kidson's, and me naked. At some point in the night, I woke up thinking I had heard a noise and found myself wrapped in Julia's arms. I did not hear anything else, though, and I found myself relaxed and comfortable in her arms, rather than resentful and trapped like I had done so recently in Laos. I went back to sleep and woke up the next morning feeling more peaceful and rested than I had in a long time.

Julia was already in the shower, and when she stepped back into the bedroom the tension had faded from her face and she looked rested as well. I told her she looked well. She thanked me for coming over.

"I am starting to feel silly. I don't think I imagined seeing Jonno and he might have had something else to do yesterday. He can't spend all day every day outside my flat. But having you here is starting to make me wonder whether I was mistaken."

"No problem. Let's hope it's nothing. It was a nice evening."

"Yes — it would be good to do it again. But I still want you to stay. At least one more day."

It was still the summer holidays and she did not live far from my flat. I could get used to her cooking. I watched her dress as she made no attempt to cover herself and appeared totally oblivious to my casual gaze. It felt comfortable rather than sordid, and we felt more like a couple now than we had at any point during our relationship. She told me to go and shower whilst she made breakfast.

"Thanks. I'll stay for at least a few days, until you feel more relaxed."

I was just getting into the shower when I heard her yelp. I grabbed her gown and ran downstairs. She was standing in the kitchen, staring at the door. There was a book on the floor and I had no idea what had startled her. Then I read the cover. It was a brand-new Lonely Planet Guide to Laos.

"Is this yours, Julia?"

"No — someone must have posted it through the door last night."

I remembered waking up because I thought I heard a noise, which could have been the sound of the book hitting the floor, but that was the middle of the night. A perfect time for someone who did not want to be seen. If it was Jonno who did it, he clearly wanted Julia to know that it was him and it ruled out the idea of a random person being the stalker. But equally, it was just a book. Julia could have left it there herself.

"Could it have been left as a present?"

"Don't be silly, it's not wrapped." She took the book from me and flipped through it. "No one's written anything in it, either. And who would give me a guidebook in the middle of the night to a place I've just visited?"

She had a point. It seemed a choice between her being stalked by Jonno or her constructing an elaborate plan to stalk me. It made no sense that Jonno would have followed us back from Laos and then followed Julia. How would he even know where she lived?

"Are you sure this isn't your book?"

"Of course, I'm bloody sure, Jo. What are you suggesting? I put it here to trick you."

That was exactly what I wanted to suggest, but I had to be sure.

"No, just wondered whether you might have bought a new one."

"And in the middle of the night it flew from my bookcase and landed here."

I did not point out that she had come down on her own to make breakfast and could have placed it there. I could feel my heart racing. Adrenaline was pumping round me and I could feel a slight sweat developing on my forehead. I felt afraid, but did not know what I was afraid of. Should I be comforting Julia or running from her?

We looked through the guidebook together, with me trying to keep slightly behind Julia's shoulder, scanning her as much as the book and ready to jump. I decided that if this was a plan of Julia's, then it would be to get back together with me, not to hurt me, so I did not need to be afraid. There was nothing written or hidden inside the book which made me suspect Julia, because she would know that I would recognise her writing. If Jonno was stalking her somehow, he would leave some clue. We kept flicking through the book and saying the same things. I suggested calling the police, but Julia was against it.

"What should we tell them — we found a book in the kitchen?"

"Yes. And that you think he is stalking you."

"Will they believe us? Do you even believe me? I can see the way you are looking at me right now, yourself."

"Of course I believe you," I said in a voice that, though I struggled to control it, hardly sounded reassuring.

"Hmmm."

To be honest, I wanted to call the police mostly to find out whether she was telling the truth. We did not know his surname or anything about him, but they could perhaps liaise with the police in Laos to identify him. Finally, we decided to call the police.

The operator was slightly bemused, but then very helpful, giving us a CAD number and telling us some officers would be round shortly. Neither of us was hungry any more, so I made us a pot of black coffee. I was almost shaking and dropped far too much coffee into the filter, but we needed something to wake us up. If it was Jonno, the idea of him stalking and watching her and then leaving the signal seemed so calculating and deliberate that it was either absurd or suggested that he might be very dangerous indeed. Maybe that was the point. If it was Julia, then either she was going mad or she was making a harmless but ridiculous attempt to get back together with me or she was stalking me, possibly taking her revenge for how I had treated her. Whatever was going on, someone was potentially stalking at least one of us. Julia seemed too lucid for me to believe that she was making it up, so I was becoming convinced that I should be afraid that either Jonno or Julia was out to get me.

The police came quickly, but were not helpful.

"Let me get this straight — we have come to look into a possible intruder or stalker and he manifests himself by leaving you a present through the letterbox. Shall I arrest all the local postmen, love?" said the older, fatter of the two.

He was unshaven and could have been any age between early thirties and late forties — it was hard to say, because his puffy features and slightly dishevelled unshaven look made him appear old, but he also looked like a man who lived on takeaway and booze and he just looked past it either way. He introduced himself as PC Whetstone, whilst constantly adjusting his truncheon belt to fit round his overhanging beer gut. He was clearly not in the mood to listen to some nervous women. When I tried to explain about the incident in Laos with drugs, all I got back was two disbelieving faces and a heavy sigh from the fat one.

"Yeah, we'll look into it — if they got him with drugs the penalty could be death, possibly by firing squad. Certainly, he'd be looking at years in prison, so it seems unlikely that he got caught by the police drug-running and is now posting guidebooks through letterboxes in London a couple of weeks later. I suppose I can get one of the specials to send them an email to find out what happened or if it was just a prank and a bag stuffed with talcum powder."

They did not inspire confidence and made no attempt to reassure us. They were not interested in fingerprinting the book and their contempt was obvious. We sat in silence for a few minutes after they left, too disheartened to try to analyse their visit. Then the doorbell rang again. Assuming it was them, I opened it. I was too stunned to react when the man pushed the door fully open and walked past me into the kitchen.

Trouble

He was bearded and the clothes were less cool, but there was no doubt who it was. As he barged past me, I was too stunned to react or even consider running straight out the door he had just pushed through. Mutely, I pushed the door shut and followed Jonno into the kitchen and heard Julia suppress a muffled yelp as he came in.

"Evening, ladies, bet this is a surprise!"

He was pleased with himself. He was wearing Converse trainers, jeans and a checked shirt, much blander than his Laos outfits, and he had a logo-less baseball cap and plain black sunglasses in his hands. As he leaned against the counter on the opposite side of the kitchen, he exuded an air of casual menace and control. Julia breathed in and out in her calming way that she taught her clients to do, and then, in a commendably calm tone, asked Jonno what he wanted.

He told us that we had caused him a lot of trouble by making such a fuss about a "small bag of coke". I opened my mouth to point out that he had just dumped it on me, but he raised his hand and dismissed me like a dog being brought to heel. I was ashamed of myself and could feel my cheeks burning with shame and fear. He had gone back to his hotel room to find some of the dealer's men waiting for him. They had already taken his watch, some cash and his passport. Even after he agreed to pay them £5000 to get the passport back and to leave the country quickly, they still gave him a beating and only twenty-four hours to leave. He had to book a premium flight and they kept his valuables and made it clear that they were only letting him leave because they did not want the death and disappearance of a foreigner to attract any headlines. He would no longer be safe in Laos and he would not be able to do business with anyone in Laos or Thailand, where he had been living and trading.

"So you two owe me a lot of money."

"What? We didn't ask to be involved," I said.

"Look, you planted the drugs on us — we had nothing to do with it," Julia said, not daring to shout but with a distinctly angry tone.

"Don't use that tone on me. I've taken a beating for you two. Don't push me to hit a woman or two. Just pay me what's due and I'll let you go."

"But we just threw the drugs away. We didn't make any money. How are we supposed to pay you?"

"Not my problem. You cost me almost £10,000 in cash, valuables, air fare and lost me my business. I'll have to start from scratch again somewhere else. Maybe here."

Neither of us spoke. We were scared what we would do if we argued, but it was not our fault.

"So there you have it, ladies. Now, I am a reasonable guy and I am sure that you feel bad for the hurt you caused me and are only too willing to compensate me for the losses you caused. We don't need to get nasty here — I don't care to hurt women and I am sure you wouldn't want any... unpleasantness. I'll settle for £20,000. I am sure you two can raise that between you. If you can't, we can come to some arrangement. If I am setting up here, I may need some jobs done."

I mustered all my courage and told him that I would call the police if he didn't leave. He grinned and dared me to do it.

"Why do you think I spent all that time freaking your girlfriend out? Just to make her sound so crazy the police would ignore her. Sympathetic, were they?"

He was right, but I looked surreptitiously round the room to make a mental note where to tell them to check for prints. Julia seemed to shrink as he spoke, clearly aware of how hysterical she had sounded, and then asked him how he found her. He was happy to boast about how easy it was for someone as connected as him to tip the hotel owner into giving the name of the person who had booked the room and that he even had friends in law enforcement in this country who supplied him with the occasional address or helped him in 'a spot of bother'.

"I have friends everywhere, always happy to help me out. You two may think you're smart and tough, but I've been playing this game for years and I'm a winner. If you want me out of your lives quickly, get £20,000 in cash ready. Otherwise, you'll have to work it off. Feel free to try and call the police and see if they believe you, but I know how to deal with them and I will put the price up if you start making things harder for me. And believe me, you only want to deal with me when I am in a good mood, so don't piss me off by lying to me or trying to get cute. I'll leave you girls to reflect and then to start counting your money. See you in a week or so, but I'll have someone keep an eye on you in between."

Then he was gone — walking calmly and affectedly slowly — pausing to straighten his hair in the hallway mirror, before putting his cap and glasses on. He closed the door quietly and made no attempt to rush as he walked down the street. Julia and I were too scared to photograph him, but what could we have done with the photo anyway? He looked like almost every other man in the area and, from the back, he could have been anyone.

As we watched him go, I could feel my knees start to tremble involuntarily. My stomach and my back felt cold and I did not feel in control of my body. I put my arm on Julia's back and it was sweaty and I could hear her breathing. I did not look at her, but I could feel her staring at me. I wondered whether she realised how much I had doubted her. I did not doubt her now. It was clear who our enemy was.

We sat down and did not move or speak for a minute or so. Then Julia said that he was right, we could not call the police again because they would not believe us. I told her we had to try, more for something to do to make me feel less impotent, so I rang them. Once again, the operator was helpful but insisted that she would send the same officers. I could have screamed in frustration and wondered whether they were Jonno's friends, but I could not see any other option, so I asked her to send them back.

I made us both a cup of tea and turned on the TV to some random house-buying or makeover show which we watched like zombies. I knew that this was my fault — I may not have done much, but Julia had been right to want to avoid him from the start. I whispered 'sorry' and was grateful that Julia replied that, stupid as I was, neither she nor I could have predicted this. Her comments were not matched by her manifestly reproachful stares, but she was more generous and forgiving than I would have been. I moved next to her and we held hands for a bit. Though we were not watching, when the programme ended, I got up to make us some cheese on toast, just for something to do.

The police came back about two hours later and looked angry even before they came in. PC Whetstone made no attempt to hide his obvious contempt for our story, rolling his eyes and sighing pointedly. The other officer looked about twelve years old, shifty and nervous, and had 'Special' on his pips. He was certainly not going to help. PC Whetstone did not even allow us to finish telling him everything before looking at his watch, yawning and replying, "Look, love, this is England and Laos we are talking about — not Hollywood. In Laos, the penalty for drugs is death, so if your mate had been caught by a gang, they would have taken him to some corrupt cop and he would be rotting in a cell now. I don't know if you're trying to wind us up or if you are still hung-over from whatever you got up to on holiday. I don't want to know. Maybe you and your friend, or girlfriend or whatever you two are to each other, need to just calm down and try not to let your imagination get the better of you. Now, I am not going to book you for wasting police time, but I suggest you do not call again unless something has actually happened and you have evidence that it did. If you do call us again, I am going to start looking into exactly why you may or may not have had a stash of drugs in your bag and why exactly you keep calling officers round to your flat just for some company when we have actual crimes to solve."

He nodded to his apparently mute colleague and they did not wait for us to show them to the door. They strode out more quickly than our previous visitor and made a point of shutting the door very firmly. We were now very much alone.

Help

When they left, we both sobbed and held each other on the sofa. There was nothing to say. I felt humiliated and powerless. Neither of us could find any words to offer solace or solutions. Eventually, Julia spoke.

"Well — I hate that bastard, but maybe we have to pay him. I have only about £5000 in savings."

"I have less than that — I am a teacher, not a banker," I replied.

"Even if we can raise all that money, he might just come back and ask for more."

That was true — if we just tried to pay him off, he would be sure to demand extra; but we were both convinced that he would not simply let it go if we did not pay. Both of us were sure that if we went down the route of doing favours, we would only get deeper into trouble and probably end up being arrested by the same policemen who had refused to take our report seriously.

I wanted to leave the flat immediately and told Julia to come with me, but Julia dismissed the idea.

"Look — I want to get out of here desperately. I love this flat, but I don't think I'll ever feel safe here again. But what if he follows us?"

"Yeah — I didn't think about that. You have to come and stay at mine. We'll just take a long route and make sure we are not followed."

"At the moment he doesn't know your address, so let's keep it that way. We need to make sure he does not get your real name, either. We have some time, probably not much, but, for God's sake, Jo, we need to calm down and think sensibly. And plan. Try not to panic."

She had not blamed me or turned on me yet, but I knew the last comment was a justified dig. And that she was right. If we panicked now, we could end up in even more trouble, but I had to leave the flat; I could feel my blood pounding and it felt like the flat was on fire and had suddenly shrunk to the size of a prison cell.

"Yes, Julia. You're right. I'm sorry. But we need to get out of the flat to talk. He may have planted some listening device or something."

Yesterday, the idea of random people planting listening devices in a flat would have been laughable. Today, it seemed likely. What had happened to my world? Julia nodded to me and neither of us spoke until we had left the flat. We walked to the common and made sure that we sat on a bench where we could see all around us and be certain that no one was eavesdropping. Julia suggested a fake identity for me so that, even if he demanded my name when he came for the money, I could pretend to be someone else and then he would not be able to trace me — all I had to do was find someone else called Joanna who worked as a teacher. I did know a teacher from a previous school, but did not want to even give him a clue as to my previous job or put someone else in danger, so we decided to just look at random school staff lists and then take a real name and fake address and feed him that.

We also decided that we would find out what type of favour Jonno wanted and stall for time before we even tried to give him the money. We wanted to get some hidden webcams around the flat, but neither Julia nor myself would be able to fit them. If Jonno was keeping tabs on our flat as he had threatened, there was no way we would be able to get someone in to fit them for us. Even going to a shop to ask for advice made us nervous in case we were followed, so we decided to research and order on Amazon Prime. If we could film our next encounter, the police would have to believe us.

"Julia, it will be at least a week before he comes back, I am sure. I have to be at work then. I won't be able to give him the slip every day. I have to go home. I can't leave you here, so you will have to come with me. We can give him the slip and get there."

"Easy for you to say. What about my clients? They come to the house. I can't just move out and arrange new premises. And what about my stuff?"

"But I have to go to work."

Secretly, I was delighted that I had a reason why I would have to escape, but I could not just leave Julia to deal with Jonno alone. I realised that I still cared for her and felt responsible for this mess. And anyway, if I did not take responsibility, she could just give my name to get rid of him and leave me on my own. And who could blame her? I assured her that I would stay until the day before school and then come back at the weekends until it was over. I also promised her I would either pay up or help with anything he asked us to do. Meanwhile, we would start looking for a new place for her and her clients, and I told her that my flat was big enough for her to stay and to see her clients in the short term. She could stay in the spare room and take over my study area during the day, but it was not ideal and would not look professional or reassuring to her clients. I knew it was my fault and felt shitty, but knew how lucky I was that my flat and job had not been compromised. I could see how taut her face had become and she had visibly paled, but she still had enough dignity and stiff upper lip to hold back the tears.

"I know it's not fair. Of course I do — but you know that if I don't keep my word you can give him my name, address and all my details. We are still in this together. I am trying. I really am — and I will do my best not to let you down."

"You always let people down, Jo. You mean well, but you just do. I can see you think you mean it, but really, whenever it comes down to making a choice — the only person you choose is you. I knew it from the first time we met. I have no idea how I managed to end up in this situation with a person who asked me out with the line: 'Can I buy you a drink because the clocks go back and we'll have an hour more tonight?'"

I couldn't resist a grin at my own clumsy cockiness. Julia smiled as well and we both got the giggles. A woman pushing her pram looked at us and then made sure to give us a wide berth — we looked like what we were: a pair of hastily dressed, half-hysterical women, desperately laughing at nothing to try to relieve the tension and feel a bit normal again.

"It was never your cheesy lines — it was your barefaced, unembarrassed cheek. You always try to be kind and never set out to hurt people, but you just manage to create chaos out of anything. It is infuriating. The life-coach in me is still certain that there is a kinder and more selfless person inside you, and I know that this isn't really your fault because how could you have known what would happen? But trouble just follows you, Jo. I'm sorry, but it just does. And other people get hurt."

I could not argue. She was right. Trouble did follow me. I had learnt to deal with it, but my friends and people I cared about had not. I was used to walking or running away and moving on, but Izzy and Julia were not my only casualties.

"I know. I think I am just unlucky, Julia. I am sorry."

"Jo, I don't blame you for this and I am saying this as a friend. It's not just bad luck. You take risks. You don't think. You... never... avoid... risks..."

Each word was spoken slowly. Not in an angry tone, but like a disappointed parent. I could feel my lip tremble and if we had not been in such a public place I would have cried. To realise my fear. For embarrassment. For Izzy.

"Julia, I am sorry. I promise I will get us out of this. I will be different. I even want to listen to your coaching. I promise, I won't even dismiss it as pretentious crap."

A smile, at last, from Julia.

"I want to be a better person. I don't want to be the kind of person who gets you into this crap and I don't want to be the kind of person who hurts someone so much they can't move on and they can't forgive me."

She studied me and then nodded. "Izzy?"

I nodded back.

"I often wondered if you were in love with her. I knew you were never serious about me, but I didn't think you were ready to be serious about anyone. You're a difficult person to love, Jo. I wonder whether you'll be able to try again with her."

And so, bizarrely, we passed an hour or so on the park bench, talking and forgetting about Jonno. In the end, it seemed perfectly natural to be talking to my ex-girlfriend about my first ex and all the other women in between and all the people I had let down and hurt, whilst hiding in a public place. It seemed irrelevant that I had, at least temporarily, driven her out of her home and place of business whilst attempting to seduce a man to get over her and another woman. She told me to try to see the good in myself.

"You know, Jo. In some ways I am glad — well, obviously not glad, but you know, glad — that this sorry situation will keep us in touch. I think you'll be a good friend. You don't have to be afraid of things that scare you like love and proper intimacy. And, basically, you are a good person and a good friend. You're just also an idiot and a bit of an arse."

"Thanks! So kind!"

I was insulted in a relaxed kind of way, but it was actually one of the most sincere, semi-compliments I had had in ages. We laughed, hugged and agreed to be friends. We remembered what we both liked about each other at the start and we had to be united to get out of this mess. Then Julia remembered that she had a client coming and we needed to get the flat tidied up. She asked me to stay, but in the bedroom with the newspaper where her client would not see me.

More Plans

As the next few days passed, the sense of danger began to diminish. There were moments when one or both of us would suddenly be imagining the sound of a door opening, or hear an unfamiliar creak, or think someone outside had already walked past a few too many times to be a coincidence. All things considered, we were remarkably calm. We were both afraid to do our usual things or meet other friends and drag them into our mess, but in the end, I had to phone Lexi. I did not want to meet her at Julia's, so I arranged to meet her in a bar round the corner. I told her to make sure she used public transport and she sounded bemused, but assumed that it was just a way of making sure she did not have to worry about driving home drunk. Julia asked if I wanted her to come and be back up if Lexi thought I sounded too crazy, but I told her that Lexi and I knew each other too well. I knew that Julia also wanted to come and be distracted, but she thought Lexi was too frivolous and Lexi found her boring. I promised that I would not be long and that she could call me back at any time if need be.

Living at Julia's was not nearly as bad as I had feared. Despite all the tension, in many ways we were getting on better than we ever had as lovers. And, as an unexpected bonus, it turned out she was pretty good at the whole life coaching. I was not explicitly her client, but we whiled away the time trying to sort out my personal life. She was a good listener, and now she no longer had a vested interest in my future, she was able to stop trying to change me and listened attentively. I had to admit that, as a friend, she offered some good advice. It was not encouraging advice, because she told me that she would not have me back if she was Izzy, but that I was right that my best chance would be to give her some space and then try befriending her friend Fay. She also suggested trying to make casual small talk to her in the staffroom and gradually build up longer conversations, making sure that I was doing more listening than talking and letting Izzy control the conversation. She did at least tell me that she believed that I was starting to grow up and thought that I was starting to be honest with myself and feel some genuine attraction and affection for Izzy. Her encouragement was barely lukewarm, but it was the one positive I could take from the last week, and it helped give me hope, which I could take to Lexi and will her to kindle.

I made sure I left early to meet Lexi — trying to scan to see if I was being followed and then grabbing a seat by the window to check if anyone was watching. I picked a seat where I would be visible from the window but Lexi would be able to sit so that she could only be seen from inside the pub. As I sipped my gin and tonic, I began to feel a little more like a glamorous secret agent and less like a mouse waiting for the house cat to toy with me. When Lexi arrived half an hour later, I had already ordered another round and included G+T for her. She threw her arms round me and immediately commented on the new location and what a dive it was.

"Don't think I don't know that this place is round the corner from Julia's — you're not back with Little Miss Prissy again, are you? I thought that you were delighted to have got rid with minimal fuss."

I tried to interject and explain, but as soon as my 'no' came out, she moved on.

"Great, darling — but then why the hell would you choose this dive? And we're sitting outside — I need a ciggie if we're drinking in a place like this."

As I steered here away from the tables at the front and to one in the corner of the beer garden, furthest away from eavesdropper, she was too distracted with her questions to protest.

"Surely it must be some girl — or are you back to men again? Do tell, but first, you won't believe the week I have had. Bloody editor and blah blah blah — too boring, but the one bright point, if you get my meaning, was Mr Duracell. So good I saw him twice, but now I know what the phrase 'shagged out' means. Are you okay, Jo?"

Normally, I would have laughed out loud and happily let her talk herself out, regaling me with her glamorous and crazy lifestyle, but I just needed my friend to listen. I told her I was definitely not okay and asked her to let me tell her what had happened in full before deciding I was mad or asking any questions. She told me that she would quickly order us another round of drinks to keep us going and then give me her undivided attention.

When I finished, she just sat there — I had never seen her lost for words before. She had already smoked three roll-ups whilst I talked, but when I finished, she took a last drag and exhale of smoke, then immediately started to roll the next one and only as she licked the paper together, did she speak.

"Well, fuck me doesn't quite cover it this time. I'm not going to ask if you are sure this all happened, because it sounds crazy, but I know you and I can see that this is no wind-up. To be honest, the only thing I really can't believe is how calm you are. That makes me wonder whether it is all a big wind-up. You definitely don't look like you are joking. Is this a joke?"

"Honestly, Lexi — it's not. Though it would have been a great one if it was. I promise."

"Okay. I'm going to believe. Next question. Are you sure that this is not Julia tricking you into her lair like a lethal attraction of basic shag-type thing?"

"Yes — I suspected that, too. But she hated Jonno from the moment she met him and it is just too far-fetched to believe he travelled over from Thailand to help her scam me."

"And you are sure the police won't help if you hassle them again? Or demand someone different?"

I assured her that it was not a joke and told her that PC Whetstone had made certain that we understood that we would get no help from the police.

"Useless pigs," Lexi said, and I nodded in agreement. "Blimey!"

She asked me what I wanted her to do and promised to do anything she could to help. I told her I did not know what help I needed, but, for now, I just needed to talk and know that she believed me and would try to help if she could. Then she started to look round and asked if I could tell if we were followed. I told her I did not think so, but advised her to swap cabs and take a weird route home. She said that she would be going back to the office later anyway and they had great security, so she would be able to ensure that no one would be able to identify which company

89

she worked for in such a large office block and she could just leave by a different entrance afterwards anyway. I was glad that she would be safe.

She held my hand and then we just chatted as normal. I told her about Julia and she claimed to be pleased that I was growing up, but I could see her nose crinkle in disapproval and was not sure if it was only because of Julia or also because she did not want me to get back with Izzy. I asked about Mr Duracell and her story did not disappoint. He sounded like the ultimate fantasy fusion of Mr Darcy's charisma with Brad Pitt looks and an eager and energetic desire to please. I hadn't had any sex since Pru, but I was not remotely jealous of Lexi's adventures and felt thoroughly repulsed now at the thought of sex with a man myself.

We could have chatted for hours, but Lexi had to get back to work and I felt bad at Julia being on her own. Lexi promised to keep tabs on me and to try to come up with a plan, and I felt better that someone else knew our story, in case anything happened to us. Lexi told me that she would expect a twice-daily text from now on or she would start to worry. Her parting words were, "Don't worry, darling. We'll think of something and we'll all be laughing about this the same time next week," she said, before mouthing, "In a pub chosen by me!"

I laughed obligingly, but was less convinced that we would be laughing together a week from now. I wondered whether I would ever laugh again.

Back to School

I moved back into my flat the night before school began. I went via Chelsea because we had found a Joanna on a list of school staff at an exceptionally expensive prep school there, so I thought that it would be good cover to go there if we later had to pretend that I was her. It was no hardship to spend a little time shopping there either, and I picked out some new clothes for school. My week with Julia had not helped my figure — we may not have eaten much, but I had done no exercise and my stomach was sagging over the otherwise very sexy trousers I tried on. I decided to buy them anyway and go home and do some sit-ups. No matter how angry Izzy might be with me, she would be sure to notice me in these.

I picked out a shirt to match and then took my time idly shopping. If a man was following me, he would surely be going crazy by now, and I made sure to linger on every floor of Peter Jones to check no one was behind me. There were too many exits for anyone to find me unless they were following closely. After a suitable diversion and laden with bags, I headed for the overground, getting off at Barnes instead of Putney and then walking through the woods. I could not stop myself turning round nervously, but there were too many dog walkers around for anyone to attack me, and I made sure I kept taking unusual paths to make it harder. By the time I had crossed the common and circled the roads around me long enough to start attracting weird looks from people who seemed to think I might be following them, I decided I was definitely safe. Besides, I doubted even an experienced gangster would be able to sneak past Doris unnoticed.

Sure enough, even though I tiptoed up the stairs with my key already out, the faintest sound of my key being inserted into the lock caused her door to open. She feigned shock and fear as she reproached me for my surprise arrival. I was also chided for not telling her I had gone away.

"I nearly called the police — I was worried you had died. You just got back from one holiday and then you go again. It would only be polite to let me know if suddenly you are just going to disappear for a week."

"I was just trying to be considerate, Doris. I know how loud you can find me when I am at home, so I thought it best to just move somewhere else until term started."

She was momentarily disconcerted as she tried to decide whether I was being rude. I had tried to pass it off in a light tone and with a friendly smile, so, although her smile was frosty, she seemed to conclude that it was yet more evidence of my general frivolousness and she gave me a sarcastic parting volley before I could retreat inside.

"Well, nice to know you are alive. Do try to be quiet when you leave for work. Please remember that I am retired and I only get up early if you wake me, and then I can't get back to sleep."

Once inside, I found myself feeling almost fond of Doris. She was every bit as alert as a trained guard dog and, perhaps, marginally more intimidating. She would certainly call the police if she noticed anyone suspicious, and nothing got past her. I considered telling her to be a look-out for me, but did not trust her. Anyway, the police would think she was even crazier than us if she called them with a story about Jonno. Even so, she would knock on my door if she suspected anything — she had before. And she had made the police come out a couple of times after she had badgered them about cold callers getting into the building. She was persistent and not to be fobbed off easily.

It felt amazing to be home and I could feel tension I did not even know I had lifted off my shoulders. I thought about trying Pru's number for some light relief, but I was too tired and not in the mood. I ran a bath and poured far more Jo Malone into it than I would normally allow myself and then sank into it with a large glass of wine. As a last thought, I grabbed the phone and called Julia whilst I gradually relaxed into the beautifully spiced, warm water. She was scared on her own but said she understood why I had to go. She had started seeing her clients again and knew she could not expect me to miss work or risk being followed every day. She said she did not expect me to call but appreciated it, and, back in life-coach mode, told me that it was a sign of my personal growth.

We chatted amicably and I almost found myself missing her. Tense as things were, it felt relaxing to lie back on the sofa together, reading or watching TV. I had never lived with anyone except as a flat share, and instead of my expected feelings of being claustrophobic and constantly being worried about annoying the other person, in the end I found staying with Julia to be very comfortable. For the first time in a long time, I found myself feeling lonely. I desperately wanted to call Izzy, but knew that she would either not answer or tell me off. Even if I told her about Julia and Jonno, I wondered whether she would think I was capable of making the whole thing up just to get her attention. In any case, I did not want to drag her into it. I nearly called Pru anyway, just to avoid being alone, but it was already nearly evening and by the time she arrived I would be far too tired to cope with her and then have to cope with what would inevitably be a day of my numbingly tedious INSET at school the next day when shagged out and exhausted. I picked up my phone and flipped idly through it. Debbie might be free for a chat, just to kill some time, and if she did want to meet, she would be much less work. I was tired and part of me just wanted to enjoy being back in my own bed, but there were a couple of hours until then and I just did not feel like being alone.

I had met Debbie when making up numbers for a cricket team as a favour for a girl I pulled at the Candy Bar. The night itself had been so-so and neither of us were going to pretend that we would call each other again. Then, whilst I was in the shower, she got a call from her cricket captain telling her they were short of players and she asked me if I would play. I had nothing else on and the game was on Clapham Common, so it would be easy to get home afterwards. I figured I might as well give it a go. It was fun and I ended up fielding at slip next to a slightly chubby and not particularly attractive girl called Debbie. She was shy, twenty-two, with mousey hair and was generally unremarkable apart from her startling blue eyes. Her whole appearance screamed lesbian even if she had not been in a ladies' cricket team — her faded Adidas trainers, scruffy whites, close-cropped messy hair and total absence of any make-up, moisturiser, deodorant, etc. She could not quite look at me and her embarrassment made it obvious that she was trying to flirt with me. Fifty overs take a long time and, shy as she was, she was very funny. She was not even particularly well-co-ordinated for a slip fielder (but neither was

93

I, and we were thrashed quite comprehensively, so I guess no one was particularly competitive), but she was a master sledger. At least a few of the wickets were caused by her making their player so distracted she slogged an edge to the keeper or was bowled having missed the ball completely. In the pub after the match, I overlooked the crassness of her clumsy attempt at snogging me under the pretence of slipping on a wet floor, and just asked her directly if she would like to come back to my place. Obviously, she said yes, and I decided the startled-fawn-caught-in-the-headlights-of-an-oncoming-truck look was one that actually seemed to work for her. In fact, it made me grab her hand and make her run for the bus. I was very eager to find out exactly what, if any, experience she had.

The answer turned out to be a long and virtually platonic relationship with a girl in her sixth form, who left her after a couple of nights when she went to university. Broken heart. Yada, yada, yada. Then a few drunken snogs on cricket nights and the occasional all-nighter. Her inexperience showed and she was far too self-conscious to be a good lover. But she was a grateful and appreciative one who forced herself to muffle her orgasms but who permitted herself to clamp her arms around me a bit like a hot, sweaty, satisfied limpet afterwards. Mediocre as the sex was, she made me laugh and was unpretentious and easy-going. I made it clear that I was not the type of lesbian whose idea of a second date was moving in together and whose third date was choosing a cat from the sanctuary. When I was clear that she was fine with that, I was happy to share many more evenings with her, without officially checking that she was fine with an open relationship.

Gradually, we drifted apart, but after bumping into her a few months later and spending another night together for old times' sake, we stumbled into a casual bed-buddy relationship and she would be fine with me calling her just for the night. It might even be good to talk through the whole Jonno business, but I didn't want word getting round and people starting to think I was some kind of drug dealer or druggie or fantasist. In the end, I decided that the TV remote could decide. I found a good film and watched that instead. I was becoming paranoid about most things and started to worry that if I had sex this evening, Izzy would somehow know or guess tomorrow. I wondered whether she would care if she did. Anyway, I was tired. I hoped I wasn't losing interest altogether, but, from what my married friends had told me, I supposed that losing my libido was also part and parcel of being in a proper adult relationship.

Tantalisingly Close

However much I might enjoy teaching, no one looks forward to the start of the Autumn term. It is fun for about twenty minutes chatting to everyone, but then two days of mind-numbing tedium only made bearable by the shared sense of disbelief and frustration at Senior Management's incompetence and lack of awareness and a freely-shared and open mockery of whatever 'new' policy had floated to the surface this year. Izzy and Fay were inseparable today and, though I made sure that I sat where I had a good view of them, I think at most I saw Izzy look my way once, and even then her glance showed nothing but reserve.

I had to keep my distance from her, but that also meant that I could not get started on my new plan to befriend Fay. It was even hard to join in on the endless 'how was your holiday?' chats. I tried reminding myself of all the adventures Julia and I had shared travelling in Asia, but all I could think about was the day at the cave with Jonno and everything that had followed. I composed myself, cleared my mind and managed to remember the good times, and by break I was able to chat happily with colleagues about Asia and their holidays. By lunchtime, it was starting to feel like a normal day. It felt great to be able to forget everything else and be normal again. Even though Izzy was not looking at me, I was enjoying looking at her.

She looked amazing. Even trying to keep a low profile and without her smile or sparkle in her eyes, she was still hot. It was a casual clothes day and she had figure-hugging jeans and had opted for a tight T-shirt with a Red Hot Chili Peppers slogan. I was sure that she did not even own one of their albums and had never been to a gig, but she looked red hot to me. It felt good to think that I had a little hand in influencing her to emphasise her best features. Being able to steal glances at the curve of her hips and watch her self-conscious head tilt as she whispered to Fay during the meeting, and imagining the nights when I got to touch her and nights in the future when I might do so again, made the endless powerpoints and speeches so much more enjoyable. Clearly, my libido had not died after all, and suddenly I could imagine how it would feel to be happily faithful to just one woman. Best of all, when we were given our final handout of the day, I discovered that my working party for the second INSET day would be in a group of ten including Izzy. There was no way she could avoid me, and that would be a great way to start my re-seduction.

I went home tired and with a splitting headache, cursing myself for never remembering a water-bottle on INSET days. I had scarcely given Julia a thought all day, but I found myself cooking a dish that she had taught me the previous week when we were bunkered in at her place. I could not face calling her, so I texted to ask if she was okay and to promise to call later, and she texted back saying all was well. I was beginning to hope that it was all just an empty threat or even that we had made the whole thing up or were the victims of an elaborate practical joke.

Time and distance had made me relax, but as I sat down to eat my supper on my own, I suddenly felt lonelier than I could remember. I have always liked my own company, even if it is nicer to eat with someone. I enjoy having my own place, so am happy with my music and my books and TV. I phoned Julia, but there was no answer. It was strange and I briefly worried that something had happened, but she had just texted to say she was fine and had probably popped out for some food or even gone out with a friend. In the end, just for someone to talk to, I nearly called my mum, but then I remembered that she would only want to know whether I was in a proper relationship yet — "I don't care if you date a man or woman, if you are going to call yourself a lesbian at least find one to settle down with." I can't remember when my phone book seemed to contain only the kind of friends I telephoned so rarely, that they had stopped phoning me and the numbers of women I may have only dated once or who I hooked up with whenever we were at a loose end.

The realisation that Lexi, Izzy and Julia were not just ex-girlfriends but probably also the best friends hit me like a bucket of ice tipped over my head. Especially when I considered that one of these friends did not actually want to talk to me ever again. I remembered being considered cool and popular a few years back and wondered what had happened to my friends. Some of us had just drifted apart with changes of job and/or addresses. Others who I had been really close to over the years had simply grown tired of not being called back or invited out. It barely seemed a year ago that I had considered myself too popular or busy to return calls. Now only Lexi and Julia ever called. It was a sobering thought and I was delighted when the phone rang and I saw Julia's number flash up.

"Jonno was here — he was here when you called."

All the happiness drained out of me and the tension flooded back in. I moved back to the table and sat down.

"Are you okay? Shall I come over? What did he want?"

She explained that she walked into the kitchen and found him sitting there. Deliberately staged so he was straight in front of the door, legs astride, with one arm lounging casually on the table and the other taking biscuits from her jar. He told her to make them both a cup of tea while they talked. She was so shaken that she mutely obeyed, cursing herself for allowing him to take control so effortlessly in her home. He commented on my absence, but claimed to know exactly where I was. Even in my state of panic I thought this must still be a bluff, and Julia was kind enough to reassure me, saying that she also thought so. She also told me that I should not visit. She wished I could and she wanted me to comfort her, but she did not want me to come back unless Jonno made me, because it was crucial that my address stayed unknown. She also said that she was going to do a thorough house clean and check for listening devices; but, for now, as a precaution, she had left the flat and gone to sit on a bench where no one could eavesdrop.

He had asked about whether we had got the money together, and Julia said that by then she had started to gain some presence of mind and had stalled him. She told him that we had discussed it and wanted some guarantees that he would not be back, what his final price would be, instalments and exactly what sort of favours he had in mind instead of cash. She said that his response was a smug grin and to ask her why she felt she was in a position to negotiate with him. He said that he would settle for £15,000 if it came no later than next week, or even very close to that if we could prove that was all we had. If we took that option, he gave his word as a gentleman that we would never hear from him again. Neither Julia nor I found any comfort in that.

Then he said that the longer the arrangement, the more risk he was taking, so the more it would cost us. We could pay in a few quick instalments, but then it would be at least £20,000. If we chose to do him some favours, we could settle our debts in a mixture of cash and jobs and he would pay us far more than the going rate of £1000 a job to clear the £20,000.

"No questions, just deliver a few packages — I am sure that you get my meaning. I'm offering a lot more than the going rate, but you could deliver parcels other couriers couldn't because you don't look my usual employees. Not to mention, once you delivered the first package, I doubt I would have to worry about either of you involving the police."

Julia said that despite never having had a violent impulse before, not even to kill a spider, she had to force her arms still to suppress the urge to slap the sneer off his face. I had not had to deal with all of his visits and stalking, but I wished that he was locked up in Laos, possibly even being beaten or ill-treated by the guards. Maybe I even wished him dead. People like him always seem to get away with things, and people like us get caught the first time anything happens.

We went over the options and we seriously considered just scraping £15,000 together by means of a bank loan, but we both agreed that if we rolled over that easily he would only come back again. Julia said that she would give her landlord notice that she was ending her lease and, if need be, just pay him the last three months' rent and move straight out as soon as she could find a place and inform her clients. I felt it was the least I could do to offer my flat and promised to keep it tidy and professional-looking until she could find somewhere else. She was not sure if her clients would travel, but I only lived about twenty or thirty minutes away and was near a station. I pointed out that Julia would be just far enough to prevent Jonno finding her again without causing any major disruptions to her clients, who came from all over South London.

If we paid Jonno or did jobs for him, we doubted there would ever be an end to things. But if we pretended to co-operate and took delivery of a parcel and then went to the police, they would have to believe us. But Jonno might test us out first and neither of us even knew the difference between real drugs and fake ones, so he could make the first job a test and then we might call the police and look even more stupid. Anyway, if we waited to go to the police until after we had taken some drugs from him, we could be found guilty of possession or supplying or something. Julia said that the police would not prosecute small fry like us if we were willing to help them get Jonno, even if they did not believe that we were forced into it. I was less sure.

"They were rubbish and hostile from the start, Julia. They might even turn it round on us and claim that our 999 call about Jonno, was just a front. After the way they acted, I really wouldn't be surprised if he was either paying them already or would be able to pay them off. And I am a teacher, for God's sake. If I even got a caution for drugs, that would be the end of my career. I could not disclose something like that and then sit in a job interview trying to explain why I was delivering drugs to people. It would be less ruinous to just keep giving him part of my pay cheque for ever."

So, after considering all the options, we decided that Julia had to move out. I felt shitty. She loved her flat and had lived there a long time, but it was only rented.

"At least you'll be saving money at mine and can stay as long as you like until we find you something better."

I was trying to console myself as much as her. And we could only hope that although he definitely had her name and details and a few details about me, he would not be able to find my flat, too. We had no plan for how Julia was going to move her clothes and luggage, but the main thing was for her to get away with any paperwork, photos, etc, that could flesh out details about her as soon as possible, and then the rest could follow. Her phone was nearly out of charge at this point. I offered to meet her somewhere, but she reluctantly declined and reminded me that it was even more important than ever before that I was not followed.

We decided that she could call her clients from my place and make quick plans tomorrow but get out of there as fast as she could. She was probably most likely to be followed tonight, so the plan was for her to meet her morning clients as normal the next day and then leave at lunchtime, when it would look like a normal lunch date. She had a client whose boyfriend ran a man-and-van company and she would call her and pretend that her landlord had suddenly decided to put her rent up massively just as she was renewing her lease and she had been forced to move or sign for another year at a ridiculous rent. She would flesh out the story by claiming his sister had just come back from Australia or something and needed a flat for her.

I hid the key under the bin in the cupboard beside my door, then spent the last bit of the evening and most of the night lying awake going over all the details of the plan. Anything could go wrong, but at least there was a chance that it might actually work, rather than simply hoping that Jonno would go away.

Plans of Action

It was not even the proper start of term; it was only the second INSET day and I was exhausted. We were busy learning about how to write lesson plans for inspection. I listened politely and pretended to share the communal sense of dread at the impending inspection, whilst inwardly feeling that the inspection was merely further confirmation that the universe hated me. Meanwhile, the only plan I had chosen for myself — to win back Izzy — seemed to be starting so poorly that it did not bode well for my ability to plan for getting rid of random drug dealers and salvage my career.

I had barely slept and was tired before I even got to work. As I waited in line, feigning interest in the usual queue conversations, I realised I was standing next to the noticeboard with the groups posted on it. My group stood out because someone had written on it, and I realised that Izzy had been crossed off my group and swapped with Fay. I was so fazed by this, I even considered going to the Deputy Head and telling on her. I wondered how serious he would take a suggestion to implement an immediate and retrograde 'no swapsies' policy. I decided that it would be wiser to just accept it and to start drinking tea instead of coffee until I calmed down. I was clearly hyped-up enough without extra caffeine, even though all the INSET drinks were cold, caramelly, insipid affairs, with the coffee mildly more drinkable than the tea, which tasted suspiciously like it was just hot water washing off an old coffee urn. In fact, as I slowly sipped my tea, I reminded myself that in some ways it was probably a good thing that Izzy had swapped groups, because I was definitely puffy-eyed and probably a bit crazed-looking and was not emitting any suave, alluring bees-to-the-honey pheromones at the moment. Besides, there could be any number of reasons why Izzy and Fay had swapped groups, and it may not have had anything to do with me.

Once we separated into groups, I only needed to glance in Fay's direction to be irrefutably convinced that the swap *was* all about me. Fay's icy stare and unabashed hostility was not what I needed today. Looking round, the other staff seemed oblivious to Fay's attempts to stare me out, so I ruled out a last-minute attempt of my own to swap groups and sat next to Ben, another English teacher, to try to get through the session as painlessly as possible. I started work on piercing Fay's armour by playing on her earnestness and minimising my reflex sarcasm and cynicism. I even tried to make some helpful comments, adhering to the strict PC jargon of the careerist teachers and talking about my preferred style of lesson planning for 'growth mindset' and developing 'resilience' and 'mindful teaching styles'. Ben kept looking at me expectantly, waiting for the snide punchline, and I humoured him and myself by discreetly whispering ones to him whenever I was sure that Fay was not looking.

However, at every break between meetings and even a couple of times during the sessions, I went to the loo just to have a quiet place to check my messages. By lunchtime, Julia was out of the flat with most of her documents and some tightly-squashed changes of clothes. She had liaised with her client's boyfriend and several movers to put her stuff into storage and to turn up with the van very shortly after she left the flat. A couple of hours later, she texted to say that she was safely in my flat and was sure that her route was sufficiently complex and that she had been vigilant enough to be sure that she had not been followed.

So far so good. And what was more, during the last session I ended up being paired with Fay. She had stopped giving me the stare and had even agreed with some of the comments I had made. Of course, I thought my suggestions were nonsense, but I knew Fay and was delighted that my plan was working. No one in SLT ever implemented anything from an INSET day anyway, so there was no harm in appearing keen. But I had never understood why Izzy liked her. Nevertheless, getting Fay on-side would be a major step in getting Izzy to give me a second chance. I congratulated myself on a minor acting masterclass and for avoiding outright sycophancy, whilst still implying that Fay's ideas about education were innovative and thrillingly original, and I even experimented with some subtle mimicking of her body language and gestures to get her on-side. By the end of the day my plan was up and running and I had impressed her so much that as I was leaving, she said, "Goodbye, Jo. I enjoyed being in a group with you today."

All that would be needed now to make a perfect day was to go home, have a nice supper and chat with Julia and not, at any point of the evening, find Jonno either inside my flat or outside my front door. What could go wrong?

My New Roomie

I practically tiptoed up the stairs to my flat and even considered taking my shoes off, but then I knew I would have to justify being barefoot to Doris when she inevitably heard me anyway. She was waiting by her door as I climbed the last stair and came round the corner. This was impressive even by her standards, and I wondered whether she spent her days sitting by the wall by the staircase with listening devices.

"Somebody is in your flat — that woman who used to come round but hasn't been for a while. She was rooting through your rubbish cupboard and found the key — I watched her through the spy hole. You shouldn't leave keys in there. It would be the first place a burglar would look, and it is just not hygienic. You and your lady friend could catch anything."

"Thank you, Doris. I only left it there for her this morning because I was expecting her."

"Well — you could have asked me to keep it. I have offered several times. That is what neighbours are for. And if you left your number, like I suggested, I could ring you if I saw anything suspicious. I have been worried all afternoon and even thought about ringing the police. You are very lucky I recognised her."

I apologised for being so inconsiderate again and decided not to mention the fact that she did not leave her key with me. Nor my suspicions that she would let herself in and rifle through my possessions whilst I was at work. It was easier to just apologise, and I promised to give her my number at some point, but pretended I was just about to change phones, so would change my number. If I gave her the number, I suspected I would be called at least weekly. However, with all this business with Jonno, I thought it might be worth a bit of hassle just to have an extra pair of eyes. Knowing Doris, she would probably call me and worry us continually up until the day he actually turned up and did something, and that would be the only time she slept through undisturbed.

I escaped into my flat and found that I was delighted to see Julia, and she looked much happier and relaxed than she had been. She had put a couple of crystals on the hallway table, which I knew she did to create positive energy and in the belief that it would protect us. I resisted the urge to point out that the crystals had clearly not worked in her house. She smiled apologetically and asked if I minded. I found that I did not and meant that even more sincerely when I discovered a few groceries in my kitchen and soup simmering next to a hearty rustic and seeded organic loaf of bread. Frankly, if Julia was going to be making supper and shopping, she could stay as long as she liked and create whatever Chi or Zen space she wanted.

It felt grown up and comfortable to have supper at home without any pressure or expectations. Julia was confident that she had not been followed and she said that the removal men were asked by 'some bloke' who claimed he knew her where she was moving and if he could pop inside to check if she had left something he had lent to her. They told him that they could not tell him her address or give him her mobile number. When they called to tell her, she gave them a cover story that she had made up on the spot, but it worked perfectly. She pretended that she had had a weird friend who could not accept that she was a lesbian and was convinced that he could turn her. She told them that she found him quite creepy and he was part of the reason why she was moving, and she definitely did not want him to get her address. When she said that she thought he was a bit of a stalker type and they should check he wasn't following them, they became all macho and protective and offered to 'give him a slap or so just to knock some sense into him'. Julia was almost tempted to say yes to this, but thought that if Jonno was as dangerous as we feared, it was best not to make him any angrier than he would be already. Just in case he found us.

Julia told them it was fine, just not to let him find out where she was. It was a perfect cover story and we decided that we would use that story again if we needed to, and then we could give a description of Jonno. It might even be worth giving Doris that description if she just thought he was an unrequited lover. Even if Jonno decided to follow the van, the furniture was all going into storage and they would not get it out until they were sure it was safe. Julia had managed to squash a few outfits into her bag and I could lend her some clothes, too.

After she had brought me up to speed on her day, she asked about my day and how things were with Izzy. She was already starting to feel like a valued friend, and having always guarded my space and privacy before, I found myself enjoying having a flatmate. Our adventures had made us feel much closer, and the mutual relief of ending the sexual part of our relationship gave us a much gentler intimacy. I felt more at ease with Julia than almost anyone. Even with Izzy at its best, we were never this comfortable. Our friendship was always unbalanced, with Izzy fancying me at the start and then being more in love and with me being more in lust. Julia and I both needed the same thing — mutual support to deal with the situation and to protect each other. We had also stopped annoying and being annoyed by each other and become comfortable with each other's foibles. For someone who was only just beginning to entertain the possibility of being in an actual grown-up commitment-type relationship, I seemed to have quietly slipped into the perfect platonic marriage at the same time.

I was almost disappointed that Julia had already made up the spare bed and put her things there, and she asked if I would rather she read in her room, so I could go to bed early before school or do some work. Normally, I would be up late planning lessons the night before term started, but instead I suggested we watch a DVD and she was clearly happy to do this. I steered clear of the racier films in my collection and we settled for a *Bridget Jones* — lowbrow and relaxing — and we snuggled up together on the same sofa, leaning against one another to share the popcorn, without any tension or awkwardness. If we really had seen the last of him, I felt strangely grateful for how the situation seemed to be reaping some unexpected benefits.

When the film was over, we both got up together and cleared our plates and bowls. My room had an en suite and we had a brief moment of awkwardness as we said goodnight. Julia broke it by giving me a chaste kiss on the lips and an almost sisterly hand placed on my back at the same time. In some ways it was the most romantic or tender gesture I had experienced up until that moment.

Lessons in Love

Julia had already had breakfast and started preparing for the day when I got up. She was putting the final touches to my study, which we had agreed she could use as her consultation room during the day. She asked whether I minded her decluttering a little and perhaps swapping some of my pictures to create a 'more positive space'. I did mind, but knew it would be churlish to say so, particularly given everything she had had to give up. I forced myself to balance the pros and the cons and realised that I would miss her when she did move out, but I was hoping to replace her with Izzy.

I wondered whether, assuming I could win her back, Izzy would want to move in with me or whether she would expect me to move into her flat instead. Izzy gave the appearance of being easy going, but she liked everything just the way she had put it. I could imagine that even if we ever got to the stage of wanting to move in together, it would put yet another strain on the relationship as we negotiated over territory and belongings. Having said that, when Julia and I were dating I had found her high-maintenance and uncompromising. I had been attracted by her surface calm and seduced by her poise and confidence, all contained in the graceful femininity of a mature lady used to being admired and able to manipulate both genders through a combination of intelligence, charm and gentle flirtation. However, as a lover she quickly took control, and whilst her dominant and controlling love-making was both arousing and addictive, I was not the kind of person who always liked to let the other person set the pace or agenda. When I had tried to talk to her about it, the woman who earned her living through discussion just dismissed my criticism with a glib "femme on the streets, butch in the sheets, honey".

However, now we were not together, I saw all her good qualities again. It was definitely a combination of her being less controlling and me being less resistant and spiky, but I was not sure how much of which. Either way, she had become much more of the confident, relaxed and gentle person I first admired. I found myself wondering what it would be like to try again on more equal terms. I also wondered how Izzy's personality or behaviour to me was shaped by her being the one who wanted me more and whether she would become more or less controlling if she felt more secure.

Would I feel the need to run away again if our relationship ever became serious? Was I capable of fidelity? And for how long? I had rejected several chances to have sex since deciding to try again with Izzy, but I was not sure if I was old enough to have the kind of libido that would enable me to stay constant. Fortunately, Izzy had a high sex drive, too, and I was certain after last time that she would not be willing to consider an open relationship.

"Don't you have school this morning? Is it a late start or something?"

Julia's words shocked me into life. I looked at my watch and realised that after choosing a movie over last-minute lesson planning last night, I should have left at least ten minutes ago. I had showered and dressed, but was just standing in the kitchen as the Nespresso switched itself off for the third time without me actually pressing the button for my coffee. I grabbed my iPad and bag and was grateful to Julia for handing me some peanut butter toast to eat on the way out.

I had a few free periods that day to cram some last-minute work into, but it was still fairly frantic, though I still managed to notice Izzy suddenly walking another way or going into a classroom to talk to a student or teacher whenever she would otherwise have had to walk past me. More encouragingly, Fay greeted me pleasantly enough and we even had a couple of brief chats about our day at the inevitable queue for the photocopiers as, one by one, they all jammed and broke during the day. The best part of the day was just before lunch when we had a year assembly — never normally anything to be excited about, but I did discover that I was in the same year team as Izzy. From the look on her face, it seemed that she had also only just realised and was rather less excited than me. There were not many year team meetings, but there would only be seven of us in the meeting and she would have no choice but to speak to me. I thought it was finally a positive step my way, but then I saw her talking to the Head of Year after assembly and presumed she was trying to swap out again. I hoped that he would not let her because the students would already know who their tutor would be. A few surreptitious glances as I left the hall as slowly as possible made it clear that he was not reacting well to whatever she was saying.

I did not want her to get into trouble, both because I cared about her and because she would blame me and that would make things even harder. I went to the dining hall and got my lunch and then made a beeline for Fay, who hesitated and looked around when I tried to sit next to her. I could tell that she felt compromised and was trying to see if Izzy was around, so I quickly said that I needed to say something to her. She started to point out that she was not going to get caught in the middle and was Izzy's friend, but I told her what had happened and told her to tell Izzy that I promise to try and make things as easy as I could for her. I asked her to tell her that, much as I felt I had changed or was changing and could earn a second chance, I owed it to Izzy to respect her wishes and I would not take advantage of the situation unless she changed her mind.

Fay was blunt:

"She is not going to change her mind, you can bet your last penny on that!"

However, she could not hide the definite softening of her facial expressions and I could tell that I had made some progress. I caught sight of Izzy and, to show how sincere I was, I immediately offered to move. Obviously, I was committed to taking advantage of the situation and determined to win her back, but by making such a show of resignation and acceptance, I was gently befriending one of my biggest obstacles. I was still not sure if it was love that I was feeling, but it was certainly elation.

I moved to sit with the rest of my department and we had an enjoyable lunch. I felt more relaxed and happier than I could remember. Given the last month, I found that feeling this at peace was genuinely unsettling and I began to get an ominous sense of doom. I excused myself for a pre-lesson loo break and checked in with Julia by text. Even though we had assumed that she was safe at mine, I felt genuine relief when she texted back that everything was fine and asked whether I wanted tofu and noodles. I thought it went without saying that there were many meals I would prefer to tofu and noodles, but none of these meals were going to cook themselves, so I texted back my thanks and wondered whether I needed to pick up some flowers for my new housewife on my way home. I suspected Julia would consider me bringing her flowers patronising, and they would probably end up thrust back at me, so I did a detour via Patisserie Valerie instead because I felt we both deserved something special.

Good Times

The next few weeks hurtled past and became months. Life seemed constantly busy but free of danger and intrigue, and there was no sign of Jonno. Things with Izzy seemed to be finally moving on a constant positive trajectory, albeit an achingly slow one. Izzy had accepted that she had to be in my year team. She and Fay had conferred after lunch and Izzy sent Fay to speak to me as her emissary to ask me to honour my promise to leave her alone. Fay also gave me a condescending pat on the back for 'demonstrating my willingness to be considerate and respectful'. I accepted the pat, held my tongue as a thousand sarcastic answers scrambled through my head, and smiled in a manner I thought looked both grateful and friendly.

"You can count on me, Fay. Of course we can be civil to each other. I'd love to be friends, but I won't press anything. But it will look bad if we can't at least act pleasantly to each other. It would hurt Izzy's career."

"Yes, of course. She has every right to be angry with you, but I'll speak to her."

Progress again. If Izzy had to pretend to be fine with me in team meetings, she would get used to it and we would be speaking again in no time. And Fay was agreeing with me. For the first time in my professional life, I was wishing we had more pastoral meetings to discuss who was not doing their homework and whose skirt never came below her knee or whose tie was only two inches long. As the days passed, Izzy continued to avoid me, but only if it was easy to, and Fay and I would at least nod or say hello to each other and even smile or make small talk.

Living with Julia was so much better than I could possibly have envisioned. Her clients came and went during the day, which, inevitably, disturbed Doris. I was too used to Doris's moaning to view that as a major risk, but I had assumed it would be another job to do — but Julia seemed to have mystical powers over Doris. Doris had come round to complain whilst I was at work the first day and Julia had charmed her and then distracted her so she suddenly paused mid-sentence as though trying to remember what she was doing. On the second day, Julia and I had laughed about Doris knocking on the door to complain, only to be answered by Julia standing at the door with a plate of freshly baked biscuits by way of an apology. Julia had brushed aside her attempts at resistance and somehow ushered in an era of peace on the landing. I used to be irritated by Julia's ability to steer a conversation away from whatever I was trying to discuss and then use it to manipulate me to question myself; but now I found myself eavesdropping on her exchanges with Doris from the hallway, marvelling at her effortless conversation deflectors and ability to win people round.

Evening meals were healthy, civilised and either tasty or absolutely delicious. I offered to cook, but Julia declined. She had offered to pay rent, but I felt too guilty for making her homeless, so she did the shopping and paid the bills instead. She was happy and we both knew that she was the better cook. Ironically, if we had still been dating, I was sure she would not have agreed to any such relationship because she would have felt demeaned by any suggestion that she was playing the part of the stay-at-home wife. As friends, however, she was happy to use her more flexible hours to pitch in, and she knew that she had both my respect and gratitude. I even managed to get used to the sight of her going in or out of the bathroom with just a towel wrapped round her or standing in the kitchen in a bra and pants, and I managed to give barely a glance at her breasts and curves. Occasionally, I felt a stirring, but I found myself gradually becoming asexual. Well, aside from the odd dalliances on a night out.

Georgie had been the most recent and although she had been fun, waking up in her flat the next morning had almost made me consider going back to men. I had met her on a Friday night post-work piss-up. She was a friend of Gabby, a PE teacher at my school, and she taught games at a school in North London. She was fanatical about playing and watching sport, but as I danced with her in the club, I did not care and barely heard whatever game she was talking about because I was too busy trying to brush against her delicious curved bottom and toned breasts. She was solidly built and with borderline gingerness, manifesting itself primarily through an exceptionally freckled face and arms.

Throughout the evening I could sense some of my colleagues staring at us as we danced increasingly intimately. Some of the men were almost leering and clearly enjoying the view and some of the women were clearly getting in touch with their inner homophobe. Gabby was alternating between pride at her match-making and jealousy because I was hogging her friend. As soon as I was sure that Georgie was as aroused as I was, I suggested that we make our excuses and go back to my place. She said that she had a dog and asked if we could go back to hers and I happily agreed — it would save having to deal with Julia, and I loved dogs. We resisted the urge to make out in the cab — the driver looked seedy enough without us putting on a girlie show, and I used the time to text Julia to let her know that I would not be home.

When we got to the flat, Georgie was lavishly greeted by an ancient border terrier called Mutley, who stalked stiffly around me but deigned to accept some fuss. He clearly did not want to be a third wheel and was keen to impress upon me that he was willing and able to put me in my place if I tried anything with his owner. Dogs always liked me, but clearly Mutley was the exception. When I felt safe enough to take my eyes off him, a quick glance around the flat revealed Georgie to be seriously lacking in even rudimentary housekeeping skills and probably any basic hygiene. Given my new mature domestic arrangements, I nearly turned and ran, but Georgie herself was still curvy and sportily toned to perfection and, given that we had barely been off the dancefloor for two hours in an increasingly packed club, she was as clean and fresh as could be expected. I suggested we turned the lights off and head straight for the bedroom; I figured that if I could not see the bedroom, I would be less put off by it. It was dark enough to barely make out where the bed was and I enjoyed having to feel my way around.

She was every bit as athletic as I had hoped and was tireless in bed. She wore me out. Though, in my defence, at one point I had to muffle a girlie yelp of surprise when I raised my head out from between her legs and out of the duvet for air, only to be confronted by Mutley's brown whiskers, semi-snarl and highly off-putting dog breath. Georgie felt my surprise and simply asked whether I minded, because he always slept on the bed and had been alone all night. Clearly, if I objected, it would kill the mood, so I moved to the other side of the bed and pushed her downwards to show her appreciation for my tolerance.

I woke up early, sneezing, and went to the bathroom to blow my nose and clean myself up a bit, glad that I had kept my disposable toothbrushes in my handbag for emergencies. Georgie was older than me, but I had not been in a bathroom this uncared-for since my days in a student house-share. The mirror had probably never been wiped and I was, frankly, apprehensive even to run a piece of toilet paper over it to see my face in case I caught something. Her toothbrush had more residual toothpaste on it than bristles and the sink was stained with stripey toothpaste and various unidentifiable residues. Even in my most bachelorette days, I had never lived like this, and it was strangely satisfying to feel like the grown-up person in the one-night stand. But when I returned to the bedroom, I looked around, feeling stomach-churningly uncomfortable at the state of what I had slept in. The bed looked like it had not been washed for weeks and there were actual tufts of dog hair around the room and on the bed. Worse still, there was a suspicious-looking white stain on the bed which I worried suggested either that Georgie batted for both teams or that Mutley had enjoyed his ringside seat more than natural. Either way, I suddenly had no desire for any early-morning nooky and dressed and made my excuses as politely but as quickly as I could, grateful for her evident desire to get back to sleep as soon as possible.

It had been fun for a night, but I was now worried a report of my behaviour would get back to Gabby and then to the whole staffroom. I cursed my stupidity and though I found myself again longing to be with Izzy, whose flat was always immaculate and who did laundry even when bedding a woman for the first time, I reminded myself that if she did not want me, I was free to sleep with whomever I chose. I rushed back to my flat, my shower and Julia. I knew Julia would ask about my night and with a gentle probing that generally made me feel bad about things. She kept telling me that I had to actually change to get Izzy back, not just pretend that I had, and that having the odd night of casual sex was no different in her mind to an alcoholic having one last drink. Certainly, my fling with Georgie was helping to convince me that, maybe, I was ready to only sleep with one woman for the rest of my life. Even, possibly, if that turned out to be the next seventy years or more.

Relationship Advice

Julia was alone in the flat, looking calm and elegant, with her hair tied back in a loose swirling bun and wearing sleeveless white cotton pyjamas with blue flowers on them that looked so crisp and clean I could scarcely believe she had slept in them. The contrast was enormous and when she offered to make pancakes for us, I could have hugged her.

"Oh, Julia, thanks so much. I'll just shower and change and join you. I've got the papers. Your *Guardian*, too — I assumed you wouldn't have been out yet."

Her eyebrow went even higher, but she looked amused.

"Thanks — yes. I have not been out, this morning or all night. I suspected you might want to shower first."

Feeling a bit like a teenager caught sneaking in through a bedroom window by her parents, I endeavoured to retain some dignity whilst scuttling off to the shower. I decided to put my pyjamas on, too. We had grown used to spending Sundays reading the papers together and I had invested in some grown-up pyjamas and started ironing them, too. I put on my stripey pair and found the table already set out with pancakes, chopped fruit, Nutella and a fresh cafetiere of coffee. Julia was already flicking through the *Guardian* and, still feeling slightly guilty and embarrassed, I spoke first.

"Wow — fab. Thanks. Anything interesting? I saw the lifestyle section when I picked it up."

"Yes, thanks for getting it for me. How was your evening?"

She only glanced at me, pretending to be reading, but I knew she was curious. I kept it brief and, whilst not lying to Julia, I tried to suggest that Georgie had flirted first.

"And the dog hair — everywhere! Really, I am getting too old for such things."

"Yes, Jo, you are."

I was not expecting the clear criticism in her tone. She had put down the paper and did not look jealous, but she looked exasperated.

"Honestly, Jo, for someone supposed to be intelligent, you can be incredibly stupid. Do you want Izzy back or not? Do you ever want to settle down and date and have a normal relationship?"

"Hey, now, hold on a minute. You're not my mum. And Izzy is not my girlfriend. For all I know, she could have spent last night with someone."

As I spoke, I realised that what I said could actually be true, and that was worse than Julia's criticism. Julia saw it, too, and her stern look softened and she spoke more gently.

"I know I'm not your mum, Jo. But we are friends and I have listened to you mope after her and counselled you as a friend. You pulled a woman you had never met for a one-night stand in front of all your colleagues. Of course it will get back to her, and you can argue all you want about being free to sleep with whoever and however many women you want, but do you think it helps your career doing it in front of the people you work with so often?"

Julia was never going to call me a 'slapper' or something like that, but I knew it was something of a joke amongst my friends. Probably there were other colleagues who did not find it funny. And it was true that I rarely got asked about my career plans and aspirations in the same way colleagues my age tended to be, and I knew that I was good at my job and was liked by my students.

"Okay. I know. Maybe I should stop doing the Friday thing. But what — am I supposed to be celibate?"

"Seriously, Izzy — it's been a few months. It's hardly celibate. I'm not your mum and I'm not telling you how to live your life. But if you are still serious about winning her back, this kind of thing is what will ensure you never do. And if you are going to move on, you could try actually dating someone else."

"Yeah, well — do you really think Izzy is just sitting around pining for me?"

"I hope not, for her sake. From what you say, she has spent long enough. But are you really trying to claim you think she was having a one-night stand last night? In her case, it would be justified. Look, Jo —

I don't want to fight with you. I care about you. It's just frustrating to see you always taking one step forward and two steps back. If this is how you want to live, fine. But you don't look happy to me."

I tried to argue with her, but there were no words. Izzy was far more closeted than me, and I think Fay was the only other teacher who even knew she was a lesbian. It was possible that other staff had guessed when we were together and I had never heard the gossip, but Izzy kept herself to herself and the only gossip about her was when she had been off school and then after our break-up. My friends joked about my drinking and my sex life, but I had definitely seen disapproving looks in the staffroom from other staff when we were talking loudly about drunken nights. I suddenly saw myself as a bit of an old letch and possibly a figure of fun. I dreaded the idea of last night becoming a bit of staffroom gossip that got back to her embellished and made even more sordid than it already was. Julia seemed to read my mind.

"Come on — eat your pancakes. It's done. I have no right to judge you. Izzy probably won't find out. I just, you know, want you to think about these kinds of things before you just run after the next one. Friends?"

I sighed and leaned forwards and put my hand on hers.

"Yes. Friends. Thanks for caring enough to say it. I'm trying. And this breakfast is too good to spoil."

We went back to reading the papers and easily slipped back into our usual routine.

On Monday, at work, I played it cool, but made a point of being extra nice to Gabby, who made only a brief joke about us leaving together, and when I did not take the bait and tell her anything, she was quick to move on. By the end of the week, I was sure that I had avoided any gossip and, what was more, when the only seat left at lunch was next to me, Izzy took it rather than foregoing lunch. We managed to have a pleasant conversation, initially about students and work and then about the news and even about each other. I desperately wanted to ask her out for a drink or suggest a bike ride, but restrained myself and simply told her how glad I was that we were starting to get on again and that I missed talking to her. She looked down and reddened slightly, but she also looked as though she was starting to waver. I had a brief moment of hope before she gathered her almost-finished plate, gulped down her water before putting it back on her tray, and then turned to me.

"It was never about not liking you, Jo. It's about not trusting you. The pain that you cause. Maybe things would be different now and I can see that you are changing. I guess I knew you were not ready for a relationship when we dated. Perhaps you are now. The past will always be there now."

She spoke gently and her voice showed that she felt almost as much regret as I did. She stood up slowly, so as to avoid a scene, and I pretended not to watch her leave and then left a moment later.

She was keeping the door firmly closed to me, but it was obvious that she still felt something for me. I was a long way away, but confident I could regain her trust somehow. Clearly, nothing I had done had stopped her caring and perhaps even loving me — she was just afraid. And I had hurt her and given her a reason to hate me. Still she did not. I felt encouraged, and so was Julia when I told her about it that evening. She reminded me how lucky I was that Izzy had not found out about Georgie and told me that it was now crucial that I stopped shagging around and started actually paying some attention to other people and make much more effort to consider their feelings. If I started actually caring about other people, it would help with Izzy and with life generally. Harsh, but I had to concede that she had a point.

Julia also had news. Her relationship with Natalie was going so well that Julia was beginning to think she had finally found someone to spend the rest of her life with. Natalie was an artist who Julia had started seeing very casually, shortly before Jonno had re-appeared in our lives. One of her friends had first advised her to move on from me and then had ambushed her in what proved to be an obvious matchmaking attempt. She had been invited to the pub by a mutual friend and both she and Natalie had been surprised as they quickly realised the obvious set-up when their friend had made excuses and left early. Despite their shared annoyance at being misled, they had hit it off and spent an enjoyable evening together, laughing and spinning a plan about pretending they had spent the night together just to get their own back. They had quickly realised that they genuinely liked each other and their friend's plan had been both well-judged and well-intentioned. Ironically, for a life coach,

Julia hated other people trying to organise her own life, so although she resisted the urge to take things further, she genuinely liked Natalie and was not going to let her pride stand in the way of such an easy and relaxed friendship and potential relationship.

The date had gone well and led to another, and they had started to date exclusively even whilst at the early stages and they were still at the hand-holding and stolen kisses stage, rather than the throw-clothing-in-a-heap-and-jump-into-bed-together stage. Some grown-up relationships were clearly beyond me. I realised that there was no point suggesting a try-before-you-buy approach to long-term relationships. I was pleased to realise that I only felt happiness for her. We were too different for our relationship to work, but I was glad that we had built a friendship instead. I felt a mild twinge of jealousy, but only because she was having what I wanted with Izzy. Seeing Julia so obviously happy took away my guilt about our relationship and about the mess I had brought into our lives via Jonno. It had been almost two months since Julia moved in with me and there had been no sign of him. Julia's exile and our shared living had been good for both of us. I wondered whether Julia was going to start looking for a place of her own again, but I was enjoying her company and quietly pleased to note that she spent less time perusing the flats to rent ads every day. Half-term had been and gone and left me feeling so rested, I was happy to go back to school afterwards, not least because I would be seeing Izzy every day.

Unfortunately, my night with Georgie came back to slap me in the face. It took a couple of weeks, but when I walked past Izzy in the corridor one day and felt almost physically wounded by the unexpected anger in her glare, I was surprised and then silenced. Before I could recover and try to speak, she had stalked past at speed. Then, inevitably, a short while later, I received an even more hostile glare from Fay when I encountered her in a corridor. At least she spoke to me.

"Why can't you just have the decency to leave her alone, Jo?"

"What? I have been. I have given her all the space she wants."

"No — you have been sidling up to her, pretending you loved her, too, and then sleeping around with whoever will have you on the side."

I made a last pathetic attempt at feigning ignorance. I was angry with her tone and her judgement and myself, but I forced myself to try and keep a civil tone to salvage some of the progress I had made.

"What do you mean? What are you implying?"

"Gabby has been telling anyone who will listen about your little tryst with her friend. Classy, Jo! I can't believe that I was starting to like you. You just don't care about Izzy at all, do you?"

Angry as I was, I took a breath and kept my composure. I knew that Fay's support was crucial.

"Hey — just remember, Izzy has made it clear she doesn't want me. We are not a couple. I can do what I want."

"Yes. And you've made sure that she knows you've moved on as publicly as you could."

"No! Look, I was an idiot. This once. I miss her, too, Fay. And I was lonely and a bit drunk. I would do anything to convince her to try again with me, but I'm not perfect."

"That's the point. You can talk the talk, but you clearly can't walk the walk. Yes, fine, you're a free agent, but then leave her alone and let her be one, too. Don't be nice to her and don't try to befriend me if you don't even have the self-control to refrain from pulling random women in front of all your workmates, so that Izzy has to hear the gory details. You owe her that."

"Tell her, I'm sorry. I don't want to hurt her. It was a moment of weakness."

I could tell that Fay was softening. There was less condescension and challenge in her tone, but she was still standing tall and angry for her friend. I almost found myself trying to confide in her how much I still loved Izzy and all the pressure I had been under, but knew that I would just be humiliating myself for nothing.

"It's always just a moment of weakness for you. That's why Izzy will never trust you again."

Fay's words, spoken more gently and with less condescension, hit me harder than the rest. I felt my shoulders slump and leaned against the wall. I struggled in vain to find the right words to say.

"Jo, if you really care about her, leave her alone."

Fay walked on and I considered following her and making her understand. I wanted to shout after her that I had not been unfaithful, I had just been a normal thirty-year-old who was single, lonely and had a one-night stand. It was stupid doing it at a work do, but where was the harm? I wanted to tell her that she had no right to judge me. But I knew that Izzy would see it the same way as me sleeping around when I was with her. But it was different then. I had just realised I was a lesbian and wanted to explore. And back then, I had been unfaithful to her. We had never officially said that we were exclusive, but, of course, I knew that that was what Izzy expected. Objectively, I had done nothing wrong, but I still felt guilty, and my night with Georgie was clearly not worth the damage it had done. I was furious with Gabby, but knew that I should have expected it. She was known for her gossip and although most people knew not to tell her anything personal, she traded in gossip, so people found themselves swapping stories about others. I was so angry that I wanted to slap her and myself.

I had probably undone a couple of months of progress in one night. I considered chasing after Fay and trying to reason with her and explain that it was just one night, but doubted she would listen, and I suspected that Fay had not had sex for some time. Fay was either wholly without libido or was an incredibly frustrated, repressed and guilty closet lesbian type. She was like a less glossy version of someone with whom I had succumbed to a one-night stand when I had been with Izzy. Veronica, a crazed hybrid of a remorseful closet case, nymphomaniac, control freak.

That particular fling had been an entirely regrettable moment of weakness that had been precipitated by a particularly bland and unsuccessful night at the Candy Bar whilst Izzy was camping on a school Duke of Edinburgh weekend. I had seized my opportunity to go cruising but was ready to go home disappointed when I realised that I was being checked out. Veronica was standing a few metres away from me, radiating uptightness through each strand of her naturally frizzed hair pinned firmly into submission in a tight and wholly symmetrical bun. It was a windy day and I imagined that the amount of product needed to keep every wild hair completely in order was probably enough to make a significant contribution to global warming. She was wearing a grey pencil skirt twinned with a blue pin-striped shirt. It was nearly eleven p.m. and she had clearly come from work, but as I moved towards her, I could barely see a ripple in its immaculately starched cotton. Her secretary glasses made her look like an almost comical caricature of a male fantasy office dominatrix, but she was a lot better than going home alone. I offered to buy her a drink and she arched her eyebrows and insisted on buying me one instead. She was clearly butch and wanting to assert herself and I knew that we would only clash, but the way she paid for the drink seemed designed to convey a kind of transaction for the night and I was happy to play along.

She took me back to her flat on Brewer Street. My mind boggled at what the rent must be. She saw me gazing round the flat in an admiring and envious way and said that she was an accounts manager, by way of explanation. She was disinclined to give me any details, but I was not interested anyway. There was no small talk and no offer of another drink before she dragged me straight to the bedroom. When her clothes came off there were very few curves, a lot of very pale skin and an immaculately plucked and moisturised body. She liberated her curls with what she thought was an enticing flick of her head, but her hair was definitely better restrained — suddenly she seemed to have a giant mane and I knew I was in for a night of hair everywhere. No matter how good the sex, I made a vow to never invite her back to mine because I would be finding gingery brown frizz everywhere for weeks.

Her chest was barely curved, with small, pert, oval-shaped breasts. Her tongue seemed abnormally long, but she was highly adept at using it to seek out the most responsive part of my clitoris. She was a perfectionist and touched me imaginatively, with great skill and naked desire. For her part, she was as insatiable as I had hoped, but she was too controlling and would not allow me to just touch her and discover her erogenous zones. Instead, she had to keep moving my hand and giving me instructions. I felt like telling her to just buy a vibrator and get over herself, but eventually I managed to sneak past her defences and she switched to a more satisfied type of moaning and I was able to show her my own skills as a lover.

Afterwards, there were no pleasantries and as I lay exhausted and about to drift off into a post-coital slumber, she got out of bed and excused herself. I could hear her washing herself and turning the shower on and off, and when she came back to the bedroom she was scrubbed and brushed, wearing expensive silk pyjamas and looking ready for an expensive boarding school sleepover.

"Look, I'm sorry. We shouldn't have done this — I'm not actually a lesbian. Anyway, do you mind leaving? I have an important presentation."

Fine. I have my pride. I was not going to argue that I was about to fall asleep, so I made one petulant comment as I threw my clothes back on.

"Well, you do a convincing impression of one."

Given how late it was, I decided that even though there might be a tube from hers, it would not be running back in Putney. I could not face the idea of making inane conversation with random drunks on the night-bus, so I had decided to splurge on a black cab home and in the back on the way home I read some texts from Izzy about how camping had been going and how she was missing me.

Izzy had never found out about Veronica and she had been a lot more fun than Georgie, but I realised how she must see me now. I was at an age and in a profession where most women my age were marrying and even having kids. Or pining for a boyfriend. On work do's now, I was one of the older women to still be in the pub at last orders, with the PE teachers and the NQTs all happy to choose nightclubs with music so horrible that even I baulked at the prospect. Suddenly, for the first time, I felt embarrassed rather than adventurous. I thought people saw me as fun and up for anything, but I wondered what they really thought. I went through the motions for the rest of the day and kept a low profile, even grabbing a sandwich for lunch rather than sit in the dining hall.

I returned home hoping to be consoled by some delicious food and a word of advice from Julia, and instead was confronted by a note and a recipe card. She had intended to cook some Thai curry, but Natalie had called and asked her to be her date for a friend's exhibition. I felt unreasonably angry, both because she was not there and at her foolishly ambitious hopes that I was going to cook a curry from scratch with actual herbs and vegetables. I should have been delighted to have the flat to myself and the chance to order a cheap, unhealthy kebab shop-style pizza, with side orders of garlic bread, extra toppings, sauces and a high risk of premature heart failure. Instead, I felt grouchy and jealous. Surely, if Natalie and her were not even having sex, she could not be a more fun companion than me? I may never have been able to invite her to glamorous openings, but I had my rugged and endearing charm and introduced her to a shady new underworld of drug dealers and extortion.

I knew I was being unreasonable and I could not have imagined myself ever playing the role of the jealous housewife in a real relationship, but suddenly, both my exes were seemingly doing far better than I was. I briefly debated consoling myself by going out on the pull or checking in with someone like Pru, but decided not to go there and, to be honest, I could not face getting tarted up and then crawling into work shagged out or hung-over the next day. I decided to cheer myself up by eating half a tub of ice cream in front of the TV. I figured that I had no one to care if my belly got a bit wobblier, so I might as well enjoy it.

At eleven p.m. I went to bed. Julia was still not home, no matter how long I dragged out my bathroom routine. Nor was she back in the morning when I went to work. I figured that Natalie had found a way to snare her interest after all.

Winter Blues

The next few weeks managed to prove even more depressing than the usual perpetual grey damp and cold that always precedes Christmas in London. I travelled to and from work mostly in the dark. When I ventured out in the cold and incessant deceptively persistent rain that blows horizontally in the wind, barely affected by the largest umbrella, it was for platonic and mostly sober affairs, as the spice and warmth gradually faded from my life. At work, I became accustomed to Izzy and Fay's ongoing coldness, but it still cast a chill and I found myself spending breaks in my classroom instead of in the staffroom. My good friends still chatted to me, but I ceased to be a regular of the Friday pub crew, going occasionally and returning home early. I started spending more and more nights in, on my own, reading Brontë and Austen. I stopped reading my Jeanette Wintersons and Sarah Waters because I was starting to see aspects of myself in their most dysfunctional characters. Julia was spending more and more time at Natalie's, but I enjoyed the three or four nights she spent at our place. I was all too aware of the irony that I had started calling it 'ours' rather than 'mine', just as she had started treating it more as a base than a home.

Julia had become the interesting one. She talked casually about Natalie and the dinner parties and soirees they attended together. I could not help being a bit jealous of the contrast between her happiness and the glamour of her new lifestyle set against the growing monotonous loneliness of my own. Nevertheless, I still managed to be pleased for her. I was glad that she was so happy and that I did not have to feel any residual guilt over our relationship and the drugs debacle. She indulged me enough to let me vent my frustration about Izzy and how my life was going generally, but stopped me when I became too maudlin and encouraged me not to dwell too much. She even told me that I was still a very attractive woman, jokingly telling me 'she would', but that it was good for me to actually try living with my own company for a few weeks and without any one-night stands or meaningless sex. In fact, in some ways it was good for me, but less so for my waistline as I became increasingly sedentary and kept crisps or chocolate on hand. Living in a world of relentless darkness and rain made it a struggle to find jogging routes that did not involve getting soaked or mugged. Running was one of my few sources of exercise, and forcing myself through the pain was managing to keep both my waist and libido just about in order.

In many ways, Julia was the only positive in my life. Our relationship was closer and more intimate than it had ever been as lovers. We were finally equals who looked out for each other with no hidden agenda or power games, and we took an unselfish joy in each other's happiness. Although the chemistry had gone completely, she possessed almost all the other qualities of my perfect woman. Of course, I still loved and longed for Izzy, but she was always going to be hard work. In her role as my informal life coach, Julia had started to tell me that it was time to look to the future and leave the past behind me. I stopped calling my friends with benefits, but felt it rude to decline when they called me. Even then, I found myself mostly going through the motions, thinking of Izzy, and was sure that Pru, or Veronica, or whoever, could tell, and I knew myself to be a poor lover.

The end of term was a massive relief and I forced myself through the endless parade of Christmas and New Year parties with huge amounts of fake bonhomie and only two one-night stands. On New Year's Eve, I rejected several women at Heaven, including two who were seriously hot, and I almost kicked myself for my lost opportunities even as I did it. I went back to my empty flat at one a.m. and sat on the sofa with a blanket and a mug of cocoa, pretending to watch a film and doing some serious soul-searching and resolution-making.

In the end, I settled for three resolutions:

1. To resume my plan to get Izzy back (maybe she was resolving to forgive me at the same time).

2. Just in case, to start also looking to find a proper relationship with someone else, perhaps one that did not involve sleeping with someone on the first date.

3. As part of resolutions 1 and 2, to have no more than one one-night stand a month.

Julia was planning to come home in a few hours and we were going out for a New Year's Day lunch to celebrate the end of a very mixed year because, as she said, "I think we need to start next year with some positive energy and our heads in the right place."

Looking to the future was raising my spirits, and I went to bed exhausted and slept well, until I was awoken by the sound of Julia trying to insert her key into the lock and the door being scraped and pushed as she struggled.

Back Again

I stretched myself awake and came out in pyjamas to greet her. I was looking forward to teasing her about still being drunk the morning after, but as she finally succeeded in opening the door and almost fell into the flat after it, I could tell immediately that she was sober and something was wrong. Her hair was wild and she had barely brushed it, let alone pinned it back. She looked anxious and pale.

"What's wrong? Has something happened between you and Natalie?"

"No, we're fine. Well, me and Natalie as a couple are fine. I am not fine. I think I saw Jonno tonight."

"*The* Jonno?" I knew the question was ridiculous even as I asked it.

"Well, who else?"

She was not certain it was him, but she had been walking home after a party in Brixton when one of Natalie's friends had stopped to buy some drugs on Coldharbour Lane. Julia was very New Age and I had almost expected her to smoke some recreational pot, but her older brother had caused a very middle-class counselling and detox intervention crisis. This had led her to being very anti-drugs, though she forced herself to appear tolerant and respectful to others. Natalie knew how she felt and although she had dabbled at university and occasionally joined in with her friends, she never did it in front of Julia. They had waited and watched on the other side of the road during the deal. As they stared idly around, Julia's eyes had settled on one of the few white dealers and realised that she thought she recognised him.

"I'm not sure — he looked much thinner and scruffier. His clothes were plain and very unlike how Jonno normally dresses. I nearly dismissed the idea and assumed that my subconscious associated drugs with him and that made me think it was him. But then I think he saw me and also thought I looked familiar. He definitely stared our way. OK, I can't be certain and I did not want to stare, obviously, and we walked away quickly after that. He may have just been looking dishevelled to fit in in Brixton."

Even though months had passed since everything had happened, I felt the old fear rising. I asked whether Jonno had followed her. Julia said she was confident that he had not. She was not sure it was him and she had not said anything to Natalie, so she did not want to make it obvious to her that she was looking behind her in case Natalie decided she was mad. All the way home, she had glanced back as surreptitiously as possible and he stayed where he was, busy dealing with a customer, until she was out of sight as she went round the corner. She had not seen him when she looked back a few times on the way home, either. When she left Natalie's this morning, there was no sign of him and she was sure that they had not been followed.

I fought back the urge to curl up into a ball and cry. I wanted to hug and comfort Julia or to have her comfort me, but even the idea of us making eye contact made my eyes start to water. I went into the kitchen to make us both a cup of tea and breathed as slowly and consciously as I could until I could feel the cold chill start to dissipate from my stomach. I was calmer as I brought the mugs back to the living room. I sat next to Julia and put my arm round her. She felt cold and stared ahead stonily, probably also not wanting to let her guard down.

"What a start to the year!" she said.

"I know. But let's try to be positive. It may not even have been him. And he may not have followed you, and we have been free of him for months now. We won last time and even if he managed to follow you, we can win again."

"Maybe. And maybe I am being paranoid. But I feel it in my gut that it was him. You don't just rent this flat, you own it, so you can't just move out without a trail. You'd have to sell it. Then he would find us. And what if he speaks to Natalie? I'll have to warn her, just in case. She might think I am mad. And let's be honest — we didn't win. I lost my home and had to move my business. We just ran away successfully."

The old guilt came flooding back. Fuck! My first thought was predictably selfish — I hoped that she was right about not being followed from Natalie's flat. But it was far more likely that she had been followed to Natalie's flat. I thought about suggesting the police again; because we were in a different area, we might get different officers, but we were in the same borough and I did not trust any police now.

We sat in silence for a few minutes to let things sink in and then we both tried to reassure each other. Time had passed and things were a bit different now. We both felt less scared of him and, if it really was him, he was clearly not doing well and was probably not the big-shot dealer he had made out. He would have to have been lying about his contacts, because no master criminal with police on his payroll would be peddling drugs in person on Coldharbour Lane on New Year's Eve. Enough time had passed for him to have moved on as well. However, if we were the reason why he had gone from staying in swish hotels in sunny Thailand, dressed in freshly-laundered linens, to being a street dealer in Brixton, then he would be even angrier and more vindictive. Had we reduced him to how Julia described him? In which case, he would be very angry indeed. We could well be in even more danger because we had escaped once before. Our attempts at consoling each other had taken a darker turn as we both realised that, if it was really him and if he really found us, he would be even more dangerous this time round. Once again, I was one step removed from the situation that I had created. Although I felt guilt, I was still sheltered. But, above all, I was just not willing to be so scared of him again. For the first time, I believed, that somehow, we would win in the end. Now all I had to do was convince Julia.

I told her that I wanted to have our New Year lunch anyway, but only if we banned talk of Jonno and did not let him ruin our day. She stared at me as though I was mad, but then her face softened and she agreed that we should allow ourselves some peace. We would only go back into plan mode if and when he showed up again, but she would casually slip the whole Jonno saga into conversation with Natalie as soon as she could.

"I feel bad for not telling her, anyway. It was such a major thing in our lives, however briefly. I just didn't want to appear a little nuts. I should have told her ages ago. She'd probably find it cool and exciting."

"Yeah — but I get why you didn't. I haven't told anyone. People already think I spend my life just lurching from one crisis to another. No one thinks that about you. If you tell it right, it will make you sound like a sexy, sultry super-sleuth."

We both stood up and I hugged her. She accepted — rather than responded to — my hug and I felt a rush of tenderness towards her. It was not even sexual — I just wanted to take her to bed and lie naked with her until we both felt comforted. As if sensing my thoughts, she shrugged off my embrace and went to shower and change for lunch, as did I.

I distracted myself from my fear and disappointment by phoning my mother to wish her a happy new year. Having to listen to her worries about my lack of relationship, my career going nowhere and the fact that I never visited was a predictably depressing start to the year, but I figured my good deed was done and the year could only get better from this point on. Obviously, it would not have helped the situation to point out that, perhaps, my lack of visits, were partly due to the fact that she only seemed to use such visits to interrogate me about my lack of long-term commitment and inability to start providing grandchildren. She knew I was a lesbian now, something that she had to acknowledge and pretend to be fine with so that she could support her avant-garde persona, and she enjoyed discussing the fact that her daughter 'was a Sappho girl' at bridge parties. However, neither the fact that I was a lesbian nor my repeated insistence that I was not ready to settle down deterred my mother from constantly expecting me to deliver babies. I had even tried telling her that, to my mind, the best thing about dating women was never having to worry about accidentally getting pregnant. Another failing in the eyes of my mother.

I was inexpressibly grateful when Julia emerged from the bedroom in some skin-tight blue jeans and a loose and flowing chiffon blouse. She had definitely lost weight, probably due to all the sex she was having, and she looked radiant. I kicked myself briefly for having missed my opportunity, but Izzy would always be my first choice. There was almost no prospect of success there (never say never!) and Julia would have made a damn hot second choice and probably one that was much easier to live with. I apologised for having wasted so much time on the phone, but she smiled sympathetically and I showered and dressed quickly.

We decided not to go to a fancy restaurant after all and just have a quiet lunch in the pub by the river, have a few drinks and then go for a stroll along the towpath. As we talked and laughed and reviewed the old year and made plans for the new, although Jonno's name inevitably kept coming up, the fear went and we even started to laugh and marvel at our bravery and adventures.

January Blues

After the initial shock and fear, neither Julia nor I could muster up the same level of panic as we had the last time Jonno re-entered our lives. When we saw no further sign of him for a couple of days, we relaxed and carried on as before. We continued to be a little on alert when leaving or coming back to the flat, but we both relaxed quickly and let the rest of the holiday flash past until suddenly I was back at school without seeming to have had any break at all.

Izzy and Fay were visibly less hostile. Fay treated me like any other colleague and though she did not acknowledge our recent almost friendship, she also refrained from commenting or rebuking me for anything else. Izzy greeted me if I walked past and stopped leaving the room as soon as I entered it, but I knew her too well and could see the effort it took her. She tensed as she spoke to me and had to force herself to be still, rather than walk away. In some ways, it was more hurtful than her nakedly angry looks and forced avoidance. Suddenly, I found myself torn between wanting to be the one to walk the other way and wanting to walk towards her and hug her or plead with her. She was far more important to me than a distant memory of Jonno and became all I could think about. I had stopped going out on dates and was avoiding most boozy nights out and was becoming something of a hermit. Lexi was still my loyal friend and was always fun to meet up with, but she had made it clear how bored she was by my constant talk of Izzy and kept telling me to 'snap out of it'. I wondered whether she was right and I found myself absent-mindedly flicking through the jobs' pages in the *TES*, wondering if it was time to change job and, perhaps, move away from London, move away from Izzy and generally just start everything again.

Julia spent increasing amounts of time at Natalie's and I found myself cherishing our evenings together, with both of us staying up much later to savour our chats. She was always with Natalie on a Friday, so I sometimes did the usual Friday night post-work pub trip, but I had stopped being a regular and never went on to a club afterwards. I did not want to be reminded of the Georgie fiasco. One lonely Saturday by myself, when Pru phoned me, just as I was going to bed, to comment on my continued absence from all the usual places we used to bump into each other and to say that she was in the area. I invited her round just for something to do. I felt guilty as I put down the phone and if she had been further away, I would have called her back and told her not to come. I knew that I was doing nothing wrong and longed for some adventure and was, frankly, starting to worry that I had forgotten how to have sex. When I opened the door to her, she was dressed in an understated but clearly expensive figure-hugging black cocktail dress and high heels. She barely wore make-up, but wore it well. She had clearly been on holiday recently and looked tanned and radiant. I ushered her in quickly, in a whisper to avoid Doris.

"Hello, stranger. Where have you been hiding? Nice pyjama/hoodie combination — I see you made an effort for me," she said.

My pyjamas were freshly-ironed White Company ones. After all, I had time to iron these days. When Pru had called, I had spent so long agonising over my decision to invite her over that instead of getting dressed, I had simply thrown my school logo-ed sports hoodie over the top half and answered the door bra-less. Pru's comments were said partly jokingly but also with surprise. Next to her, I looked a mess. I suddenly needed to get her into bed, just to try and get us both out of our clothes.

"Yes — sorry. I, erm, you know."

"And here I was, thinking you were all holed up in some deep relationship. I know what you need!"

There was no attempt to hide the innuendo and I wanted to say yes, but these days I was used to being a good host and having comfortable nights in.

"Would you like a cup of tea?"

"Oh, for heaven's sake — don't be so ridiculous. Come on."

She led me to the bedroom and started undressing. I was still kicking myself for offering tea and not wine, and instead of just dragging her off to bed. I felt unsure of myself, but Pru's casually shameless, boundless desire framed inside her effortlessly stunning body would be enough to stoke a fire in even the staunchest heterosexual woman. It was liberating to actually feel aroused and happy. Suddenly, I was back to my old self and the sex was amazing. I was exhausted afterwards and asked Pru if she wanted to stay the night.

"Sorry, hun, off on a family thing tomorrow so need to go home and sort a couple of things."

It was one a.m. and as Pru summoned and waited for her Uber, I found myself yawning and struggling to stay awake.

"Can I get you something to eat, or drink — you must have worked up an appetite?"

"Maybe I will have that tea, after all."

Pru was clearly mocking me as she spoke, but gently, and she gave me a tender bum slap as I got up and put my gown on to make it.

"What is with you?"

Pru and I were just occasional sex buddies and her life was so obviously glamorous, I did not want to bore her with the details, but she was kind and the question was genuine and we had to fill the time before her ride arrived.

"I may be in love. With Izzy — you know, the one I was with when we met. And she doesn't want anything to do with me."

She looked at me pityingly.

"Your first?"

I nodded. Pru had been one of my first one-night stands and had overlapped the end of my relationship with Izzy. I had not told her much, but she had asked the usual questions about 'how I knew' as we lay in bed recovering.

"Yes."

"Oh, darling, I never figured you for the cliché. Meet a girl, just one girl, fall in love, move in together, get cats, become vegan and play golf or hockey. Such a waste."

I looked down. I felt dowdy and helpless next to Pru.

"Oh, just ignore me. I'll never settle down, but it works for some. Apart from the divorces and the court battles over money. But you seem to have it bad. My advice, go for it. Quickly and with conviction. Either win her back or lose her forever and then move on. This — this just isn't working for you."

Her Uber had arrived and she kissed me on the cheek and left her tea half-drunk. I was glad to be alone and too tired to do anything but sleep on her thoughts.

Again

Days and even weeks began to merge. I was forced to take some stock of my life so far and it did not look promising for my thirties. My weekends became little different from my weekdays, except my planning was interrupted by trips to the supermarket rather than actual lessons. At least my career was going well. Jonno was a distant memory and rapidly becoming the only interesting anecdote I could remember, though I remained too embarrassed to talk about it. There were a couple of occasions when Julia came back from Natalie's saying she vaguely thought she had seen the man who she thought was Jonno, or possibly a man who looked like the man she thought looked like Jonno. Or maybe someone else who looked a bit like Jonno. But we had both mentally dismissed the idea and agreed that despite Brixton's gradual gentrification, there would always be shady types hanging around. So it was perhaps inevitable that Natalie should see someone dodgy who looked a bit like someone she knew. Unless she became certain that it was him or that she was being followed, neither of us would worry. So, one evening, as we finished off one of Julia's superbly cooked, ultra-health-conscious mushroom stews with Thai noodles, we were taken completely by surprise by Natalie's frantic phone calls.

Julia had ignored the first call. And the second. The third time, she apologised and left the table. She called out to me that it was Natalie, and I heard her barely say hello before being cut off by Natalie's voice. As I cleared the table, I could hear Natalie's angry voice berating Julia for something. I tried not to eavesdrop, but I could not resist straining to hear as I moved round the kitchen, loading the dishwasher as silently as I could.

"I'm sorry. Please, try to calm down. I'll come."

Silence, rushed voice, angry voice, pause, on the other end of the line.

"You have to let me explain in person. I'm going to leave now. I'll be there soon."

Another pause and a voice definitely telling her not to come and then angry voice again.

"I love you. I am coming."

Julia got off the phone, suddenly looking tense and old. I could tell from her manner that he was back. I hugged her and she instinctively pushed me away before accepting my hug.

"Jonno?"

She nodded.

"I'm sorry."

This time I had involved Natalie, too. I waited for Julia to lash out at me, but she looked broken. I was desperate for details.

"Can I get you a drink?"

My simple question spurred her into action.

"No — I need to get to Natalie's. I'll have a water and grab some things. We'll talk as I get my stuff together."

"Do you want me to come?"

"No." Her tone was sharp but softened instantly. "I'm not blaming you, but this is for me and Natalie to sort out. I kind of hinted at what had happened but played it down. I should have told her everything. He would have scared her anyway, but at least she would have known who he was and how I knew him."

She was too keen to get to Natalie to talk properly, but promised to text me details. I reminded her to be careful — if he had only just gone, he could be watching Natalie's flat to catch her when she arrived. She promised to call when she could and texted me details as she travelled. Natalie was okay but shaken. Jonno had lied to her. He claimed that Julia had been running errands for him to pay off a drug debt and had stolen some of his stock. He had told Natalie that Julia had given him her address and he would only leave her alone if she gave him Julia's real address. I texted my sympathies and assured her Natalie would not believe the lies. But Julia said that Natalie was half and half. On the one hand, she knew Julia hated drugs. On the other hand, Julia had mentioned a drug dealer in a clumsy attempt to half-tell Natalie, so she knew that there was some link. And, above all, having a drug dealer turn up at her

140

door demanding Julia settle a debt to him was enough to make anyone suspicious. There was not much to say to that except to offer meaningless words. I wondered whether I should tell Izzy, but we were definitely not there. And it was not as though he would turn up at her door any time soon.

Julia had promised to text when she was safely inside Natalie's flat and again an hour later (to check he did not follow her in and to keep me updated). But I had to wait the full hour before her next update. I called Lexi on my landline and filled her in, but Lexi was in a loud bar and though she went outside for a cigarette and to talk, I had no answers to her questions and we kept it short. I could not concentrate on the TV or anything, so I spent most of the hour pacing the flat.

When she finally texted, she explained that she would call when she could. Natalie was furious with her and had nearly given Jonno her address and almost called the police before Julia and again even after speaking to Julia. Julia said that Natalie had told her she still loved her and had listened to her, but she was still far from believing her fully. Jonno had told Natalie he would be back soon to "let you think things over", and Julia was going to stay the night, but she would be back tomorrow morning because she had a client first thing.

I texted to update Lexi, who called me back to say that she would come over. I opened a screw-top bottle of white and poured myself a large glass before letting it chill, putting it in the fridge for Lexi and dropping a couple of cubes of ice in. Just for something to do, I started munching my way through an entire bag of peanuts. I was starting to wish that I smoked and considered asking Lexi for some of her roll-ups when she arrived, but the wine took the edge off my feeling of nausea and dread. I realised that I was much angrier than scared this time. I was not going to be pushed around or blackmailed again, but I had no idea what he might do if we refused. I was scared of being hit or worse and wondered whether his threats about knowing the police and framing me for something were actually true. Once again, I was out of the immediate danger and felt ashamed of what I was doing to Julia and could feel my cheeks flush and I let my pacing led me to the freezer, where I dropped some more ice into my wine. Julia had proved to be one of the most loyal and valuable friends in my life. Possibly more so than even Lexi. And all I had brought her was trouble.

I had become a little immune to Jonno. I told myself that if he really had police contacts or a proper drug gang, we would not have managed to stay safe thus far. He had not threatened Natalie or tried to scare her, and although he had played the villain to perfection in Julia's flat, he had never actually laid a hand on either of us. Yes, it could be that he was so used to getting his way and he assumed that we were so scared we would simply obey him so he did not feel the need to use violence, but I doubted it. In Laos, he had seemed easy going and in control, but back in England he had shown a much nastier side. An important drug dealer would surely have to use violence almost routinely, and I was certain that he would have hit us at least once to intimidate and bully us. Or he would have brought someone else round to scare us. And why would he need to lie to Natalie to gain her co-operation. Surely, he could have just forced it out of her immediately.

I convinced myself that he was bluffing, but if I, or we, called his bluff, the consequences could be ruinous both physically and emotionally — I could imagine assault, rape, prison, anything. I reminded myself that I had also been convinced we had seen the last of him at Julia's, but it was just bad luck that had brought him back into our lives. His latest move had to be a desperate last attempt — though a desperate drug dealer with a grudge was certainly more dangerous than anyone I knew in my suburban teacher life. I was angry that a brief moment of stupidity months ago had led to this, and though the stakes were enormous, I was starting to feel that I had had enough and the time had come to end it one way or another. But it had to be Julia and Natalie who had the final say, and first they had to sort things out for themselves.

Girl Power

As I expected, Lexi managed to make me feel much better and put things
into perspective. She did not like Julia much. When Julia and I were
together, she told me frankly that she thought she was too controlling,
and I had thought the same. With hindsight, I suspected that part of the
problem was that I was just a bit selfish and unwilling to compromise.
Nowadays, Lexi had mellowed to her a bit, but she blamed Julia for
making me boring and "someone who stays in every night, baking
banana bread and wearing pyjamas and fleece". I blamed myself for this
and pointed out that I had never eaten banana bread in my life. I also
suspected that she felt her role as best friend and confidante was being
usurped by Julia's more accessible role of flatmate. She may have been
right, to a certain extent, but some friendships are too special and run too
deep. Within half an hour of chatting and a couple of glasses of the
emergency gin and tonics she had brought with her, we were as close as
ever.

"Look, darling, the main thing is you have to keep your flat safe."

"I know, but I feel terrible that I have dragged Natalie into things
and maybe wrecked their relationship."

"Oh, fiddlesticks. If Natalie loves her, she will forgive her. She
won't just keep going on about it like Izzy."

I started to speak, but Lexi held up her hand to stop me.

"Seriously, darling, you've been mooning after her for months now
and living like a nun. You have to move on."

"I suppose so, and part of me agrees. I just can't stop thinking about
her."

"I'm not getting into that again now. We have just talked and talked
and talked and analysed every detail of that. Back to Druggie Man. I have
a plan."

Lexi started to prepare a roll-up and I stopped her.

"Oh, for heaven's sake. She's not even here!" she snapped at me.

"No, but she's got a client in the morning so she will be back, and she says it makes her look unprofessional."

Lexi rolled her eyes, but we moved to the balcony, where we could just fit on two wobbly metal chairs.

"I won't say a word," she said, raising her eyebrows and sitting down with exaggerated discomfort as she wrapped her cardigan over her shoulders on what was actually a pleasantly mild evening.

"Actually, I have a plan. Assuming they patch things up, why don't you persuade them to move in together properly? You can be matchmaker: they get each other and then there is no risk of her being followed; you get the flat back; and Druggie Man is no longer your problem. Flat back, normality back, you become yourself again. Done."

It was a plan, but I was surprised that my first reaction was that I did not want the flat to myself again. I had been happy on my own for years, but now I missed Julia when she was not there. Normally, I told Lexi everything, but I did not want to admit to her how much I liked having Julia around.

"It's not a plan. Druggie Man, Jonno, will come back. If I don't help do something, they can simply tell him where I live."

"She won't do that — she'd have to be a complete bitch to give him your address. I'd never do that."

"Even if I just left you on your own to deal with my Druggie Man?"

"Yes. Okay. But the important thing is to keep him at their flat. And more wine — bring the bottle out here."

I was impatient that Lexi was already calling it their flat, but I brought the bottle back and we relaxed as we chatted. I needed a friend and a laugh and was glad she had come. Maybe the old me would have just tried to leave Julia and Natalie to deal with things and move away as subtly as I could, but Lexi understood that I was not going to do that now.

"You really care about her, don't you?"

I nodded.

"Blimey. You have bloody changed; but we've been friends for too long for me to judge. You know I will always be here for you, darling. Let's make a plan. And drink."

We drank, felt close to each other and laughed. There was nothing to plan until I had more details, but I was grateful for her company and conversation and I relaxed. She promised she would do whatever she could to help and kept suggesting friends of friends who could maybe follow him or threaten him. I would have forgotten about Jonno and Julia entirely by the second bottle had the alarm on my phone not beeped to remind me to check on Julia. When I texted her, she called straight back and said that things were fine. She had explained everything to Natalie, who was a little shocked but had believed her and she was forgiven. I sighed out the last of the residual guilt and tension and allowed myself to relax. She had decided to stay there overnight and they would make some plans together. Natalie's flat had a heavy front door and an alarm, so I did not need to keep checking up on her. When I rang off, Lexi, who was so close to me on the balcony that she had heard almost everything, raised an eyebrow and said, "Well, that sounds positive. She practically told you all was well. You're in the clear."

"I am responsible until he is out of their lives forever."

"Oh, aren't you a dashing lesbo knight in shining armour!"

There was only a tinge of bitterness to her tone, but more mocking good humour, and as we rehashed the whole sorry affair, we convinced ourselves that all would be well. We were sure that Jonno was not all he tried to appear. Aside from his contacts at the garage in Laos, we had never seen him with anyone. He could have been an ordinary tourist making a quick profit and putting on a swagger because he was so impressed by his own daring. He may have looked wealthy and assured, both in Laos and initially in London, but surely it would not have been so easy to escape a proper dealer? I knew that we had to be careful and try not to take any risks, but I was no longer willing to just let him dictate terms unless we saw something more tangible than his cocky attitude. If we were wrong, we could get badly hurt or worse, and I was worried about my teaching career, too. I cursed myself for what should have been just a passing indiscretion and vowed to learn from my mistakes.

Lexi was great. She told me not to keep beating myself up about flirting with Jonno and pointed out that given our mutual track records, it was both a wonder that neither of us had got into trouble before and proof that no one could have anticipated the consequences. She also had the beginnings of another, more practical plan. She knew a friend of a friend who worked on the Brixton Blog and sometimes did interviews with the police for the website, and he could try to investigate whether Jonno had any police connections or a criminal record. She also had a very casual no-strings-attached occasional fling with one of the doormen at the Dogstar, Brixton, and she said that she would give him a call, and maybe something else, and hopefully he would then be able to find out something about Jonno. The doormen knew most of the dealers in the area.

As we came to the end of the second bottle, I was not even trying to mask my yawns. We had started drinking early so it was barely ten p.m., but I had school the next day and I was already dreading the potential hangover. I knew Lexi would have happily opened a third bottle, but she stood up and held out her arms to me and we hugged tightly.

"An early night will be good for me. No need to call a cab, I'll get the train."

"Do you want me to walk you?"

"Darling, I can see that it's way past your bedtime. It's okay. I'm fine."

"Thanks — you've made me feel so much better."

"My pleasure. Thought it would be nice to have the old you back, sometimes. When this is over, or next school holiday — big girls' night out."

"You're on!"

She left, and as I cleared up quickly, conscious that Julia might be home before I was up the next day, I found myself wondering, as I occasionally did, what would happen, if Lexi had batted for my team. Would it be worth jeopardising my most precious friendship just to satisfy both our curiosity? I was not sure that we would be compatible if we lived together full-time, but I knew that I would feel like a jealous lover if Lexi ever experimented with another woman. I knew that, attractive as she was, our relationship was firmly platonic. She was, in many ways, perfect for me — exciting, reckless, loyal, but neither desirous nor demanding of any form of commitment, and she claimed, in an outrageously boastful and archly flirtatious way, to be tremendously accomplished in the bedroom. We had been friends for almost a decade and we had never argued and had barely even exchanged a sullen or angry word, despite far too many drunken escapades. I could not imagine

Lexi ever being clingy or needy, and she would be far lower maintenance than Julia or Izzy, although she could take ages to get ready to go out, wore a lot more make-up than any lesbian I knew and she thrived on compliments and had to be the centre of things. I dismissed the thought. It would be like any relationship, such as mine and Julia's. It is easier to forgive a friend's annoying habits than a lover's, because they go home and can annoy someone else. Nor have I or Lexi ever felt like trying to tame or change each other; but she has certainly tried to do that to some of her lovers. I could see myself with Izzy, but I could not see myself in a relationship with Lexi.

Still, unlike Izzy, she believed in me and was able to forgive and forget quickly, without fuss or judgement. It was enough for her that she cared about me and that we always had fun together and looked out for each other. I had let Izzy down once and now there was no way back. Well, maybe twice, but that was just being picky. Even so, if I had ever meant as much to her as she claimed that I did, she should care enough to want to have a bit more faith in me and try again.

The Morning After

Julie returned to the flat as I was having my solitary breakfast. I had tidied up and was desperate to see her and even considering calling in sick to work. She came in looking fresh and composed. I was hung-over and had slept badly.

We hugged and she said, "Oh, Jo, I thought I made it clear that everything was all right."

"Do I look that bad?"

"Erm. A little tense but not bad, no. I just know you well."

"So what happened? How are things?"

"I'll keep it brief or you'll be late for work. But come home early and we'll chat then. Natalie's flatmate is home tonight so she will be fine. He was at the gym when Jonno came round yesterday."

I remembered that Julia had talked about Natalie's flatmate, Will. Julia described him as yet another surprising part of her diverse friendship group, but I remembered that he did martial arts or something, and although she found him gentle and quite personable, he did fights and competitions for fun. It would have been interesting if he had been the one to answer the door to Jonno. Julia and Natalie had thought the same. She told me not to worry and that, once she had got over the shock of being confronted by Jonno and his lies about Julia selling drugs for him, when she went back over the incident calmly, she described Jonno as weaselly and toxic rather than dangerous and intimidating.

I wanted to stay but had to go to work. I grabbed a packet of paracetamol on my way out and explained that I had been Lexied. Julia raised her eyebrows and promised a detox supper. I still felt guilty and offered to cook, but as I left, she said, "I have a light day today and Nat's got a commission she has to finish, so she'll be busy. It's okay. We don't blame you. Not as much as you blame yourself, anyway. I'll do supper."

I was glad it was a light day for me, too, and I changed my lesson plans to include some silent unseen tests for the first couple of lessons.

The marking would be my punishment for earning some space to think in the lessons, but I had to do them anyway by the end of the week, so I just moved it forward. By lunchtime the day had stopped dragging as painfully and I had decided that if Julia was not worried then I should move on, too. I wondered what she and Natalie had decided, but distracted myself with frequent trips to the staffroom for tea and biscuits and trying to clear my marking. I was glad to get home and too impatient to pick up something on the way.

Julia was surprised to see me home so quickly and had not started to cook, so we did it together whilst we talked.

"So, why aren't you and Natalie worried?"

"We are. A little bit. But to be honest, I was more worried about how she would take things. And she was fine."

A broad smile flickered across her face and she composed herself quickly. I could not resist.

"So you've made up, so to speak?"

Julia's cheeks went a shade of pink. Although she spent time listening to others talk about their sex life and we talked about most bits of their relationship, she almost never talked about her own sex life. But it was obvious to me. I wondered whether I had ever produced a smile like that the next day.

"Don't!"

It was a gentle rebuke, but a rebuke nonetheless.

"Yes. She was cross that I had not told her properly. But she realised that I had tried to tell her and accepted that I just felt embarrassed. She thinks that he is probably harmless but we should go to the police anyway. I told her about Wetstone, you remember, the cop."

"How could I forget? He was worse than Jonno."

"Yes. I said that they wouldn't do anything. When I explained, Nat agreed with me. She doesn't really like the police anyway. Some of her friends have been hassled by them and she thinks that they find it easier to target and fine people just on the fringes of breaking the law and never really go after the dealers and the big-timers."

"So, what are we going to do? I mean, you don't seem that bothered by it."

"Well, honestly, Nat says that if she was expecting him and had been prepared, he didn't seem scary at all. We were scared of him because it was a foreign country and then he just turned up at your flat. Even from what I glimpsed of him on the other side of the road that night, he looks like he is using himself. A bit desperate."

"I know, but if he is desperate, surely that makes him more dangerous?"

"More dangerous but less powerful. Look, we are not dismissing it, but we will wait and see. You don't need to move in to Nat's and nor do I, but I might spend a bit more time there, certainly if Will is out. But we will see what his next move is and then panic. Will is happy to try and stay in for a few days until he has been and so Nat will be safe, and Will might scare Jonno off for good anyway."

It was easy to think we could solve the problem just like that. And hopefully we could. It sounded a little too good to be true, but maybe it would work.

Up and Then Down Again

Meanwhile, the first half of the spring term continued to involve leaving and returning from work in darkness every day. Jonno turning up at Natalie's door had been the most interesting thing to happen for a while. With half-term round the corner and a determination not to waste time agonising about things I could not control. I had battled through the January blues despite being confronted by Valentine's kitsch everywhere I looked. I have never liked Valentine's Day, but nor have I hated it. If people want to pin their lifelong relationship hopes on a card with a picture of teddy bears holding hands, a helium balloon and some supermarket roses, let them. Maybe the giving of a Clinton Teddy Bear to a woman in her thirties or forties really does put modern man somewhere high up on the evolutionary scale and sets them up as a potential life-mate. Good luck to them. But this year, everything annoyed me. I found myself darting into shops to look at cards, striving to find a suitable one for Izzy, only to be driven out by too many images of penguins holding hands and naff messages. I looked at joke gifts, silly gifts, real gifts, but knew that any gift would offend her. I had never looked so hard for a gift and an excuse and knew that if I did give in and buy one, it would only make things worse.

Our relationship at school was improving, albeit at an achingly slow pace. Over time we had slowly extended our "Good mornings" into "How are you?" and a brief comment about the weather. I became bolder and one morning casually asked whether she had plans for half-term. She replied that she was not sure yet but she might get a last-minute deal and go away with someone. I could not hide my reaction and, although I recovered quickly enough to resist the urge to flinch, my blinking eyebrows betrayed my fears that it would be a romantic getaway. To her credit, she did not want to hurt me.

"Don't worry — it's not a dirty weekend. Fay and I might fly to Rome or Venice for a bit of culture and warmth. Not that it is any of your business, but I am not seeing anyone. I am a bit more careful and discerning these days. And your plans? I suppose you will be dipping into your little black book."

"There is no black book. Iz, I promised I would not ask you out or hassle you again, but I don't want anyone else. I know you won't believe that I have changed, but I have. I know you don't want to hurt me, but it does. I am trying to move on, but I can't."

Understandably, she was shocked by my declaration, but she also looked apologetic, guilty and, I hope, a little pleased that I still cared for her. I walked away, embarrassed by my revelation and not wanting her to see the faint stinging of tears trying to come. I never want anyone to see any of my weaknesses, but it would be a disaster for a student to walk past us in the corridor and see or overhear something. Frustration and anger had emboldened me and I realised that I had no regrets about telling her how I felt. I hoped it would spur her into some kind of action. If I was lucky, she would forgive me; but frankly, by this point, even if it caused her to hate me even more, at least I would have the relief of knowing that she would never take me back and it would help me to move on.

Luckily for me, she responded. She texted me and suggested supper in Carluccio's on Friday. She made a point of stating that it was not a date, but merely a chance to talk and perhaps try to be friends. She made it clear that she was not offering anything else. I was delighted by the simple fact that she had kept my phone number and, of course, accepted. Carluccio's could not be considered the romantic destination of choice for anyone, unless watching other people's children scream and run round a restaurant was their thing, but it was more promising than anything I could have hoped for.

When I got home after school, I was delighted Julia was there and she was thrilled for me.

"You deserve this. We all do. We've made our own luck. Me and Natalie, progress with Jonno and now you and Izzy."

Natalie had been superb about Jonno. Will — her sometimes actor, mostly waiter and kids' entertainer, karate black belt-holding housemate — was happy to stay home more and walk her to and from the tube late at night. He was flattered at the idea of being needed as a protector or bit of muscle. What was more, when Julia had told Natalie that she was worried Natalie would leave her, Natalie had responded by saying that she loved her and would not let her down. Julia had tried, unsuccessfully, to hide their mutual joy, but seeing me making progress, too, had made her relax and we were as happy as we had ever been since knowing each other.

Julia was delighted to slip back into her role as my live-in life-coach and advised me not to be my usual glib and cocky self, but to approach the meeting without a plan and let Izzy dictate the pace wholly.

"She is not going to roll into bed with you for a long, long time, if ever, so just relax and act like a normal person. See it as a meeting with someone you care about, listen to what she has to say and just be honest. You have a lot going for you, Jo. You are kind, honest and loyal, and now that you are not just a nymphomaniac self-absorbed womaniser, you are actually very likeable and a good catch. If you cut the crap out, she will see that."

I took stock and started to believe in myself and decided that she was right, I could be a catch — I was easy to get along with and was now proper relationship material. When I went to meet her, I wore my favourite jeans and a blouse that suited my figure but which was smart casual rather than date night. I felt optimistic, if not confident, and happy, too. Even the sight of exhausted parents trying to force restaurant food down their tired, bored and irritable children before dragging them home to bed could not dim my enthusiasm. I wondered whether Izzy had suggested a six-p.m. meeting knowing that the sight and sound of over-tired, over-indulged children would challenge me. She knew I despised children, particularly since I became a teacher.

I timed my arrival for 5.58 p.m. because I knew that Izzy disliked my frequently making us late when we were a couple. Izzy was not there and arrived at 6.10 p.m. with a brief apology but with staged lateness. I knew she loved to be punctual, so it must have pained her to arrive late. She clearly thought it more important to send me a message that she was not too bothered about our meeting. I could live with that. Besides, I had taken the opportunity to get us a table by the river and to have quickly progressed to my second tension-relieving glass of beer.

She was wearing dark trousers and a loose polo-necked jumper that was probably a remnant from the days of her using clothes to camouflage her figure before we started dating. I found myself a little amused rather than offended and had to force myself not to ask whether the reason for her lateness was indecision over her wardrobe. The fact that she was so keen to show me that she was not available had the opposite effect and I interpreted it more as a sign that she did not trust herself to resist. If I read the situation correctly and was willing to be patient, for the first time in months I could see a way back into her life and her bed. It made no difference to me how baggy her jumper was: I could imagine her naked at will and the jumper helped distract me enough to stop making it obvious to her.

I stood up and offered to help push her chair, but she brushed me aside and seated herself. She was trying to be brusque, but I knew her too well. I could see the hint of flush in her cheeks and noticed her checking out her reflection in the glass panels behind me. I made a point of being friendly, attentive and solicitous, but made sure that I suppressed my natural dating instincts to be chivalrous and, frankly, a little dominant. I asked her advice on the menu and was relieved when she suggested the item I wanted anyway — it showed she remembered what I liked.

I was not surprised when she said she would rather not share a bottle of wine and I decided against a third bottle of beer, so we had a sensible bottle of mineral water and still managed to relax into a comfortable conversation. I ate my pasta hanging on Izzy's every word, over-reading and interpreting every tiny gesture, facial expression or intonation until I barely had any idea what she was actually saying. I did pay attention when she asked me about what had happened with Julia. I decided not to tell her that Julia was currently staying at my flat, nor about the whole crazy situation with Jonno. Clearly, what Izzy wanted was something simple and straightforward, rather than a whole load more baggage for her to process. I realised that there was an inherent contradiction about my showing her that I was ready to supply all that by concealing the truth from her, but I figured that Jonno was not my fault and that was why she would not believe that Julia and I had simply become platonic flatmates. So I glossed over some details and told her that we had grown apart gradually, Julia was practically living with someone else and we still kept in touch occasionally as friends. I did acknowledge that our friendship had helped me to grow up and that being in a relationship that was wrong for me had made me realise that I wanted to be in a relationship with Izzy.

Izzy raised her eyebrows and told me that I was talking nonsense, but she also seemed to sit more upright and lean towards me to hear my reply. I assured her that I was not spinning her a line and told her that she must have noticed a change in me.

"Come on, Izzy, you know how patient I have been all these months. I know you have a right to be angry with me, but do you think that the old me would have been willing to wait so patiently and respectfully? Without even a glimmer of hope or sign that you would forgive me? You know that you have had me dangling on a string, trying my level best to honour my promise not to pursue you. Why would I have done that if what I am saying is not true? I have never let anyone have this much control over me."

I could barely believe my own audacity, but I had to let it out and trust myself to fortune. I knew that Izzy had been charmed before by my directness and honesty. Now she squirmed in her seat and looked as though I had just delivered a mild slap to the face. I wished that I had kept my counsel and was just about to offer to get the bill when she took a long sip of wine and started to speak.

"I am sorry. You are right. I haven't treated you very nicely. You hurt me and I do not want to let you hurt me again and, I guess, I wanted you to hurt, too. You make me ashamed of myself and bring out the worst in me and I don't want to get involved with you again. Yes, I still love you, but I don't want to. I think I hoped that you would have got fed up of me and moved on by now and I would be free of you. I still don't want to be in a relationship with you. I don't think I will ever trust you again. I'd rather see you with another woman now than risk falling more in love with you again."

I could see her fighting back tears and she excused herself and went to the loo. I was angry with myself for pushing her, but at least we both knew where we stood. We would not have to play games any more. I figured that she would not want to stay for pudding, so I paid the bill for both of us and when she came back, I asked if I could walk her home.

"Look, we've both been more honest with each other than ever before. I heard you. But can't we try to work past things and be friends. Just let me walk you home so we can start breaking the ice and have some nice last words. I promise, even if you try and drag me inside to your bed, I will neither ask nor agree to come inside and will go straight home to my place."

She laughed and we both felt a slight lessening of tension. Her flat was only a twenty-minute walk away, but we both walked slowly enough to make it nearly twice that. I apologised yet again and told her that I would not ask anything of her until or unless she felt that she could trust me. We walked side by side and close enough to brush elbows and hands more than once, but I did not dare take her hand and, although I put my hand in my pocket and left my elbow sticking out conspicuously, she did not put her arm through mine, and its absence weighed heavily on me.

When we got to her flat, I waited for her to find her key, though she was clearly in no rush to do so. I wondered whether she was waiting for me to kiss her and I found myself asking, "Can I kiss you goodnight — on the cheek, as a friend?"

She leaned forward and kissed my cheek and moved away quickly just in case I tried to return the kiss. This was better than anything I had hoped for and I could scarcely believe it when she said, "Jo, I think you are worth one more try. Maybe. Only at my pace, and I won't promise anything. And if you let me down again, I will never forgive you. I will call you. At my pace. Thanks for a wonderful evening and I will see you after half-term."

She went straight inside her door as she finished the last word. I stared after her but did not risk ringing her buzzer. As I walked away, I felt like skipping, but forced myself to act with some grace, at least until I was out of sight. I texted her on the way home to thank her for a lovely evening and to promise I would not let her down. I was delighted to receive a thank you and a smile emoji back and I found myself as happy and excited as though this were my first ever date.

Trouble Again

My pulse was racing all the way home and I felt like a teenager again. I lay awake for hours replaying the entire evening, going over every gesture and word from the meal and then savouring our doorstep farewell, the touch of her lips on my cheek and the long-awaited progress I had made. I felt warm and drunk, but more from relief and happiness than the few beers I had drunk. I wished Julia was staying with me instead of keeping an eye on Natalie and she was clearly loving the fact that their relationship was obviously entering the serious couple phase. We had ended the night earlier than anticipated, but, whilst I was sure Julia and Natalie would still be up at ten p.m., I was equally certain that I had no right to phone and expect Julia to listen to more relationship drama from me.

I suspected Julia would be happy to help, but Natalie would not, and rightly so. To her credit, Natalie had accepted with extraordinary good humour the fact that her lover lived with an ex-girlfriend with drug-dealing debris attached. She had tried to appear casual and friendly the first time she had come to the flat, whilst unashamedly sizing me up. She had clearly decided that I was no competition, and since then she had been friendly and good company. I was a little jealous of their obvious happiness, but I only saw Julia as a friend and I could not help liking Natalie, too. She was not my type, but she was still sexy in a quirky, bohemian, older woman kind of a way. She was naturally chatty and demonstrative and treated me as a cross between a friend and Julia's project.

Once the shock of Jonno's visit had subsided, she had immediately discussed and made light of it with her trendy south London milieu; in their eyes it only served to bolster her bohemian reputation. It had made Julia and I feel foolish for being so worried initially. I had to admire her effortless cool, and her lack of any apparent jealousy was all the more admirable now it was clear that she genuinely cared for Julia. If I was not so preoccupied with Izzy, I would have found her confidence and inhibition captivating and possibly irresistible. Julia was too grown up and discreet to have ever talked about Natalie in the bedroom, but I had tried to ask, and although Julia chided me for asking, she had a definite smile on her face. Obviously, I wanted to know whether Julia had any thoughts about whether I or Natalie was the better lover, but I knew better than to ask.

After a very sleepless night constantly playing back every moment of our evening together and reinterpreting it, before finally falling asleep shortly after dawn, I was yanked from a very arousing dream by the sound of my mobile ringing at seven on a Sunday morning. I assumed that no one I knew would ring at that time unless it was urgent and I answered Julia's call.

"Hi. Sorry if I woke you — normal people put their mobiles on silent when they sleep, but I know you never do. Is Izzy lying next to you?"

I could not quite believe that Julia seemed to be so desperate for an update that she would call so early both to insult me and to ask whether I had got Izzy into bed. Moreover, if I had managed to persuade Izzy to spend the night with me, a seven-a.m. call from my ex would have probably ensured that that would have been the very last night-time I saw her. I was sleepy and a bit irritable, but I tried to sound jokey.

"Whilst I appreciate your motherly concern — is there some reason why you are calling at this ridiculous time to check on my love life? Presumably there is some reason why you and Natalie are not lying in together."

"Sorry, Jo — I am just on edge and trying not to just come straight out with it. It's Jonno again — he came back last night. I thought about ringing you last night but knew you were on a date so did not want to call you. In any case, Nat and I have been discussing it and we have the beginnings of a plan. We are coming round to your flat together now to talk it over. Call Lexi if you want and we will be there in an hour or so because we'll make sure that we are not followed. Don't worry. He has made some demands, but Nat and I both think he is not as dangerous as he claims to be. We'll explain when we get there."

We said our goodbyes and I collapsed back on the bed. I was too exhausted even to get up and make coffee. I thought about falling asleep again, but my mind was too busy to let me, so I texted Izzy to tell her again how much I had enjoyed last night and that I would be happy to wait as long as it took, but hoped she did not mind me texting her. I was delighted when she texted back within five minutes to say that she was happy, too, but to keep things slow. She signed it 'x Iz'. Sometimes it was worth getting up early on a Sunday morning. I texted 'thank you, x Jo' and then forced myself to put my phone down and lay down to contemplate the events of the last few hours.

Julia woke me up for the second time that morning about an hour later when she and Natalie came into the flat. I apologised as best I could and got straight into the shower whist Julia made everyone coffee and apologised for the lack of decent breakfast food in the house. Natalie was as cool as ever and accepted my poor hospitality with a wry smile and a comment.

"I can see how on edge this whole situation is keeping you, so I brought some pastries for us all to eat."

I was seriously starting to get jealous of Julia.

The Deal on the Table

When I got out of the shower, to my amazement I found that I had enough ingredients left in the flat to enable Julia to make pancakes for us all. I dressed quickly and followed the smell. As we all sat down, I could tell that neither Julia nor Natalie seemed particularly fazed by the situation. It felt like a relaxed girlie breakfast, rather than a counsel of action. They did, however, get straight to the point, with Natalie taking the initiative.

Jonno had followed them up to their flat when they had returned at about nine p.m. after an early film. He had caught them by surprise and they told me that both had considered screaming and refusing to let him in, but Natalie had noticed there was a light on in Will's room and had taken the lead and firmly told him he could come in if he was willing to be civil and just wanted to talk.

They both said that he was clearly taken aback by her confident approach, but he tried to appear cool and said, "Sure — whatever. You have nothing to fear from me on this occasion."

His words were still frightening, but Natalie had confidence in Will, having seen him compete in some karate competition matches. She opened the door, casually letting Jonno go inside ahead of them. When she had calmly shut the door and shown Jonno into the kitchen, she spoke, raising her voice when she addressed Will.

"Do you want a cup of tea, Jonno? William, I am making a cup of tea for our unexpected guest Jonno, do you want one?"

Natalie's pronunciation of the name 'Jonno' made his name seem faintly ridiculous and she had previously commented that no grown man who wanted to be called 'Jonno' should ever be taken seriously. She recounted how her words had the desired effect on him and that his shoulders slumped a little and his posture definitely sagged from plumped up and bristly to ferret-like and furtive. Julia added, with genuine glee, that when Will emerged from his room in just his pyjama bottoms, slightly sweaty and with muscles on display, pretending to apologise for working out for his next fight as he slowly put his T-shirt on, Jonno seemed utterly lost for words.

Julia said that he had been quick to recompose himself. He had tried to threaten and mock them for 'getting reinforcements', but Natalie had dismissed him casually without turning round from the sink as she filled the kettle, by simply pointing out that his visit was not expected and that Will lived there. Natalie laughed about how she could feel herself flush as she spoke, but gathered herself to look normal by the time she had made the tea and sat down. Julia said that the apparent ease with which she had handled Jonno had made both Will and her feel so much more relaxed and emboldened. They both described how Will was only too happy to play the role of casual protector and seemed delighted to get a rare chance to do some acting, slightly hamming up the role. Jonno reacted by being decidedly edgy and visibly annoyed. Both of them were a little worried that if he was powerful, they were definitely running a few risks by alienating him, but were reassured by the fact he reacted as though he was wholly unprepared for this, and a proper dealer would surely take much worse in his stride. He was quick to state his business and wanted to be out of the flat as quickly as possible.

His terms were that he would either take £10,000 cash or have us deliver six parcels for him. Julia asked what guarantee we would have that he would not just keep coming back for more. He had stepped closer and tried to intimidate them as he started to say that she was in no position to dictate terms, when Will, apparently in a slightly Phil Mitchell-style voice, interrupted and suggested he speak more pleasantly to the ladies. The fact that Jonno did not slap him down and became a fraction more polite gave us all courage and strengthened our suspicions that Jonno was not all he claimed. Natalie asked about the six parcels and what kind of places they would be delivered to, and was told that they would be to big clients in the city, Camden and Bethnal Green. Julia said that Will was brilliant at that point. Revelling in his role, he cut across the conversation and told Jonno that they would consider it and get back to him sometime next week. Jonno did not let Will have it all his own way and told him that he was not going to start making house calls by our appointment. They could expect to see him in about a week but at a time of his choosing and convenience. Overall, they were feeling good about the encounter but were still a little shaken by his parting words, cliched as they were:

"Don't try and be too cute or clever with me, people. You play with knives, you get cut."

When they had finished the story, they paused to eat the pancakes and pastries and to let me take it all in, silently analysing my reactions. Being one step removed gave me courage and I was just as hopeful as they were, more so for the fact that I had not had to see him again. We had expected him to return, so I was almost reassured by their account, with the benefit of a night's sleep giving them extra confidence. Jonno had initially demanded £20,000 from us, so to only ask for half that amount after we had given him the slip so successfully last time suggested that his threats of revenge were much less solid than he wanted us to believe. However, even if he was a proper gangster, we were not the kind of people that he would normally be dealing with, and if we actually went missing it would be investigated thoroughly by the police, even if they would not do anything to help us now. So his reduced demands still did not rule out the possibility that he was not bluffing; it might just be that he had decided that we were not complete idiots. Moreover, if he was not going to give us any guarantee that he would leave us alone afterwards, it would not matter to him what we paid initially.

If we were going to accept his terms at face value, then six jobs seemed manageable — Julia and I could do three each. But I had been out partying in both venues a few times, particularly Camden, and I don't think I had ever been to either place without seeing a 'murderboard' advertising for witnesses to some shooting or another. On the other hand, if we were going to acquiesce and simply pay him off, £5000 each seemed a manageable amount, and in some ways, I was tempted to just pay up and get back to becoming a boring and sensible adult and focus on my soon-to-be relationship with Izzy. Natalie pointed out that we had no guarantee that the money would buy us anything other than more trouble, and once we handed over that kind of money to a drug dealer, we could surely be breaking some law and put ourselves at even more risk. Julia was slightly wavering on the side of caution and also considering just paying up if he was able to convince us that he would then go away, but Natalie was one step removed and much more determined that we fight him. Eventually, we decided that we would stall him one more time by waiting to hear what assurances he was willing to give us and, if not, we would get Will and, hopefully, Lexi's bouncer friend to help us sort the mess out. I texted Lexi to ask her if she had spoken to him and she texted straight back to say that Rob was already on the case and making some enquiries about Jonno. He was only too keen to help and would get some of the other bouncers involved, too.

More than anything, this piece of news lifted our spirits. The bouncers at the Dogstar would be no strangers to dealing with drug dealers, even established ones, and they were trained to read a situation and avoid getting into danger. We all started to feel genuinely confident of finding a way out. Julia felt it was time to cook us all another pancake and I took the opportunity to relate my now slightly stale Izzy news from the previous night.

Julia was delighted for me, but Natalie was rather less enthused. She frankly told me that if Izzy genuinely cared for me then she had made me wait and tested me for long enough. It was true that I had spent months tiptoeing around Izzy hanging on every incremental bit of perceived progress. Natalie said that it was now time for 'put up or shut up' and a grown woman worth bothering about should know her own mind enough by now to decide, so she did not think there would be a proper future and Izzy was not worth the effort I was making. I knew that it was exactly the same advice I would have given myself a few months ago. I wondered how similar Natalie was to me and whether she would end up hurting Julia, too; but I could see that although Natalie liked to seem ultra-cool, she was clearly smitten by Julia and was a lot more loving and attentive than I had ever been.

Julia combined depositing a pancake on my plate with telling Natalie that, given how much I had hurt Izzy and that Izzy was a giver in a relationship whereas I had hitherto only been a player, Izzy's behaviour was a little more understandable and that the effect she had had on me was definitely only to be viewed as a good thing. I knew it would not be diplomatic to point out that Julia had been the one to start my reformation and help to keep me honest, and that perhaps she was not wholly disinterested in terms of wanting to see me punished for my sins. Natalie was slightly placated by Julia's comments and next pancake, but advised me that if we were not back in at least some sort of relationship by the end of the Easter holiday, I should walk away and move on. I was starting to like Natalie so much and had already grown to depend on Julia. I was almost grateful to Jonno and the whole Laos debacle for bringing us closer together and ensuring that we stayed friends. It was not as exciting as the lesbian threesome I had sometimes imagined, but it was probably a lot more fulfilling and enjoyable.

Exploring Familiar Territory

I played it as cool as I could for a couple of days, let Valentine's Day pass and then called Izzy to ask if she would like to get out of London and into the Kent countryside for a walk in Knole Park. I felt nervous and wanted to ask her by text, but knew that I had to show her that I could face up to her; and besides, it would be harder for her to turn me down on the telephone. To my surprise, she accepted the invitation easily and asked whether we should picnic or have a proper lunch. I liked the idea of snuggling up together on a picnic blanket in a private corner of the park, but Izzy had always been overly self-conscious of PDAs, so I doubted that I would be able to put her at ease on her current terms when I had rarely succeeded even in our most intimate days. Pub it was! I told her I would surprise her. After some meticulous research on Tripadvisor, I settled on the George and Dragon, which was described as quiet, unostentatious and promising and serving some excellent food to put us both at our ease. I told her I would pick her up at ten a.m. and she said that she would prefer to drive. I did not want to argue, but my plans had centred on giving her a lift home and being invited upstairs. I was more hopeful of that than her asking to come up to my place. I gently insisted that since it was my idea and that the pub was tricky to find, it was only fair I drove. She was kind enough not to point out the obvious fact that I only ever navigated using Google Maps on my phone and could not find my way out of a cul-de-sac without it, and accepted my insistence with good grace.

I considered trying to be casual and going for the 'full lesbian' of walking boots, scruffy jeans, washed-out fleece with sensible waterproof layering, but knew that Izzy would not be fooled by any form of feigned insouciance: I would look fat and unattractive and she might even take offence at my lack of effort and take it as a sign I took her for granted. So I wore my most flattering jeans and T-shirt underneath a thin cashmere jumper, complete with my recently purchased Barbour jacket.

I was delighted to note that she had also made an effort — no fleece or baggy sweaters in sight, just skin-tight jeans and a rugby top with a similarly recently purchased quilted jacket. She had pinned her hair back, too, lifting her fringe off her face in a way that she surely remembered I loved. She blushed a little as I complimented her and I had to look away to hide my obvious pleasure.

I drove slower than usual in the hope that our hands would brush as I changed gear, deliberately leaning over the centre armrest as unobtrusively as I could, disappointed that she remained very much on her side. I was beginning to wish that she had driven so I could have initiated contact, but she took her time getting out of the car when we stopped, allowing me to hold the door open for her, and then walked close beside me as we automatically followed the same path we had taken once before, when we were still lovers. That particular day had ended with some energetic and passionate love-making, but was towards the end of our relationship. I hope she only remembered the positives. Looking back, the more familiar and skilful we had become with each other in bed, the more I yearned to experiment elsewhere. I should have been satisfied with the increasingly passionate and intense sex that we shared, but, at the time, I was too eager to experience pastures new.

It was a crisp, cloudless morning — cold enough to see our breath but not so cold as to be unpleasant when walking up and down gentle hills. On the first section that we found ourselves alone, I took her hand and was delighted to find her gently circle mine back, rather than stiffen and withdraw. I dared not look at her and she let go as soon as a group of middle-aged walkers came into view. She had always consciously avoided physical contact in front of others and I took her hand back as soon as we were alone again. This time, I made eye contact and we both smiled at each other. Finally, we had found a way to be comfortable with each other again. Even the way she let go again when she saw someone in the distance started to feel reassuring and like old times, and after we had walked for about an hour, she started to take my arm when we were alone. When we entered the Chestnut Grove, I stopped, looked around to reassure her that we were alone, held her hands and kissed her. She kissed me back, increasingly deeply, and I could feel myself moisten and had to stop my hips moving towards her. She broke apart first and then we noticed that an elderly couple were walking briskly away from us, the wife looking angry and slightly propelling her husband away. He had clearly been staring at us with a mixture of shock and titillation. Izzy blushed but giggled at the same time.

"Oh dear!" she said.

"Never mind, it was probably the most excitement he had in a while, dirty old man," was my reply.

We walked on and I did not rush things, doing nothing more intimate than walking arm in arm until we were back in the car, where I placed my hand on her thigh and she stroked my hand. I wondered how far up her leg I could let it stray, but I was willing to settle for staying well within her comfort zone. I felt confident of at least an invitation inside her flat and would be willing to wait for sex now that I seemed to be so tantalisingly close. I wished I could drive her straight home, but I did not want to look too presumptuous, so I forced myself to ask, "Still want to try the George and Dragon?"

I could tell she knew that I was not merely implying that she could choose another pub, but she brushed aside the obvious implications and replied, "Yes — I looked it up on TripAdvisor and it looks nice. I think we could both do with a sit down and some food after all the exercise."

She made a point of looking out of the window as I reluctantly inputted the postcode and drove a little further away from her bed, but I suspected that although she was toying with me, it was in a good way. She sometimes used to deliberately keep me waiting for sex, casually suggesting she was ready for bed before finding something else to do or sitting partly-dressed on the bed on the phone to her mother. It drove me wild and then she would undress slowly and let me watch, before allowing me to touch her. I hoped that this was why she was still so keen on lunch rather than fear or a change of heart. Her kiss suggested that she wanted me just as much as I wanted her.

Lunch was excellent. The food was good, but the service felt interminably slow. I am sure that was mostly due to my extreme impatience, although it did cause Izzy to order an extra glass of wine and me to wish I had not offered to drive. I discovered that I was starving and the food was delicious, served attractively by friendly but un-pushy staff. Normally, we would have lingered in such a cosy place, but I was delighted to see that Izzy was happy to skip pudding and was even relaxed enough to suggest we had coffee at her place instead, because, "I have switched coffee to one I think you'll like and my mum left me a tin of those biscuits you love."

To my ears and for Izzy, this was tantamount to her stripping naked and offering herself to me on the table. I gently pressed to pay the bill for us, but accepted Izzy's suggestion to go halves with immediate grace and drove us back as quickly as I could without driving fast enough to cause any old arguments about my driving to resurface. When we arrived back at her flat, we walked to the front door without further conversation and as she let us in I could feel myself almost burn with a mixture of anticipation, longing, tenderness and fear both of rejection and anti-climax.

She shut the door and said, "I don't think either us actually want coffee just yet, do we?"

Then she took my hand and we walked to the bedroom.

Back in Bed

I felt more nervous this time than the first time I slept with Izzy, even though it was also the first time I ever slept with a woman. There was no pressure or expectation then and I was happy to walk away if it had not gone well. I felt too desperate and too afraid to touch her. For the first time ever, I almost wished that I could fast forward through the sex part and get straight to the post-coital cuddle. Suddenly, I wanted us to slow down because I was scared that we were moving too fast and that if we slept together everything would start to collapse. I was just standing there with my hand half-raised hovering awkwardly by my side, unsure whether to take her clothes off, start unbuttoning my own or run away.

"You have changed! The Jo I knew would have pounced on me the second we got in here, but you look, frankly, a little terrified. Don't tell me you've forgotten what to do."

"I just don't want to risk spoiling how things are."

"Jo — I am an adult. I've asked you back here and I want this, too. So long as you are honest with me and actually want a proper relationship, then don't be afraid. I want this, too."

It was all the reassurance I needed. I went to her and part of me wanted to rip her clothes off roughly and push her onto the bed and the other part wanted to take my time and make this a moment for us both to treasure. We undressed each other gently but impatiently and then climbed under the covers. She left the curtains open and I lay propped on my elbow, admiring her beautiful body, more toned and inviting than ever, as I took my time gradually tracing my fingers around the curves of breast and torso. My long pursuit had emboldened her. She did not hide under the duvet but was relaxed and enjoyed the gentle pace and allowed me to touch and admire her. She touched me, too, and we kissed tenderly but with increasing urgency. I was desperate to be inside her, but I made myself slow down and try and raise our desire to a greater crescendo. In the end, she was more impatient than I was and I felt her hand caress my pubic hair and then take my hand and place it between her legs as she lay back on the mattress.

I sought out her vagina and felt another wave of gratification as my fingers found her warm and moist. She was so responsive that I allowed myself to slide straight inside her and then held her in my other arm and lay against her. It was like being home and we were both so aroused that I knew that there was no point in trying to take my time because neither of us would be able to delay any climax for long. I let my fingers slip inside and outside her and she did the same, and our first orgasms came quickly and almost simultaneously. After that we took it in turns until we were too exhausted and sore to touch or be touched any more. We lay wrapped together with our legs entangled. Neither of us spoke, not wanting to break the silence, and it was only the loud rumbling of Izzy's stomach that brought us back from our satiated stupor.

"Wow!" she said. "That was amazing. But now I am starving. Can't think what has made me so hungry. You stay here and I will get us some snacks and drinks."

Her confidence and brazen nudity were new. She was naturally shy and always left it to me to be the aggressor, but her being able to finally see how much I wanted her made our relationship more balanced and gave her more freedom. All the pain and time apart suddenly felt vindicated by the beauty of our afternoon. Lying in her bed, watching the last of the daylight disappear, I found myself, for the first time in a very long time, feeling fully content and sure of both myself and where my life was going.

She returned, naked, with a bowl of chopped apple, cheese, grapes and some water. I offered to get up, but she placed the bowl on my stomach and pushed my back down, saying, "You're not going anywhere — this is just to refuel," as she climbed astride me.

She looked radiantly happy as she rested her weight on top of my hips, helped herself to some apple and placed a grape in my mouth. I promised myself that I would do my utmost to keep her that way. At that moment I would have done anything for her and I felt a rush of love towards her. I opened my mouth to tell her how I felt, but she put her hand gently over it and told me not to speak.

"Don't say anything to me now. I don't want any more bedroom declarations. Let's just enjoy now, and this time we are going to take it slowly and not rush anything. Now you need to focus on getting your energy back."

Her smile made me helpless and I allowed her to stay on top of me, feeding me as she fed herself, casually caressing me. When I tried to sit up to drink, she allowed me only a quick gulp before pushing me down again, and when the bowl was empty, she sat up and rolled me over onto my stomach. She explored my vagina and clitoris as she forced my legs apart and knelt between them and then, even though I tried to protest that I could not come again, she took her time bringing me almost to the point of climax, then stopping and resting on top of me with her fingers inside me. Only when I told her that I could not take any more and begged her to finish did she allow release and she lay on top with her hand placed firmly between my legs as I fought to close them. It was bolder and more assertive than I had ever known her and I loved it. It felt good to see her let her guard down and be daring and demanding in bed, and I felt confident that this time we would succeed.

As I started to drift off to sleep, I felt her hand move as she tried to put her finger back inside me. I started to protest, but she brushed my words aside.

"I am not going to move, I just want us to sleep with me inside you. Please."

We rolled onto our sides, her breasts pressed against my back, and I parted my legs to let her penetrate me and then slept with her around, against and inside me.

A Dangerous Business

I woke early and watched Izzy sleeping. She looked beautiful and it was a struggle not to touch her and wake her up. I slipped out as quietly as I could to the loo and took the opportunity to freshen up and check my mobile. There was a text from Lexi saying that her friend Rob from the Dogstar had found some information about Jonno that was probably very, very bad news, but which just might turn out to be a way out of the whole thing. If we were brave enough.

It was very cryptic and my heart was already pounding and I felt slightly sick. All the pleasure and happiness from the night before was forgotten and I decided that I wanted to know what he had discovered as soon as possible. I texted Lexi back and asked her to arrange a meeting and then texted Julia, too. Even before I finished typing my message to Julia, Lexi had replied saying that she had already arranged for us all to have breakfast at the Dogstar, so with a heavy heart I went back to the bedroom to make my excuses to Izzy.

I had no idea how to explain why I had to leave her and hated the idea of lying to her. She would be furious if she found out that I was lying to her, but she would be furious anyway if she knew the truth — about my being on holiday with Julia, flirting with another man, getting into this situation and then keeping it from her. It would not matter that for so much of the time she had kept her distance from me — if there was even a chance that she would interpret it as me not being honest with her, I did not want to throw away the night we had just had. That was assuming she believed me and did not dismiss it all as nonsense. I was probably nearly free of him, so I should just make some excuse and tell her everything when our relationship was a bit more secure and the whole mess had been resolved one way or another.

She was awake when I got back to bed and clearly in the mood for some sleepy morning sex, which normally I would jump at, but I did not have time and was too anxious to think of anything but what Rob was going to say. Izzy knew something was up but interpreted my mood as regret and started telling me to just leave her alone and looked as though she was going to cry.

"Izzy — don't be angry. Something has come up and I have to meet Lexi. Last night was amazing and really special to me. I am so happy to be back with you and I really want this to work, but I have to go and meet her. Is that okay?"

She looked tense and I could see her chew the corner of her lip as she struggled to control her urge to lash out.

"Really? Lexi can handle whatever she gets into — are you sure that she doesn't just want to get the graphic details on us?"

"I'm sure. It sounds serious. I'll only find out when I get there."

"I'm sure you think she needs you, but I'm not so sure she does. Go if you think she is not just staking a claim or wanting some gossip. But you are missing out and owe me big time."

"You're not angry? We're okay? I'll stay if you want, but I think I should go."

"The moment is gone. I'll be fine. We'll be fine. But it had better be genuine and not start to be a habit."

"If you let me have a next time, I promise to make it up to you."

She looked happier but she still only accepted my kiss grudgingly and barely returned it. I dressed quickly but lingered in her flat, trying to find the right words to say, knowing that whatever I said would be a lie of some kind.

"Oh, it's okay. And don't make promises unless you know you can keep them. I, we deserved a morning together. I know she's your friend, but, seriously, if we are going to work, this better not happen next time."

Her tone was gentler and she kissed me goodbye. First on the cheek but then, quickly, on the lips, and we held. I didn't want to go and she knew it. And our kiss lingered, but as it became more passionate, she pulled away.

"Go — it's okay. You're just meeting a friend who might need help. It's not as if you're running off for some tryst or secret liaison. Go — quickly, before I change my mind and keep you here."

I left quickly to avoid blushing with shame. I took the tube to the Dogstar and was the last one to arrive. Julia, Natalie and Lexi had started

173

breakfast and Rob was doing some jobs, but he came over to join us when I sat down and started his story before my breakfast had even arrived, and what he had to say left me with very little appetite at all.

Not Good News

Rob was striking. His jeans were torn and faded from old age but they fitted his lean, toned body perfectly and he made them look like expensive boutique jeans. He completed the look with his logo-less T-shirt, still wet from the shower hair, and his face had at least two days of stubble. He managed to look effortlessly handsome and he was toned in a casual manual work kind of way. His affable manner reflected what seemed to be a genuine good nature and desire to help out. The frown on his face as he sat down and started to talk was the only sign that he was anxious for us.

He had visited the street where Julia had seen Jonno a couple of times and on the second occasion he had spotted him. Rob was hanging around watching him and deciding what to do when Jonno took out his phone to check a text message and then walked off round the corner. Rob followed him discreetly as he walked a bit further down Coldharbour Lane, into Electric Lane and then straight up to a solitary policeman who appeared to start questioning and searching him. But Rob had been intrigued by the way they had appeared to recognise each other and watched closely enough to see that as the policeman appeared to pat him down, he put a package in his pocket. Rob took out his phone, pretended to answer a call and kept walking, pretending to be preoccupied, but switching his camera to video and filming them as he walked past.

The video was erratic, with Jonno and the policeman switching in and out of the picture as Rob walked. There was no useful sound, but when he played it back it was clear enough for Julia and me to gasp with shock. The officer in the picture could only be the one who came round and mocked us when we called them the first time.

"It's PC Waterfall, Wetsuit — I don't know. What was his name?" said Lexie.

"Whetstone; such an unusual name, I definitely remember it," replied Julia.

So he did have police friends after all. Not only that, he had a dodgy cop who was a dealer and could make sure that he was sent to a routine house call. This was becoming a very nasty mess. Jonno looked dishevelled and out of his depth, but it was clear that he had not lied about his connections in the police. He had also dealt with dealers in Vietnam, so we knew that he was not to be underestimated, and we definitely could not expect to just bluff him out. A dodgy cop could plant something on us and accuse us of anything. I hated the idea of just complying with everything he said, but I was now more scared of the policeman than Jonno.

"We just have to pay him. I am a teacher and I can't mess with the police. I could lose my job. I just want this over," I said.

Julia, Natalie and Lexi had been there longer and although I could see that part of Julia wanted to agree with me, Natalie and Lexi had already convinced her to fight. It was Rob who spoke first.

"I hear what you are saying. You don't want to mess with a bad cop. But remember, the video may be a bit shit, but it still shows the connection between the two of them. And look at the cop — he even looks like a lazy bent copper in the video. I think this is your way out. But you, we, will have to be careful. This sort of thing pisses me off, so you can count on my help. But the police protect their own and we'll need to get a good cop on our side if we are going to win. If we get the right cop, they will be keen enough to get rid of a fat, bent cop like this. It probably won't even matter whether or not he thinks you might have done something first."

I was terrified and the idea that the police might even suspect me of being involved in taking or dealing drugs made me worry for my job. Julia would be okay, even if it came to being accused of being involved in a minor drugs offence. It wouldn't hurt her job at all, but I would have to go to my Headmaster and declare everything. Even if he believed me, it would be horrendous and embarrassing and probably mean the end of any career prospects at my school or possibly any school. I didn't even know if he knew I was a lesbian, but he was an old-fashioned and slightly prudish head who struggled with any form of personal conversation, and this made me look like a reckless and irresponsible fool. Private school heads hate scandal or gossip more than anything, and even if nothing came of this, he would be furious. But I had to believe that Rob was right, that even the simple fact that his video linked PC Whetstone to both attending our call out about Jonno and then to Jonno himself meant that a decent police officer would want to help. But how would we know who to report it to? If we reported it to another corrupt officer, they could simply claim it was a coincidence and how could we possibly know how many other officers were involved? Rob answered that question as well.

"We have to deal with the police pretty often in my line of work and you get all sorts. Officers who ignore some dealers and then make a massive issue of personal-use drugs, lazy officers, careerist officers and then some really good cops who genuinely care and want to help. Some of them are bottom of the ladder and would be too scared to take this on, but I know a good sergeant who comes in and is blunt enough to push through the crap here and honest enough to do what needs to be done. If you are fine with it, I will speak to him, test the water, and if he is willing to help, I'll give him your details. Okay?"

It was some hope to cling on to. I had met Rob casually before on nights out with Lexi and she had told me that he was the kind of man who could always be relied upon and had helped her out in the past. We were putting our faith in his ability to judge someone's character; but, to be frank, we were all out of our depth and he at least had a plan which had a reasonable chance of working.

Rob offered to leave us to think it over, but Jonno would be coming back to ask for our decision in the next day or so anyway so we did not really have anything to think about. Calling the police and getting them to help was what we should have been able to do from the start anyway. We all exchanged brief glances to confirm our decision and Natalie said, "I know that this has to be Jo and Julia's decision, but I think we all know that Rob's plan is our best hope. If I am being honest, I still had some doubts about why you couldn't have convinced the police to help at the start and make it go away, but this video makes it make sense. I think his plan will work. Thanks, Rob — I don't know what we would do without your help."

We all nodded and thanked Rob. Julia asked him to contact this sergeant as soon as he could. He told us he would as soon as he could but right now he had get back to work to get the pub ready. He gave us breakfast on the house despite our protestations and offers to pay. Lexi and I had always just assumed he was one of the many bouncers at the Dogstar, but it turned out that he had gradually become one of the managers there and even owned a tiny percentage. He knew that she thought he was just a bouncer but had never cared enough to correct her. He was just a genuinely nice, genuinely decent guy, and I felt lucky to be surrounded by a circle of people who had my back and added Rob to the list of people I needed to start giving back to.

We did not rush our breakfast and gradually, as we ate and talked together, the fear subsided. We were in a potentially ruinous situation and every time I thought about what could go wrong, even surrounded by my friends safely at the table, I would almost gasp from shock. But I was in the mood to count my blessings and was gradually extending my circle of eccentric and surprising friends. Natalie and Lexi had hit it off immediately and were chatting away like old friends. Julia and I were so relaxed and close to each other now that we were practically sisters. I wished that Izzy was there, too, and felt guilty for lying to her earlier and texted her to tell her I was thinking about her.

I told the others how I had left her this morning and about last night. They were all pleased for me, but their advice about what to do was just as unhelpful and conflicted as my feelings. Julia, of course, told me to tell her the truth, whilst Lexi was adamant that I should wait at least until we knew what was happening with the police. Natalie said that she understood why I did not want to tell Izzy at this point, but that finding out about Jonno from him and not Julia had made her furious at the time, though she did understand and forgive, so perhaps Izzy would, too. I admitted that I was also worried about Izzy being jealous of my friendship with Julia and that I had glossed over still being in touch, but did not want to stress the point in case I upset Natalie. They all understood, but Lexi dismissed my concerns by saying that Izzy had to learn to trust me or there was no point us continuing, though Julia and Natalie reminded me that she could not be blamed for not trusting me if I didn't tell her the truth. Of course they were right, but telling the truth now also involved me admitting that I had not told Izzy that I was living with Julia. I had definitely misled her on that and wished I had been honest, but would we be back together if I had been? As soon as I invited

Izzy back to my flat, she would know Julia was living there, so I had to tell her soon. On the other hand, Julia seemed to be on the point of moving in with Natalie and Izzy had always preferred to stay at her flat because mine had always been too much of a bachelor pad for her before Julia, so she might never find out.

I longed to be able to be honest with Izzy and wished that she could be part of this group, but I was so afraid of losing her this time. I knew I was pushing her away and lying to her, but I could only hope that it would be fine in the end.

Time to Think

After breakfast, Lexi had to leave to 'mentally prepare' for Sunday lunch with her mother, and Natalie invited me back to her flat. I needed some time to reflect and be alone, so I declined. I decided to walk back to Putney. I hadn't done that walk for a long time and even then, only after some shocking nights out when, having taken the tube to Brixton, I had decided that the night had already cost me so much I was too miserly to spend any more on cab fare, drunk enough to not think about the danger and in need of a long walk to sober up.

It was a lovely February morning — a little chilly, but cloudless and sunny enough to enjoy the walk along Clapham Common, down the ugly bit of the South Circular as I tried to follow the river as much as possible. It took about three hours including bench breaks, people-watching and reading Izzy's text, which seemed to suggest that I was forgiven, but which also made me feel guilty. I wished Izzy was beside me, holding my hand, but I was using my time to think about how much to tell her. By the time I got home, I had decided to be honest with her. I would try to tell her everything but keep gauging her reactions and downplay the craziness as much as possible. I would admit to the holiday with Julia and the mess with Jonno. If she asked questions I would elaborate and even admit that I had misled her a bit about Julia. Julia and I were only friends now, and if I was going to be honest, I had to do it properly. Her words about never forgiving me if I let her down again kept coming back to me, but this was too big a secret and Izzy would surely understand and accept that this was such an unusual situation that I could be forgiven for not knowing how to react.

I even thought about walking straight to Izzy's flat instead of going home, but I was almost grateful to remember that Izzy had asked to set the pace, so I had a reason or an excuse to delay my confession. Besides, at some point I had to tackle the marking that I had been forced to bring home for the weekend, being too preoccupied with catching up with Izzy during my frees and then everything else in the evenings. I wondered when Jonno would go back to Natalie's and when and what we would hear from the police.

An Inspector Calls

I was expecting Sunday to be a day of grocery shopping and marking, with Julia coming back to help clean the flat as a potential highlight. Lexi's phone call was an unexpected high point even before she spoke, but she had genuine news. Her Brixton bit of muscle, Rob, had got a call from his police contact first thing in the morning and he wanted to see us as soon as possible so that he could talk to us before Jonno came back to Natalie to collect his money. Rob was convinced that he would help and had already passed on our details as we had agreed. As soon as I got off the phone to Lexi, I got another telephone call. This time from Detective Sergeant Robbins, briefly introducing himself and arranging a time to come and speak to all of us. I texted Julia as we spoke and we agreed that he would come at two p.m. to my flat, just in case anyone saw him at Natalie's. I hung up and immediately called Julia to talk it through and tried to play down the reason he wanted to meet at my flat, but a policeman suspecting that Natalie's flat was under surveillance shook us all. Her flatmate, Will, was there and quick to point out that Jonno had been rattled by his presence, so they felt a bit better; but, without saying anything at all, we knew that we were all feeling a sense of rising drama, stress and excitement. Natalie had plans but promised to cancel and they agreed to come over after an early lunch to catch up and talk things through.

It was impossible to concentrate on my marking, so I decided to get the shopping done first so I could think whilst I walked. Obviously, we needed the police help and I was grateful to Lexi and Rob for their contacts and for acting so quickly. I could feel my old nerves ebb and flow and I was even worried that this new policeman was rushing to speak to us to avoid us talking to anyone else because he was also working with Jonno. Rob had assured up that this was a good officer, but was he as sure as he claimed? I even wondered whether we could trust Rob — Lexi was astute but an out-and-out thrill-seeker — she had known

Rob a long time but never particularly well. The DS had sounded pleasant on the telephone and he had been keen to reassure me that he would help me. His manner had been the very opposite of PC Whetstone's, which was encouraging in itself, unless this was a classic good cop, bad cop scenario.

I was already at the supermarket without having decided anything, but my decision to go shopping proved to be a good one because Izzy was doing her shopping at the same time. She was clearly as pleased to see me as I was to see her. She was trying to play it cool, but I was clearly forgiven and we did our shopping together. Izzy raised her eyebrows as I took us into the cleaning aisle and commented that she was not aware that I had ever used such products before. Although I had resolved to be honest with her, the supermarket did not seem the appropriate place, so I smiled and replied, "All part of the new, grown-up me."

"I hope it lasts — it may even make me want you to spend more time at mine! And what was the crisis."

She laughed flirtatiously as she spoke, but recovered herself quickly as she asked about Lexi and I had to get my mind working quickly:

"Oh, nothing. Well, no, not nothing. She met this creepy guy in a bar and she think he slipped her a Rohypnol, she woke up completely out of it with no idea how she got home."

"Oh my God! Did she call the police?"

"Well, no, she had her knickers on and everything, so we think it was ok."

"Hmm — so more of her usual night out kind of thing. And I trust she kept her knickers on the whole time too?"

"Iz — you know I only have eyes for you."

I meant it. And I wanted to kiss her immediately by the Dettol wipes, or at least take her hand, but she sensed this and looked around self-consciously and took half a step back, but smiled to show I was forgiven. She was in old jeans and a Lacoste T-shirt she had often worn when we had dated before but which was showing its age a little now. It still fitted her perfectly and she looked fantastic and her clothes made it clear that she had no plans with anyone else for the day. I wanted to ask her to lunch, but that would only lead quickly to more lies and excuses as I had to leave abruptly to meet DS Robbins at two p.m. There was definitely time for coffee. I did not want to break our agreement to let her set the pace, but I figured a chance meeting could be followed by coffee, and when I asked, she replied that it was a great idea.

We went to Café Nero and our chat about work, shopping and the weekend flowed naturally, with neither of us talking over the other or rushing to fill potential silences, just relaxed in each other's company. Occasionally, I felt an almost physical need to confess everything, but I could not do it in a café. I wanted to talk about our relationship, but knew that she would get self-conscious about anyone over-hearing us. The fact that we were together and so relaxed with each other meant that I had not blown it. We both allowed our knees to accidentally rub into each other under the table and kept discreetly touching hands. For the most part, we were as relaxed and comfortable with each other as we had ever been. The only tension came when she asked about what plans I had for the rest of the day and I told yet another lie.

"Oh, you know, just marking. And more marking."

"Oh, so you don't fancy a walk."

"I can't. Really. I am so behind on my marking, I've taken their books in, given them back again and recollected them. If I don't mark then today I'll get a complaint. And, as you saw, I have to clean the flat. If you let me take you out to dinner next week or weekend, you will have all my attention."

"Well, I wouldn't want to distract you from your important plans."

She started gathering her bags as she spoke and picked up her coffee to gulp it down, but I touched her hand to stop it.

"Izzy, please don't be like that. I am really behind — not naming names or anything, but someone keeps distracting me at work. You know, with their stunning outfits and inappropriate texting. I'm trying to be an adult and responsible and everything and I can't just hand back their unmarked books a second time. I was respecting your boundaries and taking it slow. Please, let me take you out to dinner — any time next week or the weekend."

I could see her forgive me as I spoke. I had no pride left when it came to her, so was happy for her to know that I had no other plans with anyone else, but even as I spoke, I worried that it would be almost inevitable that whatever day she chose would be the one when Jonno turned up. She put down her coffee and spoke.

"Okay. You always have the right words to say. I'm willing to believe you are not just saying what I want to hear. I'm distracted by you, too, and could do some marking of my own. But you won't be taking me out to dinner. It is my turn to take you. You can get me flowers to apologise. I'll call you or speak to you at work to suggest a date next week. Thanks for coffee. I really enjoyed it and, you know, last night."

The way she looked downwards, just for a second, before forcing herself to calmly look up again made her even more irresistible to me. I could not resist a very wide grin and kissed her on the cheek in a casual, friends, kind of way and managed to walk, not skip, out of the café. This was already one of the most eventful Sundays in a very long time, but the signs were distinctly promising.

I took the shopping home and had only enough time for a quick sandwich and hasty clean-up before Julia and Natalie arrived. We talked in the kitchen as I made tea and agreed to be totally honest with the detective unless one of us signed to the others not to trust him. We thought about agreeing a code word and a back-up plan, but thought that one of us might say it by accident, and a back-up story would be hard to memorise at this point. If we decided not to trust the officer, we would probably all agree and, if it really came to it, we decided we could just excuse ourselves from the room and talk to the others, or if needs be, send a text. We agreed that if someone left the room, we would check our phones, but we were all hoping that we could finally be honest and leave it to the professionals.

DS Robbins arrived at exactly two p.m. He was fortyish with slightly thinning hair, but still basically handsome and a little athletic. His physique helped contribute to the idea that he was basically an anti-Whetstone. The opposite in every way, and he appeared charming, amiable and far more 'cool dad' than police officer. The signs were encouraging and we started to relax. I offered him tea, but he asked for tap water and declined biscuits or anything else.

"So, Mr Turner gave me an outline of the situation and mentions that you had liaised with PC Whetstone before and…"

DS Robbins tailed off when he saw the blank looks on our faces when he mentioned 'Mr Turner'. We realised that he meant Rob, but it was embarrassing to think that we had trusted a man whose surname we did not even know. With hindsight, I think Lexi may have told me, but I could not remember and we had just taken everything on trust. We were still not on our guard and paying enough attention to detail.

DS Robbins clarified that we knew him, but although he remained friendly and reassuring, we had clearly lost some ground in his estimation. He asked to start at the beginning and let us tell the story in our own words. We all spoke simultaneously and DS Robbins was about to stop us when I acted decisively and said to Julia, "It was my fault we got into it, I'll tell it and you can correct or add anything that I miss out; and, Natalie, you can describe the bits in your flat."

DS Robbins took notes, but he was also surreptitiously checking our story with the notes he already had taken from whatever Rob had told him, and, to the relief of us all, as we told the story he seemed to believe what we were saying and, what was more, he seemed genuinely sympathetic and to be the right person to help.

Initially, he barely interrupted us, only asking for minor clarifications and details as we went through. He was disappointed we could not remember more about the officer who came with PC Whetstone, but pleased that I had stored the CAD number on my phone so was able to give it to him to check the details. He had already tried to find it on the system using my full name and could not. DS Robbins told us that he had done a search on us. This unsettled us all, but at least it meant that he was thorough. Julia told him how good it was to be taken seriously, and he said, "My pleasure, ladies. But this is a difficult situation here. You haven't broken the law and you shouldn't be afraid, and the police will help you, you have my word on that. PC Whetstone is a long-serving officer — influential with some officers and perhaps a bit intimidating to others. Obviously, I can't say anything, but he has never had any serious disciplinaries or been found to be at fault or involved in any dodgy dealings. I am speaking a little out of turn here, but I am going to be honest with you, but this is between you and me. There have been a few too many occasions when he has been the officer attending an incident involving drugs and something has gone wrong with procedure or drugs have been lost and then we have not been able to proceed. I and a few of us dealing with drug incidents have been wondering whether it is more than coincidence. But we have no evidence, and he may be an honest and decent officer who keeps being in the wrong place. I also want to assure you that I get what you are saying about him being a bit unpleasant when he wants to be. It's not easy to describe and unlikely to amount to anything in court, but I understand that he would be able to make you feel very uncomfortable and afraid to speak to the police. That is why I want you to know you can trust me."

He explained that all this would mean that he and his inspector wanted to proceed and investigate further. He reassured us that we should not be afraid of working with the police, but that it would not be easy and they would need to be patient and make things watertight. He also asked whether we would consider wearing a wire to record any meetings. I think we were all relieved that we had a police officer who would be taking over, and Julia agreed immediately. If he wanted us to tape things then he must be honest. DS Robbins then gathered his papers and told us that he would confirm things back at the station and be in touch tomorrow. He also told us that he very much doubted that PC Whetstone or Jonno would actually be watching Natalie's flat, but, just in case, he would meet at my flat and set her up with recording equipment that she could easily operate herself to ensure that, whenever Jonno turned up, she would be ready. He gave her his direct number and told her to call him as soon as Jonno turned up. He urged us to only contact him directly to avoid tipping Whetstone off, but if we felt afraid and could not reach him, to call 999 for our own safety without needing to worry about being arrested ourselves.

When he left, Julia and Natalie decided to stay at my flat for the day so that Jonno could not visit them before they were able to record him, and we felt that things would be fine. DS Robbins telling us to call 999 if we could not contact him made us trust him more, but the fact that he thought that Jonno's threats could be credible was a frightening thought. Still, we always had Will and would make sure that he would be there to open the door when Jonno returned. Soon this would be over and then I could tell Izzy the truth.

Preparation

The rest of Sunday was perfect. I called Lexi, who promised to pass on my thanks to Rob. I got on with my marking after Julia had helped me finish off the cleaning. She and Natalie stayed and we cooked an excellent supper together and watched a film. Izzy and I exchanged a few 'thinking of you, x' texts. DS Robbins called to say that his inspector had approved this operation and they were confident they could get enough evidence to use, so he would come round the next day with another officer to sort out a listening device and go through the procedure. Everything was moving positively and though we still had doubts, it seemed that everything was turning out for the best after all.

Monday started even better, with Izzy coming over to sit with me at break time and Fay even catching me in the loo to say, "Well, Jo, I am not often surprised, but I haven't seen Izzy this happy for a long time. I think you have me convinced as well; but know this, if you hurt her now, you are even more stupid or more selfish than I thought before. Just saying. No one will think well of you, so don't string her along unless you mean it."

The way she said it did not make it clear whether she was giving me advice or threatening me, but as she finished speaking, she gave me a quick pat on the back and left before I could gather my thoughts to speak. To be honest, what she said was fair. Given my past with Fay, I was even willing to see our little chat as a sign of progress. At the end of a day when for the first time in a fortnight I had been able to return all my students' homework marked and up to date, I was feeling so good about myself that I practically skipped to the car park.

When I got home, DS Robbins and another plain-clothed officer were just finishing going over things with Julia. He introduced his colleague as Detective Inspector Mark Buttler. DI Buttler was also mid-forties, with gently receding hair, and looked as though he spent a lot of time behind a desk. He was not fat, but he looked like a once-athletic man who now enjoyed good food and wine and who was comfortable with the small but distinct amount of middle-age spread as a result. He told me that he was pleased to meet us and was keen to help sort things out, but that, as he had already explained to Julia, he wanted to investigate properly, and PC Whetstone was a long-serving officer who was entitled to be presumed innocent unless there was clear evidence to the contrary. He promised to pursue and investigate any evidence of impropriety and that he wanted the integrity of his officers to be above reproach; but he also explained that, in the unlikely event any officers did not meet this standard, it could be a long and difficult process to resolve fully, and we needed to understand the seriousness of what DS Robbins was going through with us.

He then gestured to DS Robbins to take over again, and he made Julia demonstrate how to record to show that she understood and that I could help if she forgot. He told me to stay at Natalie's for a few days because it would be better if we were all there when Jonno returned. Then he briefed us how to handle the conversation and meeting with him. He explained that we should not provoke Jonno in any way in case he was dangerous, but we needed to try to record him trying to extort money from us and to admit handling drugs in this country if we were to get any usable evidence. He said that any admission about drugs in Laos would not be enough on its own because the death penalty there meant there were no extradition treaties, but it would provide background to a court case about extortion and dealing here. In order to get Jonno prosecuted for something more substantial than extortion or threatening behaviour, we would need to try to get him to explicitly talk about drug deals in this country, so we should ask him what kind of packages he would like us to deliver now. If we could get him to mention police contacts again that would be useful, so we could try to get him to make a link between himself and Whetstone by mentioning the lack of police help when we first called them. He told us it was important to try and just let Jonno speak and incriminate himself, with just a few subtle prompts and attempts to steer the conversation rather than make it obvious and keep asking questions that we obviously could already answer. Above all, we should appear scared and compliant and not put ourselves in immediate

189

danger or do something that would lead to him tipping PC Whetstone off before they could investigate properly.

Although it sounded dangerous, I could see Julia warming to the task, and she pointed out that getting people to talk about things was part of what she did for a living. Both DS Robbins and DI Buttler were quick to stress that we should try to keep things as simple and natural as possible. It would be normal for us to want Jonno out of the flat as quickly as possible, so any obvious attempt to prolong it would be suspicious. Any questions should appear to be part of us deciding whether to comply or pleading with him to let us off. They wished us luck and promised to support us, whilst reminding us that they were not offering full-time surveillance and any police response would be at least minutes away, so we must not antagonise him. Then they left and I packed a few belongings and drove us back to Natalie's flat. We spent the evening rehearsing how the conversation might go and by the end we were almost looking forward to Jonno's next visit.

Press Record

The first night at Natalie and Julia's was fun. They were welcoming and Will was surprisingly good company. Despite his weird martial arts hobby and almost obsessive fitness routines, he was surprisingly good natured, relaxed and funny at other times. We had gone to bed far later than I was now used to on school nights and as I lay on Natalie's sofa bed, I felt that either she had never opened and tested the bed herself or she was trying to punish me for the trouble I had brought to her flat. I barely slept and decided to get up early so I could beat the traffic on my extended journey to work. I helped myself to some toast and left a note, only to re-remember that traffic never stops in Brixton and on the South Circular, so managed to arrive slightly later than usual, feeling irritable and tired. As I went to make myself a coffee, I found Izzy already there, chatting to some other teachers. Although I was glad to see her, I had to force myself to show it, trying to avoid eye contact so that she would not see my puffy eyes, and I only managed to cheer up as I tasted my first sip of the school machine latte — a ludicrously thick and frothy version which tasted okay until you had seen the machine being refilled with yellow-looking beads of milk.

Tuesday was my busiest day at school, but Izzy and I still managed to have lunch together, so I ate slowly, suppressing any thoughts of last-minute lesson prep. We chatted about meeting at the weekend and she told me she had decided on a place but would pick me up and surprise me. I knew she was trying to show that she could take control and I was delighted and excited, but as soon as we finished and went back to our classrooms, I found my mood dip as I started to think about the traffic home and the prospect of another sleepless night trying to find some position where the wafer-thin mattress would not allow the metal bars and springs to either jab into my limbs or leave saggy gaps to fall into. Obviously, I had to stay at Natalie's until Jonno showed, which would be soon, but I was beginning to think that I would be more comfortable sleeping on a prison bed. I also wondered what would happen if he had still not shown when I had to meet Izzy on Friday and how she would react if I had to cancel again.

As expected, my five-mile journey home took nearly an hour. As I sat seething in stationary traffic, I decided that it would probably be better to walk tomorrow. If I overslept, I could take a bus in and walk home, but I hate bumper-to-bumper journeys and I had reached the point where I was trying to practise mindful breathing to calm down and avoid snapping as I knocked on the door of Natalie's flat. There was no answer and I waited about a minute, realising that because I had left before they were up, we had not discussed keys or whether anyone would be home. I knocked again and called out through the letterbox, feeling foolish and irritable, so was surprised when I heard Julia's voice saying that she would have to let me in "because it is Jo". As soon as she opened the door, I knew he was there by her tense expression, and her exaggerated mouthing of the words "he's here" only confirmed it. She whispered in my ear that she was recording but he was not saying anything.

Much to my relief, when I walked into the kitchen it was clear that he was as tense as we were, despite his attempts to appear cool and collected.

"Ah, Jo, perhaps you will stop wasting my time. Have you brought me my little present or are we doing something else instead?"

"You mean the £10,000?"

"You know exactly what I mean. I am not here to make small talk. Are you giving me a thank-you present or are you going to do me some favours to say sorry for the trouble you have caused me?"

"Can you tell me exactly what favours you want — I need details. When, where and is it illegal?"

"So you don't have the present?"

Julia said, "My account has a seven-day notice period, so I cannot get my half of the £10,000 you are demanding from us."

We all knew that none of us had attempted to withdraw any money, but I was impressed by Julia's clever attempt to slip the extortion into the conversation, and Jonno bit.

"What about you? And I don't care who pays."

"I can get it, but I want to find out more about the jobs you want us to do instead before I decide."

"You don't find out until you do the favours. You'll get the details then. In or out? I'm not discussing it any more. I'm offering you two choices; you are lucky we aren't discussing a third, but we soon will be. I need an answer now and I'm going."

I don't know what came over me. He had given us something on tape but it was like he knew we were stalling and he was becoming suspicious, tetchy and possibly actively dangerous. Without looking at the others for confirmation, I answered him.

"In — I'd rather do the jobs. But I want a promise that if we do six jobs for you that pays both our share. And I'll do the jobs alone. I won't put myself in danger for your drug deals."

Julia gasped and Natalie looked furious, as did Will, but Jonno laughed.

"Atta girl — I'll be in touch. I've said six and that is all you get as a promise. See you, ladies."

As soon as he left Natalie started on me, but Julia tapped her on the shoulder and put her finger to her mouth before switching off the tape. Then she turned on me, too, pointing out that the police had told us to keep it simple and now I was ensuring another visit and more complications.

"Will you never bloody learn to keep some control of yourself? Even now?"

I was flushed with guilt, but knew that this was different.

"Look, I know I got you all into this mess and I know that you tricked him into at least not denying that he was taking money from us, Julia. Well done. And sorry again. But at the end of the day, we were the only ones who mentioned money or drugs. You only need to walk round here at night to see how many people are openly dealing and getting away with it under the police's nose. We need something solid or this will not go away. And none of us even mentioned PC Whetstone, we have nothing on him, so even DS Robbins might lose interest in helping us."

"I think she's right."

Will had remained silent throughout, so I gave an involuntary start at the sound of his voice, but was grateful that he had spoken and he smiled at me and touched my arm to reassure me.

Natalie nodded and agreed that maybe I had a point.

"I feel guilty about this for part of every day. This is not just me being reckless, this is me trying to clean up my mess and get you out of it."

"Okay. We have forgiven you, Jo. You can't have predicted this. No one could. But you have to work with us and not just steamroller through this without at least looking at us for agreement," said Julia, her voice softening with every word that she spoke.

I nodded and found myself starting to well up with tears. Julia put her arm round my shoulder to comfort me and as I glanced nervously at Natalie, to see how she would react, she and Will joined the hug. The feeling of family and togetherness almost made me cry properly, but I fought it back and we broke apart. We agreed to support each other and move forward together, so we called DS Robbins and were relieved that he was working that evening and said he would be round in a couple of hours.

In fact, he came more quickly than that, but the wait seemed interminable. Julia made tea and we all drank it in silence, lost in our thoughts, until Natalie spoke.

"Jo, we have been forgiving and we have been supportive. But once again you have acted alone and on an impulse. You didn't consult us and you didn't even think this through properly for yourself. This is how we all got embroiled in this mess in the first place. Going forward, I am only going to be part of this if you include us first. You have agreed to do jobs for him and if you don't do exactly as we and the police tell you to, I may just leave you to it."

Of course Natalie was right, but it hurt to hear her say it. I tried to point out that I had only offered myself to do the jobs to keep them out of it, but Julia cut me off.

"I know you feel guilty and I know you have changed. This is why you have us all supporting you. But you clearly don't always make good decisions and you have to consult us before you make rash decisions. None of us agreed that you would offer to do jobs for him."

Suddenly, it felt as though the whole weight of the situation was starting to crush me. I knew it was my fault and yet both Natalie and Julia were the ones whose homes were invaded, whilst mine was safe. I kept telling myself that I could never have foreseen that flirting with a man on holiday and wanting to sleep with him would lead to this mess. But I was certain that Natalie and especially Julia deserved it even less and had been unbelievably patient and understanding with me. I was scared, starting to regret my decision and feeling very much like a third wheel in the house.

"I will. I'm sorry. I just wish I could do more. Let me at least cook supper."

"No, thanks. You don't know where anything is in Nat's kitchen. We can order something."

Julia had never been so short with me, so I offered to order and pay for some Lucky Star Chinese, but she and Natalie insisted on sharing the bill. We hugged again and as we waited and ate, began to calm down and discuss the way forward. The atmosphere improved, but if we were a family, they were the parents and Will was the sensible older brother, whilst I was the wayward teenage daughter. We forced our way through strained small talk to a more relaxed togetherness as we ate, but we were all grateful when DS Robbins arrived.

He was polite but business-like, making it clear that he wanted to hear the tape before hearing our thoughts on it. We cleared up and made tea whilst he listened to it. He agreed that there was not enough on the tape to incriminate anyone, but he told me that whilst I should have consulted him first, it might prove useful that I offered to do the job. I resisted the temptation to point out that there was no time to consult or to say "I told you so" and no one else reacted to the idea that maybe I had been right, so DS Robbins continued, "Look, Jonno's been smart and may even have considered that you might be taping him because he has been careful not to incriminate himself at all. You can't do a job for him unless he gives you details, but he may just parcel it out and you'll be in danger before you know anything. That could be our best chance of pinning something on him. If we can incriminate him, I am sure he will trade evidence of Whetstone for a deal. It goes without saying that you could be in a lot of danger if you agree to work with him, and that will require man hours and equipment to protect you, so I will need to ask my inspector whether he will authorise it. I am sure he will, but if not... Hmm. Well, let's hope he goes for it. He'll only do that if he thinks it is a pretty sure thing and whether you, Jo, are up to the challenge of keeping your head, acting as instructed and not doing anything rash or dangerous. Do you understand?"

As he spoke, particularly the last couple of sentences, he spoke more slowly and the look he gave me was a proper TV police interrogation stare. Natalie glanced at me and then looked away, and Julia's first glance seemed impatient and then wavered back to nervous. It was obvious that after meeting us and hearing the whole story, he would have preferred to work with Natalie or Julia.

I took a breath and summoned up my regain-control-of-a-classroom sense of calm and authority and said, "I know. But the fact is that this is my mess and I have been the least affected so far but have the most to lose now. I want to do this and I think I am capable of it."

Robbins nodded, took his time and then replied, "Thanks. That's encouraging. But you volunteered to do this job totally off-script — I don't think you even knew you were going to do that until you did it yourself. Yes, you may need to think on your feet, but we do not want some wildcard going in and thinking they are a trained officer. I want to catch Whetstone and I want to help you three. So does my inspector. This must be very difficult for you and we want to get this over with quickly. But as a drug bust goes, this is, unfortunately, very small for us and we do not have the resources to fund large operations for every drug deal. If we did, we might be able to actually improve the situation rather than simply chip away at it. Catching Whetstone and dealing with a corrupt officer at the same time makes this more of a priority, but we are only going to be able to do that if you can act calmly and as directed. It may be dangerous, particularly if you don't act within the absolute boundaries we tell you, and if it does work you will almost certainly be involved as a witness in a long drawn-out trial and will have to tell your work about this. You have to be ready for that and my inspector has to believe you are, too."

His simply stated and deliberately sobering message was designed to impress upon us the seriousness of this operation. We looked at each other and did not need to ask what would happen if we did not proceed. There was no evidence, so we would get no help of any substance — he would probably advise us to refuse to pay and say that the police would protect us, but basically, we would be back on our own and in limbo. This was our only hope and we all knew it, though it offered very little actual hope.

"I am ready to do this. The last few months have made me stronger and certainly made me consider the consequences of my actions. Let me do this. Train or brief me as best you can and I will do it."

Julia and Natalie both put a reassuring hand on me and Robbins nodded.

"Okay. I'll put it to Inspector Buttler and say I think you are up to it. We'll brief you as best we can on the operation, but if Jonno keeps things vague it will be very hard to prepare. You will have to wear an earpiece. The main thing will be to follow any instruction I give you. Do not think that you know better than us. Can you do that?"

"Yes."

"Great. I'll get back to the station and confirm that we are okay. You need to contact me as soon as you hear anything."

We were shocked but hopeful when he left. We knew we were safe for now, so I left quickly so Julia and Natalie could have time together and I could sleep in my own bed. I got back to my flat just after nine p.m. and texted Izzy, who said I could call her. I just needed to hear her voice and it was great to chat, even though I could not possibly talk about all this on the phone. We chatted about our date on Friday and promised to have lunch together at school the next day.

Fast Forward

I woke up feeling surprisingly refreshed. Even as I had climbed wearily into bed the night before, I expected my mind to be swirling with thoughts of drug drops and being worried about Izzy, but I was asleep almost as I lay down. Now, I felt calm and rested. Although I was apprehensive about the Jonno thing and slightly worried about whether the inspector would okay the job, I was quietly confident. I was looking forward to working towards a solution and, more importantly, finally being the one to solve the problem instead of just heaping stress and anxiety on Julia and Natalie. And Izzy had agreed to have lunch with me for the second day in a row, which was also encouraging and meant that she was even becoming more relaxed about the possibility of people at work finding out about us or at least suspecting we were a couple. I wished I could tell her about everything, but I would start trying to pave the way and test the water — maybe telling her during our date on Friday or, if not, at least soon, when it was over.

When I got to school, Izzy was the first person I saw as I entered the room. Although there were other staff around, I barely noticed them — she looked beautiful today. She had her hair tied back and when she smiled her eyes twinkled and the beginning of crow's feet round her eyes was endearing and made me feel a warm surge towards her, helped, at least in part, by her figure-hugging green dress that managed to stay respectable whilst still accentuating her curves and athletic body. Although it was a lovely dress, the Izzy I used to know would have been too self-conscious to wear something like that in front of a class. Today, she radiated confidence and smiled at my compliment and raised an eyebrow when we greeted each other in the kitchen. She told me she was looking forward to lunch and Friday as she picked up her jacket and left the staffroom. I had to force myself not to stare after her as she walked away, and feigned exaggerated interest in the usual coffee-making chat to distract myself from trying to picture myself taking her dress off.

It was a good start to the day and I could feel my mood and positive energy transferring itself to my students, who seemed to pay extra attention and actually engage with the text, rather than just roll off random talk of simile and metaphor like a blanket tick list with no semblance of interest or motivation. Just before lunch, DS Robbins left a voicemail saying that the job and surveillance operation were authorised and he would be in touch soon to give me more details. I texted the good news to Julia and Natalie at lunch and the afternoon seemed to fly by. Despite everything, I was as happy as I could remember and feeling as though I could handle anything. My lessons went brilliantly as my students seemed to pick up on my upbeat mood, and when I received a text from Julia saying that DS Robbins had arranged to meet at our flat with a surveillance specialist at five thirty p.m., I was happy to leave promptly and go straight there.

As I drove home, I ran through imaginary versions of conversations where I told Izzy about the whole Jonno and Julia developments. I decided that the fact that Julia was now with Natalie would ensure that she would not mind my hiding the fact that we had intermittently lived together as friends whilst hiding from Jonno. Ignoring the small details of having to pretend to be a drugs mule, it would be all plain sailing from here. Even the traffic seemed to be making way for me and I arrived with plenty of time to spare and was delighted to be greeted by the smell of fresh baking. I found myself happy to see Natalie there as well and didn't even question where Julia had conceived the idea of a 'molasses and ginger traybake' — what was wrong with a simple chocolate or coffee cake? But it tasted almost as good, all the more so because I took it as a sign that I was definitely forgiven, and whilst we ate and waited and chatted happily, Julia even quipped, "We should have thought to buy lashings of ginger beer to go with it — now we are kind of the Famous Five or Terrific Three or whatever!"

We giggled but instinctively clinked our coffee cups in the air and, as one, toasted, "The Terrific Three!"

The doorbell rang as we took our first sip and Julia let them in. DS Robbins had brought a man who looked far more like an accountant than a policeman, whom he introduced as DC Jack Bishop. Bishop was clearly in his forties, slim and with hair that was both greying and receding. He was neatly dressed in a newish but cheap-looking blue suit with a white shirt and blue striped tie. He spoke so quietly we had to strain to hear, and it was difficult to imagine him ever being in uniform or policing a drunken Friday night. He declined our offer of tea and looked at us as though it was only his natural politeness that stopped him from openly refusing to help. He clearly looked sceptical about our ability to be part of a police operation, but he dutifully showed us how to wear and use the equipment. Robbins said that he would try to be there when I put it on for real to check the device was concealed, but asked me to model it in this outfit. We found a way to hide it and to make it comfortable, but the knowledge that it was there made it feel much heavier than it was. Everything got serious again and suddenly I was starting to regret my impulsivity. Natalie, Julia and even Robbins sensed this and he was quick to reassure me.

"We wouldn't let you do this if we didn't think you could. We'll be listening and we'll be nearby. It's natural to feel nervous and I'm glad you are. You have to believe in yourself and stay calm enough not to draw suspicion and blow the operation. If you do, you might get hurt and you will definitely not get a second chance. So, if you don't feel up to it, don't do it. If you do do it, we will back you up."

This whole situation had gone on too long and we had come too far for me to back out now. Despite my fear, I was determined and I knew that, this time, when under pressure I would be able to do whatever was needed. I took a deep breath and I almost felt myself grow taller and could feel some steel and confidence calm my nerves and give me the focus that I would need. Even before I began to speak and reassure the others, I saw them exchange glances and nod. Even Bishop stopped looking sceptical and we finished up the formalities quickly. Julia and Natalie were going back to their flat so they could be there to get job details from Jonno, but were meeting friends who lived locally first. They asked me if I wanted to join them, but I sensed they were being polite and I was happy to be on my own and call Izzy from my landline instead of my mobile for a change.

After they left, I ate a bowl of cereal for supper as I checked over my lesson plans for the next day, showered and then settled down in my pyjamas to call Izzy, who sounded as though she had been hoping for my call. We chatted for half an hour and I felt closer to her than ever. I felt confident that I could tell her everything and even felt resolved to tell her on Friday night or Saturday morning, before I had done the job, if I felt that the conversation and mood were right. When I got off the phone, I felt more tired than I realised and retired early to bed and slept deeply and contentedly.

Time to Step Up

Thursday rushed past. I barely saw Izzy except to smile and say that we were both looking forward to Friday. I texted Julia to check on her, but there was still no sign of Jonno. I slept early so I would look and feel my best for my date with Izzy. When I saw her at school, she had had a haircut and was wearing a short green wool skirt with velvet trims and a fitted patterned shirt that made her look gorgeous. I told her so after following her into the staff loos and checking no one else was there. She was so emboldened by this that she even allowed me to sneak a quick kiss just before the door opened and we almost jumped apart, causing Georgie, a twenty-something Art teacher to look oddly at us, wondering what we were gossiping about. It was all shaping up brilliantly for our date this evening until I got a text from Julia saying that Jonno had just been to the flat when Natalie was on her own and told her to tell me to meet him outside Millbank Tower at seven p.m. dressed as though for a party. He had made clear that she and Natalie were not allowed to come with me and Julia had got the impression that he had been watching her flat at least to check that Will was not there.

I did not know whether I was more scared about the impending danger or angry about it meaning that I would have to lie to Izzy and cancel another date last minute. Of course, he could not know anything about my date with Izzy, or even the fact that she existed at all, but it seemed that every time things were looking good for us, Jonno was there to make it harder. Why had I been so stupid as to arrange our date on Friday when any idiot would guess that Friday or Saturday would be the busiest nights for a drug dealer? Hopefully, it would be the last twist and I could reveal all afterwards, but I had assumed that about the last meeting. I was teaching all day but, luckily, Julia agreed to tell DS Robbins, leaving me the small matter of acting calm in front of students and finding a way to cancel Izzy without lying too much or making her angry. When DS Robbins texted about an hour later, I openly checked my phone in front of my Year 10s and saw that he and a team would meet me in a van by the Tate at six p.m. for a final briefing and to check the equipment.

I hated the idea of lying to Izzy but knew that she was as excited about this evening as I was, so I could not just cancel without a reason and I could certainly not tell her everything over lunch at school. Eventually, I decided my best option was to pretend that my mother had told me I was urgently needed at home. She knew my mother was prone to sudden summonses from when we dated before, but she would also know that they were normally false alarms and that I could probably go on Saturday morning instead of Friday night. If I overplayed it and made her worry, then that would be even worse when I told her the truth in a few days, so it would be better to say as little as possible and hope that she would not be too angry.

I let my class out a few minutes early before lunch, telling them to walk slowly, deciding that the worst that would happen would be a terse email reminding me to adhere to lesson timings. All things considered, I could live with that today. I knew that Izzy had a club and was not going to lunch, but I caught her on the way and hated myself all the way through my lie about needing to go and see my mum.

"Do you really need to go tonight? You know your mum probably doesn't need you. She seems to summon you away every time we are due to meet."

The intense stare she gave me to accompany her comment made it clear she was still undecided over whether I was lying or my mother was sabotaging.

"I know, and it is shitty timing, but she is on her own and even if she could manage physically, she is exaggerating because she is lonely and just gets very down sometimes. I'll be back by Sunday and will make it up to you in any way that I can if you will see me then."

"I'll think about it. You'd better not be lying to me, Jo."

"I promise that there is nothing I want to do more than spend this evening with you. I am so happy to be given a second chance that I would not blow you out if I could avoid it."

"Does your mum know we are back together?"

"No — it's not that I wouldn't want to tell her. It's just that you know what she's like. She likes you. She's just been up and down and needy lately."

"Well, last time was a false alarm, but I suppose you must do what you think you have to do. Good luck with your mum if she needs it and I'll let you know about Sunday."

Her tone and face suggested that she was still not convinced, but she seemed okay and I was fairly sure that she would calm down and we could get over it. I would have to find time to at least text her tonight, because she would know that if I was really with my mum, I would do that and probably call as well.

Having sorted Izzy, all I had to do now was force myself to eat something, teach two more lessons and mentally prepare for tonight. Now that my initial worries about telling Izzy were over, I was able to properly process what I had to do tonight. I sat silently amongst a group of staff pretending to laugh at their jokes and eating my Friday chips as a minor wave of panic started to wash over me. I imagined scenario after scenario, each one becoming more dangerous and frightening than the last, including mobsters, rival drug gangs, guns, shoot-outs. I told myself not to be ridiculous, but when a casual holiday flirtation and drink had led to all this, then who knew what an actual drug drop could lead to? And, I reasoned, there must be some reason why Jonno was going to be at the scene but not do the drop himself. It might be just to supervise me doing my first job for him or because he needed a woman to deliver it to keep it discreet, but it might also be because it was too dangerous even for him.

My mind continued to torment and terrify me all afternoon, and as I made my way home, I knew that if I did not calm down I could either give the whole thing away or get into worse trouble that evening. I called Julia as soon as I got home and she helped me to calm down.

"I can't imagine how you must be feeling. I would be the same, but I don't think Millbank is East End gangster territory — even if it is an organised gang, it must be a rich one as it will be teeming with rich bankers and politicians at that time, so not the kind of place where you are likely to be in danger. Jonno is not a mobster, he is a small-time dealer with a police minder, and PC Whetstone seems too stupid and petty to have mob links. He asked you to dress up — it could be because he just wouldn't look the part. The only thing Natalie and I were worried about is somebody, who knows, trying to take advantage."

I realised what she meant. Suddenly, I had visions of being raped or being forced into the sex trade. Julia understood my long silence.

"Sorry — I didn't mean to worry you. I just want you to be careful. He said to dress for a party, not like a... well, you know. Just wear something evening-ish but that is not revealing or flattering. And be careful —and you know you can back out at any time. DS Robbins has the details and he is letting you go ahead."

"Yeah — but he is not in danger."

I realised as I said it that it was me who had put myself in danger and he was just there to help me. Julia and Natalie had told me not to do it.

"It's okay. This is new and scary and I don't like not knowing. But I will be careful. It's good for me to be a little nervous."

"Jo, Nat and I love you. You are like a prodigal sister to us and I wish we could be there, but daren't risk spoiling things. We won't blame you if you back out."

"No — it's time to finish this. I'll be careful and do exactly as Robbins tells me. But I can do this."

I had to be strong. I composed myself and began to feel confident. Then I remembered how good Jonno had looked when I first met him. He had gone downhill since then, but he was definitely capable of mixing with any crowd. This might just be a simple drug drop and he was afraid of being caught on camera in a club or somewhere which had cameras. Anyway, cameras would keep me safe and I had police back-up, however minimal, so I would not be in trouble if I was stopped. Anyway, I had no choice but to believe that it would be okay.

I decided not to wear a dress but smart trousers, loose evening top and a jacket that would enable me to conceal any listening device and the parcel of drugs I assumed I would be delivering. I took a bag as well to put the parcel in. I wanted to wear trainers or something to help me run in, but settled for the flattest shoes I had that could be worn to a party. Then I took the tube to Millbank to meet DS Robbins. Natalie and Julia texted last minute to offer to meet for a drink on the way, but we agreed that there was a risk of them being followed, so decided against it. I had texted Lexi for moral support but knew she was covering a big event for work, and though she offered to be in the area a bit later, I told her I was okay and had to settle for just a text to give me courage.

The Job

When I got to the Tate I was surprised to see a marked police van, but delighted that when I walked over to it with feigned casualness I saw DS Robbins. I had assumed that the surveillance van would be undercover, but DS Robbins told me that, actually, a marked police van on a Friday night would be the best undercover vehicle to park in Millbank because people just ignore uniformed officers and it was the only way to park anywhere in London. He and DC Bishop were not in uniform, but he said that he had four uniformed officers who were attached to the team but also just patrolling the area routinely anyway.

He talked me through the equipment: two hidden microphones — one attached to my bra under my top and one that looked like a cheap disposable pen to keep in my jacket pocket. He also gave me a cross necklace with a tiny camera and airpod-style headphones for me to listen to him. Although the individual pieces looked a lot less designer than in the Bond films and there was certainly no Omega timepiece or DB car, I felt very secret agent and the calm, matter-of-fact and almost bored way DC Bishop went through what was clearly a standard spiel of instructions made me feel confident that they knew what they were doing.

They sent me to the rendezvous early and told me to expect Jonno to spend at least a few minutes watching me before showing his hand, so not to do anything stupid like talk into the microphone and make it obvious that I was being listened to, but if I really needed to say something I could pretend to be using my hands-free phone. I went to the meeting place, waited, paced and waited some more. I kept scanning the people around me, wondering whether he or Whetstone or someone was spying on me. If he was watching, I was sure he could sense my discomfort and was probably enjoying it, so I forced myself to stay as still as possible and feign boredom. A couple of times I could see pairs of the officers from the van walk past and casually look over in my direction, and this gave me the strength to keep my composure a little better. Eventually, ten minutes late, Jonno came up behind me and smugly introduced himself.

"Hi, there. Good girl for coming alone. Ready for action?"

I could not suppress a tiny shriek of surprise and, caught between the sudden fright and a simultaneous desire to either hit him or run away, I stepped back and let him see how on edge I was. My obvious fear and dislike were such that a couple of people glanced over, but at this time on Friday at Millbank people were too focussed on seeing in the weekend to give a more than passing thought to a random stranger. I reminded myself that this time I had the secret and some of the power, so I forced myself to step back towards him and meet his gaze.

"You're late — just give me the details and let's get this done. Some of us have things to do."

"I like your spirit, Jo, but we both know how scared you are. You do this how I tell you or else."

"Or else what?" — I wanted him to incriminate himself quickly.

Jonno paused and leaned in, and then the way he spoke, in an almost conversational tone, made his words even more menacing.

"Do you want me to threaten you? Don't play games with me, you have no idea what you are doing. Are you going to behave yourself?"

I desperately wanted to try and make him mention drugs and Whetstone, but DS Robbins had stressed to me that in order to stay undercover, especially in case Whetstone was also around and because this was a small operation, they were hanging back. If I needed help it would be at least a minute or two if not longer if I was inside the tower, so I should avoid provocation and keep things simple and unsuspicious, even if it meant not getting anything useful. I had always been confident and would rather put on a show of bravado than lose face, but my experiences since Laos had taught me to be cautious.

"Okay — let's just get this over with."

I think Jonno knew me well enough to take this quiet and submissive answer as proof that I would do what he wanted and, perhaps, that I was not being followed or trying anything. He immediately appeared more confident and I hoped that this was why he started to speak more freely.

"Good girl, good girl. Right, now listen! The snowcones are in this cake box."

"What are snowcones?", I asked to partly to make him state it explicitly and partly because I had no idea what snowcones are.

"Snowcones! Jesus, how green are you? Dust, the white stuff!"

"Oh — drugs?"

"Yes. Whatever — your job is to deliver, not ask questions. Shut up and listen."

I managed to suppress my involuntary smile and desire to look over to the van to see whether they had heard him mention drugs out loud. He opened the box and there was an obviously supermarket-style cheap cake on top of a cardboard platform which must conceal the drugs. The box looked impressive from the outside, but only an idiot would be fooled by the ridiculous cake inside. It was almost more obvious that something was going on than if I had just walked in with a plain cardboard box. He saw the disbelief in my face and said, "Don't worry — the security guard is ex-job and one of my associates, so if he does check it, just show him this card and he will know that you work for me. No one else has any reason to look if you act naturally. Don't screw this up by trying to draw attention to yourself."

He handed me a card from 'Magic Muffins' which looked very amateur, but he was confident it would work and then gave me instructions about which floor and party to go to. I tried to get my microphone pen out to write it down and he started to tell me not to write anything.

"Look — if you are expecting me to remember it all the way up in the lift, I can write it down at any time later. I'm a little on edge, I don't get forced into delivering drugs for people every day of the week. I might forget where I am supposed to go — okay?"

He nodded and spoke whilst I wrote slightly shakily and was so relieved that the cheap microphone pen actually worked as a pen, too, that I almost forgot that I was recording him as he spoke.

"Yeah. Okay. But calm down. Just do as you are told and you will be one step closer to paying your debt to me. You do this job properly and five more jobs and then I'll let you off for the drugs you lost me in Laos. You screw up and you will pay. Take a deep breath, act natural and get on with it."

As I put the note in my pocket and Jonno passed the cake box to me, I could feel myself starting to sweat and could hear a kind of dull pulsing in my ears as my blood rushed round my body. I was almost more surprised than Jonno when DS Robbins, DC Bishop and the uniformed officers suddenly appeared and started shouting at Jonno to stay where he was. Suddenly, everyone was looking and things seemed to happen as though in a dream — there was a haze of noise and people seemed to be everywhere and phones were pointing at us with cameras out. The police dispersed them quickly and although Jonno started to run, he was caught immediately by Robbins and Bishop, who seemed to have appeared from nowhere without me noticing. I almost dropped the cake box in shock, but DS Robbins had his arm out and his voice snapped me out of my trance.

"That was first rate — handled like a pro. We could see how nervous you were and when he first came over, we worried you would do something stupid. I daren't risk speaking to you because he was so close to your earphones. But you stayed calm and got him to properly incriminate himself. Great that he mentioned Laos and making you do jobs for him — I just hope that there are drugs in here to be sure of an arrest. Then he may incriminate Whetstone to get some time off his sentence."

As Robbins and Bishop gently handled the cake box and confirmed there were drugs inside, I was grateful that I had remembered to bring water. I leaned against the wall and sipped slowly, still sweating but feeling my heart slow down and the fear subside. I saw Jonno being led away in handcuffs to the van. He tried a brief angry and intimidatory stare which made my heart pound for a second, but he was half-threatening and half-pleading with the officers walking him to the police car that had suddenly appeared with two more officers and the sight of him in cuffs being put in the back was enough to calm me down quickly.

Robbins and Bishop had taken the cake box to the van and seemed to have forgotten me briefly, leaving me alone to face curious glances from people who were still hanging around to see what all the fuss was about. I could see people taking surreptitious pictures and was suddenly worried about my students finding out about this on some form of social media, so I walked to the van, too.

DS Robbins and DC Bishop were hunched over the cake box talking, but invited me inside. Bishop was holding a camera and Robbins was examining a parcel of white powder in a transparent bag. It was about the size of a bag of sugar.

"Is that the drugs?"

"Yes — I checked and it is genuine cocaine, which is class A and there is enough for him to be charged with dealing rather than possession. A few £1000s and coupled with the tape, he will not be bothering you again. Well done."

"Great — but I sense a but?"

"Yes. We've got Jonno, but there is nothing on Whetstone. Jonno may well decide to try to trade information on Whetstone because he could even face life imprisonment for dealing and extortion, but Whetstone won't face anything to incriminate himself, so it would be good to maybe carry on with the job and get the security guard."

"What? So — I still have to deliver it?"

"You don't have to do anything. But it will help us get Whetstone. If the man upstairs really is ex-cop, he could be another link to Whetstone. We'll need to get him to incriminate himself on tape, otherwise he won't speak; but since we're here already and he's expecting you, if you're up to it, I'd like to carry on."

"But won't he be tipped off by this?"

"No — too far away. Jonno didn't get a chance to call. Whetstone's on shift tonight so definitely not around, so we could just go ahead. Robbins and I can go up ahead of you if you like so we can be there to help quickly if there is a problem. If we don't act now, Whetstone will be tipped off and we won't be able to catch him."

I wanted to just walk away and forget about Whetstone. Surely, he was not my problem? But I remembered his rudeness and arrogance and wondered how many criminals were working with him and victims were being ignored. And I wanted to help Robbins.

"Okay — but are you sure I will be safe?"

"We can't be a hundred percent about anything. But you did well. We are so close, just a little bit more. I believe in you. But if you do this, we have to do it quickly. They will be expecting you to make the delivery now."

I could feel myself start to shake. Seeing Jonno arrested felt like the end, so I had stopped feeling the need to be brave. Now I had to summon back all my battered courage. Part of me resented Robbins for making me do this. Catching Whetstone would be good for his career and it seemed unlikely that Whetstone would come after me. But Robbins was a good officer, willing to risk his career to catch a bad one. He had come through for us and made us feel confident in him from the moment he took on the case. I liked him and felt reassured by him and I wanted to see this through to the end for him and his career, too. And I wanted revenge. I remembered Whetstone's patronising and bullying visit to our home when we first called him and I wanted him stopped. I took a couple of deep breaths and composed myself, and with a steady voice told DS Robbins that I wanted to do it.

He did not wait to process Jonno or give me any further instructions except to tell me that since he and Bishop were the only non-uniform officers, he would no longer be able to listen and talk to me through my earphones, and handed control to one of the other officers. He handed back the cake box, which looked even more suspicious inside with the cake icing slightly damaged from being moved round. They replaced the drugs with a similar-sized package made up with a bag of flour brought back to the van by one of the other officers and poured into a similar bag.

"We need the real drugs as evidence, so we have replaced it with flour, so if anyone tries it when you are still there, make sure you either get it on film or tell Acting PS Brennan through your microphone so we know to come and get you immediately."

Then he just told me to go up exactly as Jonno had told me and to try to get an image of the security guard and everything on the necklace camera, but to be discreet because the guard might know about such devices. I put the airbuds in and proceeded into the tower.

Magic Muffin Lady

I had barely had time to process what had just happened as I started to cross the street to Millbank Tower. As the knowledge that DS Robbins had Jonno in the back of a police van with video footage of him started to sink in, I felt a rush of elation and I found myself almost starting to skip my way across the road. I paused on the pavement to compose myself, not knowing how soon I would meet Jonno's security guard. I knew that I could never have predicted the chain of events that had led me to this moment, but I still felt responsible for getting Julia and Natalie involved and Jonno's arrest helped lift the weight of guilt off my shoulders. I wanted to stop and phone them immediately, so I reminded myself that my work was not finished. The security guard I was due to meet next was an ex-copper who would know how to spot anything suspicious. I had no idea where he was or what he looked like, but I had to believe that I could get something for the police to use against Whetstone. The idea that any back-up would be minutes away in the event of a problem almost made me shake as I considered how dangerous things could get in that time. The only thing I had going for me was that he would expect me to be nervous and, as with Jonno, it might prompt him to be over-confident and let something slip.

There was nothing suspicious in the lobby, so I took the lift up to the twenty-eighth floor and saw a man in a suit by the door. He asked me for my invitation. I could feel myself starting to sweat and as I answered him my voice came out partly as a croak and I had to clear my throat and breathe to sound normal. I told him I had been sent to deliver a cake. He asked who I worked for and I showed him the card and he grinned and told me to go right in. I paused, hoping to get him to say something, but he was holding the door open and was in no mood to chat. I forced myself to walk into the room, at least making sure my necklace could get a good view of as many people as possible, handed the box to the person Jonno had told me to ask for, and then left. I could feel myself starting to shake even as I closed the door behind me and I could see the barely-supressed smirk on the bouncer or guard's face, but this only made the drop look more convincing. Still shaking as I rode the lift back to the lobby, I texted Julia and Lexi that Jonno had been arrested, the deal was done and I would call them when I could. Lexi was at a job, though she texted immediately a dozen smiley faces and 'brave girl, well done you!'. Julia and Natalie also sent smiles and thumbs-up and a 'well done. Glad you are safe. Do you want us to meet you?'.

DS Robbins was right outside the building and he started to give me a handshake, but when he saw me shaking, he broke protocol, gave me a hug and congratulated me. He told me that I would not have to go back to the station with them as they already had statements from before. One of the officers had recognised the security guard and the picture and sound from the delivery were great, so hopefully they would be able to get something on Whetstone directly from him. There was still no direct link yet, though they would review the footage again. I suddenly realised how badly I wanted Whetstone arrested and punished, too. When we called him for help, we just got more fear and mockery. But Jonno had already been taken away and the footage of the cake delivery meant that they had a clear drug-dealing charge to trade for information about Whetstone. DS Robbins even arranged a ride back to Natalie's in a police car because two officers were heading that way and he could see that I was shaken up. I was so grateful I almost wanted to kiss him and accepted the lift without hesitation. As I cruised through the Friday night traffic swiftly back to Natalie's, I considered what to say when I phoned Izzy from their flat.

Celebrations

As I was driven back to Natalie's in the back of a police car, feeling like a cross between a criminal and a celebrity, my mind was buzzing with euphoria and relief and trying to focus on what to say to Izzy. The officers who drove me were polite but clearly unimpressed to be put on chauffeur duty on a Friday night, driving fast and constantly changing lanes. They were chatty, congratulating me on my role and wanting to know details, but I wanted them to concentrate on driving and to allow me time with my thoughts, and eventually my taciturn answers led them to talk to each other instead. I sat quietly in the back like a good criminal, feeling self-conscious at every traffic light. When we finally reached Natalie's and I was let out of the back I could almost physically feel people staring at me, even the ones pretending not to. I could sense them appraising me and deciding whether I was a criminal, informant or victim, and I was glad that I would not need to visit Natalie's again for a while after tonight. I thanked them awkwardly and deliberately loudly and then made my way up to the flat.

Julia opened the door and hugged me. Natalie was standing behind her with a huge smile, brandishing glasses of champagne. She was the first to speak.

"Well done! I thought you might have bitten off more than you could chew, but you have done it. Brave girl! Such a relief. Tell us everything."

Julia pulled me by the hand into the living room, which had plates of nibbles arranged, and Natalie saw this without jealousy, also putting her arm round me as I breathed my thanks and we raised a toast. As I swallowed the first sip of champagne, I felt a surge of adrenaline relief and exhaustion come over me as though the fear in me was lifting and all the sleepless nights and tension hit me. I knew that I had to tell them everything after all I had put them through and all of their support and grace in not blaming me, but what I really wanted was a cup of tea in my own flat and to start planning a future with Izzy.

It was nine thirty p.m. and if I had really gone to see my mother, I would have phoned Izzy by now. Julia and Natalie were eager for gossip, but I told them I wanted to text Izzy first, and though they said they understood, I could feel their impatience as I hastily typed: 'Sorry again about tonight but I can get away first thing tomorrow and don't need to stay the weekend. Bit awkward to chat here right now so sorry for texting. If you are around at all this weekend, I would love to see you and make it up to you. Any time that suits you or come to mine and let me cook for you. Sorry. So happy to be back with you. I wish I was there now.'

I was barely five minutes into the story when Izzy texted back: 'Cook for me? You? Okay — brunch at yours, 11am? Only if you are sure I won't get food poisoning!'

I wondered whether the five minutes had been spent typing and deleting 'I told you so' and making it business-like. Despite the lack of a 'xxx' or 'looking forward to it', which made it clear she was still cross, she was meeting me first thing tomorrow, which was positive. Her brunch suggestion was very ambiguous — maybe she was too keen to see me to wait and maybe she just wanted to pick a time that made it clear that she would not be spending the night at mine. I wanted to text back but had no idea how to politely clarify whether sex would or would not be part of our date. Julia and Natalie were in no mood to be distracted, so I replied a quick '☺💅xxx' and felt lucky to just get 'x' back.

They wanted every detail, constantly interrupting to question things and comment. They were impressed with the spy gadgets and my having to go and film the bouncer or bodyguard man. We all agreed it was very James Bond and I thought that when I was finally able to tell Izzy, hopefully tomorrow, she would be so impressed that she would forgive everything else and be dazzled by my daring. As we moved to speculation about what would happen next with Jonno, whether we would have to give evidence and what would happen with Whetstone, we realised that we had casually finished a bottle of champagne and eaten the whole contents on the coffee table between us. They had been too nervous to eat until I returned and we had all been starving, so we had all been cramming in food as we talked. I was feeling more than a little drunk and light-headed and in no mood to take a taxi back home tonight, so we agreed to try and get up early enough for them to give me Izzy advice and then quickly cleared up and set up a bed in the living room. Their flatmate, Will, had decided it was safe to take a night off from protecting us and had gone out, and they offered to let me sleep in his room instead. I did not know Will particularly well, but from what I gathered he seemed to divide his time between working out, going out and putting out, so I did not want to speculate what had gone on in his bed and said I would be more comfortable on the sofa. I was so mentally and physically exhausted that I knew I would sleep quickly wherever I was, and as I lay down on the tired and sagging cushions, I barely had time to replay any of the details before I was fast asleep.

Confessions

I awoke with a stiff neck, back and basically everything. It was just after seven a.m. and I was the first up. I decided Natalie and Julia would be glad to have the place to themselves, so I did a quick clear up, left a note, made myself just presentable enough for the early-morning London crowd and took a bus back to my flat. I was ravenous when I got home, but settled for a distinctly soft apple before quickly showering, putting on my best jeans and most flattering T-shirt and heading out again to shop for my brunch with Izzy. Izzy had done most of the cooking when we had dated before, so although my new skills were basic at best, I felt confident I could impress her with my pancakes and flipping skills. All I needed was an impressive array of toppings, Izzy's favourite coffee capsules and fresh oranges to juice. Feeling pleased with my brunch ingredients, I decided to also buy stuff for supper. Izzy had always liked my risotto, so I could make her something she would like without making it obvious I was expecting her to stay. I would just casually happen to have the right ingredients in the fridge with some Häagen-Dazs in the freezer to round off the meal or save for another time. I got a paper as well for us to read companionably over brunch if I was struggling to tell her the truth or for us to fail to do the crossword together if she stayed.

I got home and gave the flat a quick once over. It was tidier than it had ever been in my pre-Julia days, but I knew that the cleaner the flat was the more relaxed she would be. I knew I could have used the time to start writing reports and that the following week was promising to be filled with frantic deadlines and hastily-written worksheets for barely-planned lessons, but I had bloody earned this weekend and was not going to let work or anything else spoil it.

She arrived almost perfectly on time, which was a positive sign, and the kiss that she gave me, brazenly on the doorstep, was brief, but warm and loving.

"Well, you'll certainly have shocked Doris if she is peering through her spyhole," I said as I closed the door.

"I bet she was and it's good for her!"

She looked amazing and she clearly wanted me to think so. I told her how good she looked and she reddened slightly but smiled and deliberately did not return the compliment. She was feigning crossness, but I could tell she was just as happy to see me as I was to see her. She raised an eyebrow at the sight of me putting the first pancake on and I pre-empted her comments.

"Woman of many talents, me. I told you I have grown up. I have spent less time drinking and more time cooking since you left me to pine for you."

It was all going perfectly to my unscripted idea of how it should be, so as I served the first two pancakes, I decided to broach the subject immediately. A wiser person than me would probably have had the sense to let us savour the moment first.

"So, Izzy, sorry again for last night. But let me tell you all about everything and I think you will understand why I had no choice."

She started to say that she understood about my mum, but I told her that there was something I needed to tell her about and, please, would she hear me out in full before asking anything? All the warmth seemed to leave her face and she looked for a second as though she was going to cry, and then she looked angry.

"Look, it is nothing about us, and I haven't been unfaithful or anything. I have just been dealing with something for the last few months and I have wanted to tell you but it was never the right time. It doesn't mean I don't want to be with you. But I want to tell you everything and to be absolutely straight with you."

"So you haven't been straight with me until now."

It was definitely more of a statement than a question and it almost felt as though each syllable was a little recriminatory tap on my head at the very least. I blurted out a "Yes, no, look, just listen" and started my story with very little confidence in my ability to convince her. She pushed the pancake aside, but at least took it back and listlessly added maple syrup when I asked her to try it. It was too late to take the words back, so there was nothing left to do but to tell her everything and explain why I could not be honest before.

I went through all the details in chronological order but adding justifications and trying to explain away or seek understanding for my mistakes by telling her that I was a better person who had learnt some harsh and scary lessons. As she listened, her face alternated continuously between shock, disbelief and anger. She started to ask questions a few times and stopped herself, and then she just seemed stunned into silence, which continued after I had finished speaking. When she did speak, it was quiet and as though I had winded her.

"Is this really all true now, Jo? Is this everything"

"Yes. Really. I have wanted to tell you for so long but I did not know if you would believe me and it was crazy, and shitty. And I did not want to drag you into my chaos and I did not think you would believe me. I can't believe it all happened. But the worst has to be over now. I have wanted to tell you for so long and I know I lied to you, but not about anything important to us."

"It was important. It was important to me that this time I could trust you and I was sure I could believe you, and it turns out that you are able to keep some pretty massive things a secret from me and I still don't know you. For fuck's sake, Jo, you managed to hide the fact that at one point you were living with your ex-girlfriend while seeing me. And then helping her move house and being part of some weird threesome. You clearly trust her more than me."

"Izzy, it just isn't like that. I was wanting to leave her because I wanted you even before this whole thing started. When I came back to England all I wanted was you back and I hung on even as you made it clear you might never take me back. And as I have explained, Julia and I were involved because he found her flat, not mine. And it was my fault, so I had to be there. I was like a reformed addict paying my dues, and I wanted to actually become the kind of person who solves problems rather than makes them. So I could deserve you. And you know I have become better."

"I thought you had become better, Jo. But you have kept this from me this whole time. Again, I trusted you and again I discover you have lied."

"Izzy — when it started, you did not even want to speak to me, you swapped groups to be away from me. I couldn't tell you then. And then when you agreed to be friends and to give me a second chance, I was so happy that I was scared. I kept thinking it was over and I could scarcely believe it was happening to me and so I could not expect you to just accept it. And I admit, I knew you would not be happy about Julia, but she is a good person. We were never a proper couple and we were totally unsuited to each other and she is very happy with Natalie and I am happy for her. I like her, as a friend. And she knows how good you are for me. I knew I wanted you back, but then this and having to put her up here and getting to know her and Natalie has helped me. The state of the flat, my cooking, my taking responsibility have been helped by our friendship. I will never lie to you again, I swear. And lying to you and knowing that we would have to have this conversation was probably the hardest and most scary part of the last few months. Please, Izzy. What we have is too special to lose. You have no idea what it has been like."

"I have no idea because you kept me in the dark. I didn't want to get involved with you again because I didn't trust you and I did not want to allow myself to love you only to get hurt by you again. And you were keeping all this from me the whole time. How can I trust you?"

She paused, composing herself, and I had no words to say to make things better.

"Look, I'm just going to go. Before I say or do something that I might regret. I need space to think. Have the decency not to contact me unless I contact you."

"I can't promise you that, Izzy. I love you. If you don't call me, I can't just do nothing. At least promise to talk tomorrow night before we have to both be at school. This has been scary and harrowing for me. I am exhausted and spent. I honestly felt I had no choice."

"You had a choice. I am trying to understand, but this was a big deal and you made sure I knew nothing about it. Confiding in another woman instead, who I had no idea was living with you and who seems more important to you even than Lexi without you even mentioning her. If I stay here now, I will say something that cannot be unsaid. If there is any chance of us moving past this, you need to leave me alone until I am ready to talk."

And that was it. She left so quickly that I barely had time to even stand up. I fought back the tears and sat down at the table, staring at her half-eaten pancakes and all the things I had laid out so hopefully on the table a short while ago. Eventually, I cleared away all the uneaten delights, mechanically loading the dishwasher. I consoled myself that at least she had left rather than say anything too hurtful and at least part of her was considering saving our relationship. My rumbling stomach reminded me that I had still barely eaten and I cooked up a couple more pancakes, eating at the stove and staring at my phone, unable to type anything. Eating calmed me down and helped me realise both that however eventful my morning was proving to be, it was still too early for me to call Lexi. Also that I was friends with a counsellor who had forgiven me for being shitty, so I decided to phone her for advice.

"Hello, my little heroine! We wanted to make you breakfast but you left too early. Hope things went well with Izzy, but I am guessing that you are phoning me either because they haven't or because you don't know how to tell her."

Julia had always had an annoying habit of reading me a little too well, but it would have been nice if she had made an effort not to make me feel like a case history the morning after we were all so happy.

"It wasn't good, but I haven't screwed up entirely."

I gave her a quick summary and despite her normally default response that talking things over quickly was always the best thing to do, she agreed that, on this occasion, Izzy leaving was positive, though it could also mean, she was too upset to stay or think calmly. She said that I should not call and that I could only send one brief text without expecting a reply and to be careful because a misjudged text could provoke her, so keep it minimal and admitting I was wrong and telling her I hoped I could make it up to her. She also said that she would understand us keeping a bit of distance for a while because if Izzy was angry about me not telling her about us living together, then it would not be a good idea for us to meet up today. She was right and I thanked her and then got off the phone.

I decided that although I would call Lexi a bit later to catch up about both our nights and this morning, it would be good for my career and prospects of staying employed if I actually started the reports, got round to marking the books I kept transporting to and from school, planned a few good lessons and produced some resources. It was a mild day and May had been dry enough to make Richmond Park fairly clean on the outside loops, if I went for a run first. I could almost hear myself reciting from one of Julia's self-help books about the first step to being loved is learning to love oneself, but I told myself that actually it was making the effort not to look puffy, untoned and with ever-deteriorating skin.

I changed into my jogging gear whilst I composed my text.

'Sorry. I was too scared of losing you. You are too precious to me. It hurt so badly to lie to you but it was all so crazy. You are the best thing in my life and I have been becoming a better person so that I can deserve you. Sorry I hurt you.'

I considered leaving my phone behind as I did not expect a reply, but then had to take it with me just in case. I drove to the park and she had texted back.

'You are precious to me too but that also means that you can and do hurt me. I need time and I will call you when I am ready.'

I had not run for a while, but I think Izzy's text helped me almost to the top of Spanker's Hill before I decided that it would be a good idea to turn and jog back to the car rather than to attempt to run the whole lap of the park. Lexi phoned when I was nearly back at the car and, though I was happy to hear from her, I was even happier to have an excuse to stop running. Although she claimed to be phoning to find out all about the drug drop, she barely noticed how out of breath I was as she told me all the gossip from her glamorous work do and we arranged to meet to talk properly in person. She wanted to meet in the afternoon, but I was determined to get on top of all my work. She had a hot date that evening, so I agreed to go over to her place for a very light supper and drinks whilst she went through her outfits and we caught up.

I earned my freedom by marking, planning, cleaning, sorting, even filling a bag for the charity shop to drop off on my way to Lexi's, and I felt less guilty about snacking all afternoon when I discovered that Lexi's idea of a light bite was a couple of dips, two very small and very stinky cheeses and half a packet of water biscuits. She explained that she was having trouble fitting into the right dresses whilst fixing herself a second gin and tonic and I resisted the urge to point out that she could have had a sandwich instead for the same calories. Even thinking enviously of a sandwich instead of gin had me imagining myself surrounded by cats, hopefully with Izzy, but curled up, fat, wrinkled and in an oversized hand-knitted sweater, dipping crisps in hummus and guacamole, barely scraping off the pet hair whilst listening to *Woman's Hour* on the wireless.

Even without the gin and somewhat distracted by having to suppress my stomach from rumbling, we shared an invigorating couple of hours giggling, mocking and congratulating ourselves and sorting out our mutual love lives. She told me she missed our nights out but was happy for me. I knew that she found Izzy a bit dull (and me, too, at the moment), but we had been friends for too long to not be able to just take things as they are, and she put up with the new me with only a few mock yawns and raised eyebrows. I was starting to rely on her to let me live vicariously, a little envious of her adventures, but mostly happy that I could be warm and comfortable in my jeans and trainers and go home and have a warm meal, watch a film and try and get a healthy eight hours' sleep. When she had to go, we hugged and set off together — me to my flat and her to Islington. It was probably the gin, but I felt strangely happy and optimistic. Jonno was done, I had some of the best friends anyone could wish for, and I was sure I had found and would keep a woman who was good for me and with whom I could share a life. A text from Izzy would have cemented a perfect evening, but this was good enough for now.

Dykes on Bikes

I had a great night's sleep and I woke up feeling energised and confident about the future and my prospects with Izzy. She had still not texted so, unless she did, I had a whole day with nothing planned. I contemplated actually visiting my mum, but I had also not told her about Jonno because she would have gone completely paranoid and probably also then permanently believe that I was a drug dealer. I did not need to sit around with anyone else from whom I had kept this whole story secret. I could not see Julia because it would just cause extra stress with Izzy at the moment. I realised that over the last few months I had become ensconced in a very narrow but safe go-to group. I used to feel surrounded by people and would always have someone to call or meet up with for a drink or a night out or friends with benefits, like Pru or Debbie, but I realised that we had simply stopped texting each other without even thinking about it and without any regrets.

It was barely a year since my life seemed so busy and so fun. Now, suddenly, I was into cleaning, cooking and nights in pining for a lover. For the first time I was able to count my friends on one hand. It was depressing, but these friends were real. Lexi was the one constant in my life. Julia, who initially I lusted after and then grew bored with, irritated and cramped by, had become my friend, unofficial counsellor and, above all, the person who had stuck by me no matter how shitty I had been to her. I could not give her up for Izzy and I doubted Izzy would even ask this once she calmed down. Natalie, too, had become someone I cared for, who cared for me and was another rare soul with whom I could be totally honest and who also had never had any recriminations for the mess I had dragged her and her girlfriend into. I wondered how I would have reacted if some random drug dealer had turned up at my flat because of Julia. Thirty was a good age to become a grown-up and, despite everything, I decided I could be pleased with the adult I had become. Though I was still too young for the middle-age spread that was no longer being kept at bay by dancing and shagging all night. It was definitely time to either join a gym or to diet or start to eat genuinely healthily every meal, with no snacks until I was trim. Or, possibly, until Izzy and I were secure enough for a little bit of spread just to show that I was happily coupled up.

There was still no text and it was too early to go to the supermarket, so I decided the choice was run or cycle. I had not cycled for months, but I decided that this had the added advantages of being less effort after my jog the previous day and potentially involving a route near Izzy's flat. I went to my building's bike store and, on balance, was relieved to see that my bike had not been stolen since I last used it, but realised that this was probably mostly because it was covered in dust, cobwebs and both tyres needed reflating. By the time I had gone back up and down with bike pumps, cleaning gear, then washed the dirt and grease off my hands, I nearly decided that I had done enough exercise for the day, but I was warmed up with the effort and the sun was coming out. It was a clear and crisp day, which would be perfect for a gentle ride through the park or Wimbledon Common. I went back to change into my favourite red sports top and lighter hoodie which made me look thinner and decided to try my luck cycling to Izzy's to persuade her to come out with me.

Cycling up the hill to her house was tougher than I expected and when I spoke to her via her flat's intercom, I was afraid that I had wasted my effort because she did not seem pleased to hear from me and reminded me that I had agreed to give her space. However, when I mentioned a bike ride and told her it would just be nice to have company and clear our heads together, she softened immediately and told me she would be ready shortly. She did not invite me up, which was not positive, but, rather gallantly, I offered to check and prepare her bike for her and then she invited me up just to hand me her garage keys and a cloth at her open front door. She was still in pyjamas but had been up for a while reading and she looked perfect. She was embarrassed to be in her nightwear but accepted my compliment and asked if I would wait long enough for her to have a quick shower, too. Wanting her to look her best and be comfortable, I was happy to wait and quietly went downstairs to sort her bike out. She was ready when I came back upstairs to return everything and wash my hands. She was wearing Lycra pants and a running top which accentuated everything and were certainly worth the wait. Once I was clean, I received a kiss on the cheek, not the lips, for my efforts, but it was tender and accompanied by a gentle hand on my back which did not wander but did linger, and I knew that today could be the day we cemented our relationship.

We cycled in single file, struggling up the hill, neither of us wanting to be the first to give up and walk. When we both somehow pushed over the hill at a speed that made it an achievement even to stay upright, we grinned at each other and felt a mutual sense of pride and relief. We were grateful for the gentle slope of the underpass towards the car park. Although it was a crisp and bright day, it was still late March and the paths were fine in places but wet enough to be messy, tough or even bog-like in others.

Just as I was considering suggesting dismounting and sitting on the nearest bench for the rest of the morning, as though reading my mind, Izzy said, "It's not exactly easy going and a bit mucky, though you were right to choose here because Richmond Park cycle trail is like a velodrome on Sundays. This is more relaxing. Though I am already tired and dirty!"

I resisted any comments about tired and dirty, and replied, "Me, too, and starting to get a bit saddle sore. We could sit on the bench for a while or push on for a few more minutes to the Village for brunch or head back to the Windmill café."

"The Village — a fry-up would destroy what little exercise we have done! If we have something trendy in the Village we can both feel virtuous before we do the long straight and downhill back."

The idea of Izzy even suggesting I could feel virtuous after yesterday seemed amazing progress, even if I was taking her comments a little out of context. I was penitent enough to have agreed to whatever she said, but her answer was perfect and I felt incredibly close to her. I still dared not reach out to touch her first.

"You always say the right thing — thanks for coming with me. This, and you, are exactly what I need."

She half-whispered and half-mouthed, "Me, too," as she looked momentarily awkward on her bike. I could see that she also felt close but was deliberately keeping her distance. We cycled mostly in silence, only speaking to comment on the scenery or warn each other about sudden potholes and puddles. As we approached the Village, we decided on Gail's Bakery, but as we peered through the window at shelves of weird sourdough combinations, we decided that we had both earned one or maybe two really indulgent cakes and a latte from Paul's instead, which looked much quieter anyway.

We sat opposite each other in a quiet corner and made easy conversation as we chose our eclairs and macarons — which were delicious, full of calories and wholly unfilling. We both knew that a third cake would probably mean we had eaten an entire day's worth of calories before lunchtime without actually feeling any fuller. If we had tried to eat our fill, we would both have needed to max out our overdrafts and the waiter had raised enough of an eyebrow when we had ordered four cakes between two of us. When Izzy suggested cycling back to her flat for a sandwich, I was almost as delighted at the thought of actual food as at the progress it signalled for our relationship.

It seemed to take forever to cycle back and both of us were discreetly trying to lift our now painful sore bums off the seat for as much of the ride as we could. If the last stretch had not been downhill all the way, no matter how stubbornly neither of us wanted to be the first to suggest walking, we may not have made it home. I had been considering suggesting taking our bikes back on the bus from about half-way along Park Side Road, but I was too proud to suggest it to Izzy and was keen to improve my fitness. When we finally got to Izzy's, I think I was happier about not having to cycle home than I was about Izzy making me lunch. My legs were not happy about being made to take me both running and cycling over the same weekend and I chivalrously let Izzy go up the stairs first so that she would not see me wince and struggle up behind her. I gratefully accepted a glass of water and she rejected my offer to help with the sandwiches. Gingerly, I made my way to the table, grateful to be on a seat that was as wide as my bottom.

She had clearly also decided to spend the weekend catching up on marking, keeping the work in orderly piles. I carefully kept each pile together, pushing them onto the chairs at the end. She thanked me as she brought the food after a quick scan confirmed that they were still in the same order. She brought sandwiches, dips, crudités and crisps. It looked lovely and I suddenly felt famished, but I was not sure whether she had kept lunch light because she had nothing else in or because she wanted me to eat and go. I suspected that she was still undecided herself. I ignored the fact that my stomach rumbled pointedly at the sight of the food, which made her smile at my embarrassment, and I forced myself to eat slowly. We made small talk about how much we had enjoyed the ride, but now we were in Izzy's flat, every word we spoke seemed to make the subject of Jonno and my lies to her loom more oppressively between us. I was too scared to broach the subject myself, but unable to do anything to diffuse it. My mouth became so dry I could barely swallow my sandwich. Eventually, Izzy, with obvious effort, was the first to talk about the thing we were both not saying.

"Oh, Jo, this has been a perfect morning, but you have always known how to make me happy and how to make me sad. Right now, I feel happy, relaxed, and even though I ache in places I don't even think I used cycling, I feel a little bit horny for you."

I opened my mouth to speak, but nothing came out. I knew there was a but, but I was so surprised and happy to hear her say something encouraging, I froze whilst I took it in. Izzy spoke again quickly, before I could interrupt.

"The thing is, I don't trust you. You hurt me so badly last time and I think it would hurt even more if I let you do it again. I've been asking myself what I would have done in your position and I don't know. But the simple truth is, I would never have been in your position because I am not so reckless. I want us to be together so much, but I had no idea what was going on with you and you are just someone who will always act so impulsively. Recklessly."

"I'm trying. I've really changed."

"I can see that. But you have always just been that little bit wilder than me. Than most people. Trouble and bizarre situations just follow you. And you thrive on it. I used to think that you were some kind of sex addict or something. Now, I just think you have a short-attention span and whenever you are comfortable and safe you have to change things."

There was too much truth in what she said, but the last year had made me value safe and boring in a way I never had.

"Please. I want safe. And I want you."

"I need to protect myself and I don't know whether, as soon as this is passed, you will get bored again."

Maybe she was right, but I had known what a mistake it was to lose her from the moment I betrayed her. I wanted her even before there was Jonno and Julia. I knew I had changed and was more sure than I had ever been, that I could make it work with her. Yes, I had let so many people down that I was afraid to promise never to hurt her in case that proved to be another lie. So I had no words to say to defend myself or to try to woo her. Partly to reassure her and partly to seek comfort for myself, silently I moved closer and put my arm around her as we both looked ahead, side by side. She made to push me away, then put her arm round me, too, and we held each other. Gently at first and then tighter. I turned to face her and we looked into each other's eyes. She let me kiss her, gently, and then as I started to kiss her more passionately, she withdrew.

"Can I trust you? Do you even know the answer to that question, Jo? Do you trust yourself?"

"Yes. I don't know. Izzy, I am so different from the person who casually hurt you. This situation was crazy and it made me crazy and I couldn't think straight, and in the middle of it all, you agreed to give us a second chance and I clung to that."

"I can forgive you for lying as I have forgiven you before for so many things, but I can't keep forgiving you for one last thing for ever. And then another thing. Be honest with me and yourself for once, Jo. Are you ready for a proper relationship or are you just going to find another way to hurt me or leave me?"

I could feel tears starting to roll down my face, but at least getting control of myself gave me time to gather myself. I was still learning to trust myself, but I also wanted to scream that so many marriages ended in divorce because people can't see the future and make mistakes, but it didn't mean that we shouldn't try. Anything I said now could push her away for ever or give us a chance of a life together.

"I love you. I have for almost as long as I have known you. The difference is that now I know what that means. I hurt you and I don't want to hurt you, or anyone, any more. I've learned that. And I won't ever lie to you again, I promise; and now I am almost too scared to promise you anything, but it hurts me to hurt you. I can promise you that

I will do everything I can to be with you and to deserve you and to just not screw up this time. Please. Please."

"Okay."

We kissed, at first with relief and love and then with desire. Then she pulled away again.

"I am not doing anything with you whilst we are both so sweaty and smelly. You shower whilst I clear up and then I'll shower and join you."

She did not say "in the bedroom", but it was clear what she meant. I took the plates to the kitchen with her and she handed me a towel and kissed me again.

Neither of us took long to shower and we spent most of the afternoon in bed, showing each other just how much we loved each other. I wanted to stay all night, but eventually she told me to go, saying that we would be okay and she would give us another, final, chance, but that she needed to keep things slow until she really believed that she could trust me.

Pretty Good News?

Normally, I hate Mondays, everyone does. This Monday felt different immediately. I woke up after a blissful night of sleep and quickly shook off the disappointment of not having Izzy beside me. I felt lighter, as though multiple weights had been taken from me, and even the bathroom scales agreed. I showered and then dressed in a pair of trousers which had been so tight a few weeks ago I had been worried about them ripping open, exposing my bum to the world as I sat down in assembly. Today they were pleasantly snug in a way that tucked in my waistline and went perfectly with an old polka-dot blouse that I knew Izzy liked, complemented by an open grey cardigan to look casual and, I hoped, cool, sophisticated and attractive.

I had texted Lexi and Julia the good news about Izzy the day before and Lexi had sent me a series of intentionally lewd and suggestive emojis which included a bizarre selection of vegetables which made me seriously worry about her relationship with food! Julia had replied that she and Natalie were delighted but urged me to be careful and let her set the pace. There were no more messages from them that morning and, heeding Julia's advice, I resisted the urge to text Izzy, but could not stop myself checking my phone hopefully every few seconds as I ate my cereal.

I left early for work and as I drove in, the sun was just rising, creating a stunning backdrop to my journey. I saw two magpies instead of my usual solitary omen of sorrow. Then Izzy was the first person I saw when I got to the staffroom. She was with Fay, but still definitely pleased to see me. And Fay smiled, too. That meant that either Izzy had not told Fay about Jonno and everything or that Fay had accepted it. I suspected the former and that meant that Izzy felt loyal enough to me to not go straight to her friend to complain about me when she was upset. Another positive — it was the day that kept giving. Even my lessons seemed to go particularly well and my students seemed more engaged and even willing to laugh at my jokes. I wondered whether this was a feature of my new-found confidence or, perhaps, because I had actually returned all their homework marked and planned some pretty good lessons that day. I had lunch with Izzy and Fay and a few others. Fay had asked Izzy if she wanted to be alone with me for lunch and Izzy had eagerly pressed her to stay, which made me feel obliged to also tell her it was fine. I wanted to be alone, but it was nice to be near her and welcomed by her and everyone else seemed happy, too, and we laughed throughout the meal.

When we finished, I noticed that I had a missed call and a voicemail, so I set off back to my classroom to find somewhere private to listen to it. Izzy came over to me and told me conspiratorially that she had to ask Fay to join us so that people would not start to notice us together and that she just wanted to keep our distance at work but not out of work. She told me again that she was glad we were working things out. I could not contain my grin and looked around and she told me that my grins and general demeanour would alert the students and other staff and that was exactly why she was keeping her distance. Despite her concern, she looked amused and flattered rather than genuinely angry or worried as she headed off towards the staffroom with Fay and the others.

I went to my room, made sure I was alone and listened to the voicemail. It was from DS Robbins, asking me to call him on his direct line. I phoned him back and was delighted when he told me that they had enough to charge Jonno and that he was willing to admit to petty drug deals and even to trying to extort us to do the drug drop, once he had heard my recording. However, he was continuing to deny any knowledge of Whetstone or even having ever met him. He also told me that he had reviewed the footage of the security guard with his inspector and some drug squad officers, who confirmed what Jonno had said about him being an ex-police officer. They had all agreed that whilst the film made him look suspicious, there was nothing that could be properly used as evidence. One of the officers who had known him and knew that he was friends with Whetstone, had also said that he would be too wily to give anything away if brought in for questioning. They would make some more enquiries, but it was definitely looking as though it would be better to keep a low profile and continue to monitor Whetstone than start actively questioning people and alert him properly. They would probably just keep the footage on file and use it as potential future evidence if they caught him for something else.

It was galling to know that Whetstone would get away with everything, but I consoled myself with the knowledge that Jonno was the reason why I, Julia, Natalie and now Izzy had been scared and battered emotionally for almost a year. Whetstone had scared us and given Jonno some power, but he was someone else's problem now and surely this would ensure that he was out of our lives. DS Robbins reminded me that I would still need to testify, but that would be much further down the line and they would probably have enough evidence to lock him up awaiting trial because he was definitely a flight risk, having spent long periods abroad in places notoriously associated with drugs, like when I had met him. The word 'probably' made me catch my breath and briefly feel cold and clammy and as though my lunch might come back again. If he was let out on bail when he was angry, that could be very, very bad for us. DS Robbins sensed my fear and he immediately started to reassure me. He told me that he would argue that letting him out would put us in danger again and he was sure that would be enough to ensure that he would not make bail.

"Even if the worst comes to it and he makes bail, you have nothing to worry about. He crumbled under pressure. The only reason he would not give up Whetstone was that it was pretty obvious he is afraid of him and that he still hopes Whetstone can somehow get him off. Which he can't, by the way. He'll be too afraid to try and get to you. And if we have to let him go, I'll have a word with him first myself, just to remind him not to do anything stupid. You're okay now."

His words calmed me a little, but when I got off the phone, I could hear my heart pounding in my ears. I forced myself to breath slowly, sat down at my desk and looked out the window at the clouds drifting past until I was calm again. I reminded myself that DS Robbins had opened by saying that he "had some pretty good news" and that he seemed pleased. I wondered cynically whether it was good news for him that he had made a drugs bust, and there was certainly no risk of Jonno or his friends going round to his flat to get revenge. Or mine, for that matter — it would be Natalie's flat he targeted. Jonno aside, I could generally read people well and I believed that DS Robbins was an honest and decent guy. I could not function as a teacher without my built-in lie detector, which occasionally failed to pick up the diehard liars who had spent a whole childhood convincing mummy dearest that valuables spontaneously broke and invisible mice raided any sweets or chocolates stashed around the house, but unless DS Robbins was a genuine sociopath, I decided I could believe him and trust that he was telling the truth about us being safe. I needed time to process this, but I only had twenty minutes until my next lesson. Much as I wanted to share this with and be comforted by Izzy, I had to tell Julia. I figured that she would probably be with a client now, so I texted her:

'Good news from Robbins. Well, mostly. He thinks they have enough on Jonno but not Whetstone. Jonno could make bail but he hopes not. Will talk tonight or free for 10mins now.'

And I also texted Izzy:

'Hi — great lunch. Where are you? Update from the police. Some good, some bad. In my classroom.'

I added a heart and kiss emoji for Izzy but did not hear back from either. I wanted to see Izzy or get a cup of tea, but I would have to walk past lots of children and I thought I looked too flustered. Besides, I needed to get my paperwork and room in order for my next lesson so my bottom set Year 10 would not be the final nightmare that pushed me over the edge.

About five minutes before the end of lunch, Izzy appeared looking slightly breathless, apologising for just getting my text because her phone was on silent. She kept her distance physically but told me she wished she could hug me to comfort me and asked what had happened. I told her as quickly as I could and she told me to focus on the fact that Jonno would be charged and that even if he was released, he would not dare threaten me or Natalie (there was a definite edge to her voice when she mentioned Natalie and Julia, but she was more worried about me than angry about them). She asked whether I would like her to come over after school and I told her that I would love that. She told me she had things to do but would come round at about six p.m. and help me to cook, or we would get a takeaway. We both had lessons and it was frustrating not to be able to kiss or touch, but she had made everything seem a bit better and given me the strength to cope with whatever new way Year 10 would find of killing my enthusiasm for *Jekyll and Hyde*.

Year 10 were better than I hoped and some were so engrossed in their work that they did not notice my phone buzzing its supposedly silent vibrations or me discreetly checking it and trying to appear unconcerned, as though sending some work emails. It was Julia, who was even more rattled by the idea that Jonno might get out than I was. Of course, it was her flat that he had first appeared in, and I remembered how crazy he had made her initially. I promised to talk properly in the evening. It was a measure of how stressed and worried we had all been that it had not occurred to any of us that even if Jonno was arrested and charged he would not be in jail for long, if at all. We had to hope that now we had good police on our side, he would accept that he had no leverage over us and be too afraid to strike back. Whetstone was not implicated, so he would also surely keep away. As I walked round trying to read student attempts at different letters in the style of Dr Jekyll or Mr Hyde, I managed to compose and reassure myself a little. By the end of the afternoon, I was more worried about Izzy being in my flat when Julia rang than Jonno turning up. I decided to make a quick getaway and call Julia as soon as I got home and then tell Izzy about it when she arrived, rather than have her sitting in the flat listening and analysing every word. The flat was tidy and we had agreed to cook together, so as long as Julia was not with a client, I would be fine.

I was in luck. I got home with over an hour to spare, she was free and Natalie was back from her studio. They also thought we should have realised that Jonno would not be imprisoned for long, if at all, but had jointly decided to be positive and that the very fact that he knew we had a good officer working with us and he had been caught for something would be enough to keep him away. I understood why Julia was so in love with Natalie — arty and bohemian, she thrived on being eccentric, and the way she was able to take everything in her stride had kept all of us going. She summed up the situation perfectly.

"Look, we always talk about rehabilitation and it could even be better if he does not spend time in jail because then he will stay small-time. This could teach him a lesson and save him. Either way, he will know that he has no leverage over us, and we were not as scared or stupid as we pretended. Even if he is so angry that he just wants revenge, Robbins seems to know his stuff and he would have to be crazy and a lot braver than he seems to go after us. Sure, he makes a good threat, but if he was going to be violent, he would have done it by now. We will just have to be watchful for a while if he gets out. The main thing is, we ask Robbins to keep us informed. We will be okay. Time to move on."

She was right. And we all wanted her to be right. The future was looking better, and we had achieved something. Even if he got off, we had evidence and he had lost his hold. He knew that an honest officer had believed us. We doubted whether Whetstone would care enough about Jonno to do anything to help him. He probably had a dozen other Jonnos to work with, and all the evidence suggested that he was too lazy, arrogant and stupid to outwit DS Robbins to help get Jonno off or hurt us now. There were loose ends to tie up and I would probably have to give evidence in court, but it was over. And Izzy was coming round to comfort me and this horrible year was going to end a lot better than it started.

Staying In

I had time for a quick shower and to change. I decided that it was safe to assume we were now dating properly, so I needed something casual but which showed I was not taking her for granted and had made an effort. Black jeans, obviously, but several tops later, realising the diet and exercise still needed to be stepped up, I opted for the most flattering top that I had not yet worn on a date with Izzy, turning up the heating so I would have no comedy visible-nipple moments.

Next! The fridge. As part of my recent get-fit kick, I kept filling the fridge with fruit and vegetables which seemed to remain long after the good bits had disappeared. I realised I did not have anything exciting left to go with it. There was no time to go to a shop, so I decided that a healthy vegetable and tomato pasta dish followed by a fresh fruit salad would improve my prospects of being able to fit into a different top for the next date and would help convince Izzy of how much I had changed. I also found an unopened bar of Green and Blacks which I forced myself to save for us to eat later.

When Izzy arrived, slightly late and carrying my favourite lager, chocolates, she also had a small bag that still looked big enough to contain clothes for the next day. I forced myself to keep my eyes on Izzy rather than the bag, desperate to sneak a look inside to confirm the contents, but sure that she would not appreciate me so obviously presuming anything. The way that she tried to discreetly push it away made me even more hopeful and curious, but I assumed that even if it was an overnight bag, it was probably more of a 'just in case bag' than a definite plan.

I took her gifts and pulled her safely in away from Doris's prying eyes in the hallway, before pulling her close and kissing her. I was starting to feel entitled to do this — we were a couple and allowed to hold each other, casually hold hands or put an arm around each other, and I did not have to worry or seek permission before leaning in to kiss her. I knew that technically we were still going slowly and Izzy was still holding back, but so much had happened in the last few days, and being honest with her had been horrible at first but had brought us closer. I held her for as long as I could and she held me back, but then she looked over my shoulder to the kitchen and we separated as she went to look. I had already chopped everything and left it ready to go in the pan and I could see that she was surprised and a little impressed and a little disappointed, too.

"Wow — so many vegetables. I didn't know you even knew what all these were. And I was hoping for a China Chef tonight."

"Oh — sorry. These can keep — I'll just put them in a box for tomorrow."

"No — this is much better. China Chef's probably closed on a Monday anyway. This is much healthier and probably why you are losing weight and looking so good."

I smiled and looked down and she stroked my arm. It took an almost physical effort to turn myself around to face the stove.

"Well, I'd better start cooking if we want to eat. Can you open the beers and keep me company?"

"Of course. I'm frankly too intrigued to miss the sight of you cooking with actual vegetables."

"Little harsh — I always ate vegetables."

"Always ate — but not really cooked, except in a microwave or as a salad. Anyway, I want to hear what happened with, you know, everything."

I wanted to stay like this forever and was still nervous about doing anything to spook her, but I decided that I should tell her about talking to Julia first in case she reacted badly.

Her eyes briefly hardened and her tone went crisp, but she softened, particularly as I told her about Natalie's thoughts. I realised I was tense, too, about how she would react, but she thought I was worried about Jonno and rubbed my arm and relaxed and told me that they were right and things should be fine. I felt taller and lighter. I was delighted and started willing the food to cook more quickly so that we could eat and be free for the rest of the evening sooner. She clearly felt the same because although we chatted, we ate quickly. We talked about Jonno and everything, with her asking questions, clarifying, commiserating and being appropriately shocked and scared for me. She said that whilst she was still mostly hurt and a little angry about me not sharing this with her earlier, she could not imagine how I must have felt. But she understood! She understood how frightening it must have been and how the fear and anxiety must have weighed me down and made me unable to think or act properly. She told me how strong I was and how many people would have been broken by it.

I told her that, even though I had not told her about it, it was probably her who saved me anyway. I had to be honest and to be fair and say that Julia, Natalie and Lexi helped. She frowned a little, but quickly composed herself at that. I said that a massive part of my staying composed and dealing with everything had been my desire to win her back. My need to stop making the same mistakes again and again. My wanting to be the kind of person who solves problems and who other people can depend on, so she could depend on me, too. In my whole life, I had never spoken so honestly and completely to someone. I allowed her to see how vulnerable she made me, and I could see that she knew that and understood. By this time, we were standing in the kitchen drying up dishes, and we put them down and kissed. Tenderly and then passionately, and we held each other. I did not want to be the first to move apart but, emboldened, I gestured towards the bedroom. She pulled back.

"Jo, it's not even eight thirty p.m. I've brought my toothbrush and some clothes and I will stay over, but let's just try to be relaxed together first. Slow, Jo!"

We went into the living room and flicked through the channels. I considered an episode of *L Word* to set the tone, but we decided to watch some comedy on Dave, just to relax and have a chance to sit snuggled together without pressure. It was perfect. And she stayed over. If this was to be the future, everything that had gone before was worth it.

Trouble is Just Around the Corner

It took barely a week for the bubble to burst. Things with Izzy were great. I let her set the pace and was delighted when that quickly meant that we spent almost every other night together. We were comfortable and intimate together. When we had been together before, I had been frustrated that she never wanted to go out to clubs, particularly gay clubs, and always preferred cafés to pubs; but now I found our nights in natural, comforting and relaxed. I was happy, but more than that, I was content for the first time I could remember. And I felt I deserved to be, after everything that had happened. It was not to last.

Izzy was staying at mine again when the doorbell rang. I was cooking, so she offered to go to the door. I could not see the door or the hallway outside my flat, but I could see her answer it and quickly be pushed back as a burly officer walked in. She was briefly flustered, but had no idea who he was as she spoke.

"I was about to ask you in. I suppose we need to thank you for your help, but there was no need to push!"

She looked at me for back-up and gasped as she saw how pale I had become as I stared, wooden spoon in hand. I glanced at the chef's knife on the chopping board in front of me, but knew that I was never going to use it. I was jolted back to life by the familiar sound of his voice.

"I'll walk in however I like, pet. This one knows who I am. Took me a while to track you down, but here I am. What are you cooking? I might stay for supper."

I could not control the tiny jump I gave at the sound of his voice and I could see him smiling even as he spoke at the sight of my fear. Somehow that gave me the anger I needed to compose myself and screw my courage together and I took a breath before speaking. I scanned the room and cursed myself for leaving my phone too far away to try and record anything. If he had come to Julia's, we still had some recording equipment in place just in case Jonno had shown up again.

Izzy was still very close to him, looking confused but angry, so I had to warn her. I started to say her name but did not want to give him any information on her.

"This is Whetstone — you know, the dodgy policeman."

"It's PC Whetstone, and I think you'd better watch your tongue. I have come to give you a friendly warning, but you need to be polite to me. You wouldn't want to offend an officer of the law."

I started to argue, but decided that for once I would keep my cool and try not to inflame the situation. To my relief he seemed to be completely ignoring Izzy and focussing on me.

"Just say what you want and go."

"I'm the one who's telling you what to do, not you. I'll decide when I am ready to go — you get me?"

He stepped towards me as he spoke and I made myself stay where I was, in the doorway between the hall and the kitchen. My phone was about two metres behind me and the landline the other side of him. I was scared and could feel beads of sweat appearing on my forehead, but I hated his arrogance, contempt and corruption enough to hold my ground as he moved within half a metre of me and stared me in the face. I could see that my courage had him rattled. His physical size was intimidating on its own — both height and beer belly, which jutted out over his belt, straining to burst through his enormous protective vest. His demeanour was patronising and he clearly had no respect for women, and although I was trying hard to concentrate and appear composed, part of my mind was too preoccupied with finding a way to record him so that I would have proof to give to DS Robbins. I wondered whether officers had their movements recorded, because that would be incriminating enough.

"I said, do you understand?"

This time his tone was more menacing and I stepped back, but made myself step forward.

"Yeah."

I swallowed before I spoke and spoke quietly. I felt humiliated, especially in front of Izzy. I was desperately trying to come up with an idea, but he was right in front of me and watching everything I did, so it would be impossible to even signal to Izzy without him noticing. I consoled myself that at least he was ignoring her.

"That's more like it. Now listen up and listen good!"

There was a pause whilst he adjusted his belt back up and whilst I noticed that he, too, was sweating. Then he continued.

"You need to stop working with your DS Robbins. I can log in and access your file and details any time I want, so I'll know if you don't do as I say. It seems you are harassing a young man I have helped to rehabilitate who used his phone call to ask for my help. And I will help him get out and back on his feet. I think you understand me."

"Oh, I understand about your idea of rehabilitation."

"I didn't tell you to speak. You think you can make trouble for me and you have, a little. But it is nothing compared to what I can do to you. I hear any more from you and I might just have to make enquiries at your fancy school. Have a word with your headmaster about your tendency to make things up and target innocent people. Mention that you were probably dealing drugs abroad. That kind of thing. Do you want that?"

I just wanted him out. There was no point trying to argue or defend myself, I needed him out of my flat and away from Izzy so I could think.

"No. Okay."

"Good girl. You'd better hope I don't have to come back and discuss this again."

As he turned to leave, he almost bumped into Izzy. Neither of us had noticed that she was standing almost directly behind him, almost as though she was about to hit him.

"What's wrong with you? Bloody crazy women everywhere. I suppose I'd better take your details."

"Leave her out of it!"

I raised my voice in a mixture of fear and protectiveness. I knew it was a mistake, having forced myself to be calm thus far. He turned back to me, but this time kept his eye on her, too, and his voice was even angrier than before.

"You... don't... tell... me... anything. Get it?"

I nodded.

"You — I'll take your details, too. I just need my pad."

As he started to root around in his pockets, I spoke.

"I said I'll do what you want. I won't speak to DS Robbins and I'll leave Jonno out of it if you leave her alone. I'm not threatening you, but if you take her details, I'll be more likely to go back to him. You have enough to keep me quiet now you know where I live and work. You don't need to threaten her, too."

He paused. He seemed to have patted down all his trouser and vest pockets unsuccessfully anyway.

"Well, I suppose so. Save me more writing and noting stuff down. But you need to be clear, I will find out and come after you if you speak to the police about me or Jonno again. You, too."

He turned to Izzy as he spoke and then left, leaving the door open. I scrambled to shut it behind him and found myself starting to shake. My head seemed to pound and I felt sweaty and my legs could barely support me. Izzy had her back to me and I tried to put my arms around her, but she shrugged me away. I didn't know what to say, but she brandished her phone at me. I thought she was calling a taxi and started to beg her to listen, but she shushed me and showed me her photos. Then I understood. Whilst Whetstone had been focussing all his attention on me and keeping me away from my phone, she had quietly been filming it. The video was not great — it was mostly of his back and clearly when he turned round, she had quickly balanced it on the radiator behind her so the view was of the ceiling and, intermittently, of her hand moving over it to conceal it. The sound was not great, either. She turned the volume up full and we played and replayed it.

When he spoke quietly and most of what I said was lost, but there were several occasions when he raised his voice and where his tone was clearly intimidating, even though his words were not particularly incriminating. She had crept as close as she had dared, but when he was speaking to me with his back to her, she got barely every other word, with snippets like 'school' and 'headmaster', but nothing about Jonno or the threats. However, when he turned round, although the phone was only videoing the ceiling, it clearly recorded his angry "You don't tell me anything" and his final threat about speaking to the police and referencing Jonno.

We thought it was enough, but were worried that if we went back to DS Robbins and it was not enough, he would really come after us. Izzy told me I had to go back to Robbins, but I persuaded her to let me call Julia and Natalie first. Julia picked up immediately and I got straight to the point, painfully conscious that Izzy would be listening and analysing my every word, even now. Julia was going to put me on speaker, but we decided to Facetime instead. Huddled round mobiles, I quickly told them what had happened and they said that we had to risk it and to call Robbins immediately, but only on his direct line. As I hung up, they shouted out "hellos" and "pleased to meet you" to Izzy.

I could not believe my luck when DS Robbins answered his phone. He told me not to worry but to write everything down and to send the video to his email account to analyse with his inspector, promising me that nothing would be added to any accessible files. He apologised for Whetstone getting my details and not thinking about that, but said that he had had to log Jonno on the system and it would have looked very odd if such a minor case had not been logged properly. He swore audibly and uncharacteristically as he cursed himself for not leaving my details off the log.

He would not be able to come round that evening, so advised me to write everything down so that I could fill in the gaps in the recording with a full idea of what Whetstone was actually saying and that he would be in touch tomorrow or the day after when he had a plan. I knew I should have been relieved that I had even got through to him on his direct line as I wanted some reassurance. For the first time this was my home and Izzy and my work. She had been standing beside me, listening to every word as I spoke to Robbins and she could feel how cold I had become. I forced myself to be composed for her, but part of me just wanted to run straight out the door.

"We could go back to my flat instead, you know, if you feel scared here. I know I do."

"Thanks. I am scared. But there's no reason why he should be back tonight, though we can go to yours if you like."

"What do you want to do? Wait — let's not panic. I'll make us some tea and we can sit down and then decide. It's a bit late to move, but I'm not far and we probably won't get much sleep wherever we stay after that."

"Thanks."

Whilst she made tea, I texted Julia. I did not want to spend hours on the phone to them whilst Izzy was there and I needed peace to think, but

I told them I had got through and he seemed helpful and reassuring but was busy and would be in contact the next day or the day after. I could almost hear Natalie's anger in Julia's texts about Robbins having a duty to protect us that should make me his first priority, and I could feel my fear turning to anger or at least indignation, too. Izzy brought in the tea and sat down beside me and put her arm around me. I could see that she was irritated by my texting, but restrained herself. I put the phone down and leant my head against her breast and she hugged me. My phone pinged repeatedly as I did.

"Look — just Facetime them or whatever and discuss what you need to, otherwise your phone will just keep buzzing anyway."

"Sorry — we're all involved in this and we agreed to work together."

"Oh, I know."

There was no mistaking the resentment in her voice, which was a clear reminder of how long I had kept this secret from her, but almost as soon as she spoke her body softened again and she kissed my head.

"It's okay. I'm over it, almost. But now is not the time for us to argue. You, we, need all the help and support we can get."

"Thank you — I love you, Izzy."

"I love you, too, Jo."

Izzy put both her arms round me and we held each other and kissed. It felt comfortable and comforting and I only pulled away reluctantly as my phone pinged again. I leaned over and grabbed my iPad and Julia answered my Facetime almost instantly. We greeted each other and Natalie cut straight to the point.

"I think it's not on — he let Whetstone get your details and he should come round and deal with it or get someone else to now."

"I kind of agree with you, Nat, but I think he was honest about having to do something. And I would not trust another officer coming to the house right now. I only want to deal with him. He can't be working with Whetstone because he helped us and arrested Jonno."

Julia waited for me to finish speaking before quickly being the first to retort.

"I agree that he helped and I do trust him as much as anyone. But you have to remember that he is not our friend, he is a policeman with a career to protect. Catching Jonno was an easy win. Taking down

Whetstone could make him some enemies or it could help his career more. He's probably taking his time whilst he weighs up what's in it for him."

Julia was always careful, but she tended to look for the best in people. I knew that she was being cautious for all our sakes and her words made me think carefully. Izzy was nodding and whispered that she may have a point.

"Okay, you are both right. But he is the only one who can help us now. And anyway, if he's not on our side, then we are even more at risk from Whetstone. I don't think we have any choice but to trust him. And if I hassle him, that will only get his back up."

"I hate to admit it, but you're right. We can't afford to start complaining about him to another officer and we have to keep him on our side. But we record everything. Even phone calls to him if we can, and discreetly record his visit when he comes round. Don't trust anyone. Before you answer the door, set your phone to record and keep it plugged in and charged. Both your phones and your iPads and laptop, too, if you can. We can trust each other, but that's it."

I agreed with Natalie, but her words made it sound like we were spies or secret agents. I could still feel waves of fear coming and going, but they were more like ripples now and I was no longer visibly shaking. Izzy and I held each other tightly, and in some ways, it felt exciting to be going through this together. They offered to come round or for me to go there, but I reminded them that he knew where they were anyway and they needed to be on their guard in case he visited, too. Izzy and I agreed that his main threat to me had been about visiting me at work rather than hurting us physically, so it could only make things worse if he returned to find four of us trying to work as a group.

Julia and Natalie tried to comfort me, and Julia said, "Look, he can try and mess things up for you at work and he can embarrass you for a bit, and I agree you don't want that. But if he tells the head you are unstable, or makes anything up, you can get Robbins to tell him about Jonno and sort it out. It won't look great, but he'll have to listen and you won't lose your job or anything."

"He won't start promoting me to head of year or department in case I do anything weird on open days. I'll probably be put in charge of supervising the tour guides for the day."

"Do you even want promotion?"

"Now that I have started marking books and preparing lessons, I figure some kind of pay rise should be in order."

I was part joking and part serious, but even as Izzy laughed, she said, "You know, pupils have started saying good things about your teaching and not just your lessons being fun. And Fay said that you were a lot more professional than she thought. If you can impress her, you might just be on to something."

Julia and Natalie turned to each other and did fake sighs and smiled and said in unison, "Oh, look, our little girl has grown up!"

"Right, well, if we're at the take-the-piss-out-of-me part of the conversation, I'll end it there — goodbye."

"Don't forget to record everything and stay in touch. Good night."

And then Izzy and I were alone again. We stayed on the sofa holding each other for a few minutes, but Izzy reminded me about listening to the video and filling in the gaps and we forced ourselves to move.

We replayed it and there were frustrating gaps but bits which were definitely usable. His visit had been surprisingly short — barely five minutes — so we played and wrote and played and wrote and agreed our version was good enough and that we could not keep rehashing it and needed to switch off. Izzy sent me the video and I typed our version up on my computer and emailed it to Julia to share it with her and, in my paranoid state, just to ensure that if he broke in and killed Izzy and me and then raided the flat, there would still be a record of what had happened. Then we cuddled up on the sofa, pretending to watch a random panel show on Dave, barely concentrating, just taking half an hour to calm down and enjoy being together. Neither of us was in the mood for romance, but we went to bed quickly and lay in each other's arms all night. I even managed to sleep fairly well, but was woken by the first plane of the day flying low overhead and then lay listening and imagining footsteps outside the door. Izzy slept better, but also drifted in and out of sleep and gave small involuntary starts. At least when she was awake, we could hold each other until we fell asleep again, and we made it through the night getting what sleep we could.

Police Presence

I was awoken the next day by Izzy's breasts in my face as she leant over me to turn off the alarm. The brief stifling of oxygen was better at rousing me than the harsh bleeping of my bedside clock. It did not bode well for the day that the one bit of sound and deep sleep I had managed was just as I was supposed to get up, but at least Izzy apologised with a kiss for squashing me.

"That's okay. There are worse ways to be woken. Or even suffocated."

"Thanks, but we need to get up and get ready. I meant to do some work last night which I never got round to."

I could see that she would not be persuaded to stay in bed a bit longer and I told her to use the shower first. She kissed me and walked naked to the shower. I savoured the view as I considered going back to sleep and leaving her to get breakfast by herself. I knew there was no hope of persuading her to take a sick day and knew she would be cross with me if I did. Things were going too well to give her any reason to think that I was back to being irresponsible, so I dragged myself up and got a few things ready for breakfast until she finished in the shower.

She was not ready to let anyone at school see us arrive together. I told her that we lived close enough to each other that no one would think we were anything other than friends if they saw us, but she told me that she was not ready for "those kinds of conversations yet". So we had a quick breakfast together after my shower and kissed tenderly as she left. I dressed quickly and followed her almost immediately, reflecting on how comfortable we were together, barely remembering Whetstone's visit.

I was too busy sorting and photocopying my stuff for my lessons and then early morning friendship crisis in my tutor group to even check my phone for messages from DS Robbins. I was teaching both lessons before break but was free afterwards, so I cleared up my classroom quickly and headed off to the staffroom, hoping to grab some time with Izzy. As I walked down the corridors, swerving in and out of students who walked three or more abreast, oblivious to other students and even teachers, I came to an abrupt stop and gasped at the sight of a policeman in reception. One of the Year 7s following me walked into my back and there was a sudden babble of conversation, laughter and concern around, which caused the officer to turn towards us. He was definitely not Whetstone, but I was sure I recognised him from somewhere and maybe I had seen him with Whetstone or somewhere.

"You all right, miss?"

It was one of my tutees, Tim, who was a kind-hearted boy who was also a popular member of the rugby squad. Even as I was trying to keep an eye on the policeman in reception, I could see him trying to discreetly elbow kids who were giggling. The Year 7s were stammering apologies and I apologised to them, thanked Tim and tried to send the rest away. Paul Boyce, a head of year who I had spoken to a few times, got on with but did not really know, came over and the rest of the kids dispersed and he checked whether I was okay.

"I'm fine, just forgot something and a kid walked into me; it's nothing. Wonder why there is a police officer here — hope nothing serious is going on."

"Glad you're okay. He's my officer. Well, not my personal officer. PSHE cyber safety talk man. I have to greet him and get him a quick cup of tea before his talk."

"Thanks for stopping."

I walked on and was glad to see Izzy, who had saved me a seat beside her. Even though Fay was next to her, I was about to tell her how silly I had been about the policeman when I saw her give an involuntary jump. As I turned to look round, Fay asked her what the matter was.

"Oh, nothing. Just saw the policeman and got a fright until I remembered he's Cyber Cop."

"Why on earth are you suddenly afraid of policemen? Guilty conscience?"

Fay looked at me and caught Izzy and my surreptitious and guilty glances at each other. Her eyes narrowed and she turned to me.

"What have you got her into?"

"Nothing."

I knew as I spoke that I sounded like a naughty student, and Fay looked even more suspicious.

"It's okay, Fay. It's not her fault. And I'm not scared of policemen. Just one particular crooked one. I'll explain later."

Izzy looked at me as she spoke. Fay looked crossly at me and then at Izzy with a look which managed to convey pity, exasperation, crossness and sympathy in one go, before going back to anger as she looked back my way. Izzy, meanwhile, had mouthed to me that she would not say anything to Fay without talking to me. I had nothing left to say to anyone. In twenty-four hours, this disaster had suddenly relocated to my home and now Izzy and I had brought it to my work. Our suspicious behaviour had already attracted attention from students, and now Izzy was thinking of telling Fay. At least Whetstone would lose his ability to blackmail me if we simply told everyone at work ourselves and then I got sacked for just generally being irresponsible and a bad role model who dragged disasters around with her like a string of comedy tins tied to a 'just married' car.

Fay was no gossip. I had to give her that. But she was a know-all. As she and Izzy tried to restart a conversation without talking about what had just happened after Izzy promised to tell her "soon, but later" and she kept asking whether Izzy was okay, I was again plunged into a whorl of imaginary chains of events which began with Fay deciding to help by going to the police or going to the headmaster to try and solve the problem. There was a reason why all students, including her own tutor group, knew to go to another teacher if they had a problem they wanted to talk about and to go to her if they wanted to get someone into trouble or some quick action taken. She had an ingrained sense of society and an assumption that everyone would act just as she would, or, given enough of her style of encouragement, could be made to do so.

I had to get up. I was sitting in the staffroom surrounded by colleagues and Paul, another English teacher, was saying something to me.

"Penny for your thoughts? You seem a bit out of it. I know questions about moderating coursework aren't everyone's favourite conversation, but normally you at least acknowledge them."

"I'm sorry, Paul. Didn't get much sleep and I just zoned out. Is it important?"

"No — just making conversation, and it can wait until the meeting tomorrow. Are you okay?"

"Yes, well, no. I'll be fine, but I need a bit of quiet just now."

"Ah — I see. Bit of a hangover. Fair play — what did you get up to last night? You haven't had a wild one for ages. I've missed your break-time recap of adventures. I was starting to think someone had come along and tamed you. Come on, spill?"

Izzy and Fay had stopped their stilted attempt at conversation to listen.

"Oh, wouldn't you like to know? A lady never tells."

"When did you become a lady, Jo?"

Paul was being funny, but Izzy and Fay looked rattled. I liked Paul, but needed to leave.

"Sorry, Paul, would love to spill, but maybe I just spent the night by myself with *The Unconsoled* and that kept me up too late to sleep."

"Oh, don't be so ridiculous. Nobody was ever kept up late by Ishiguro's complete non-page-turner novel. You only get through a book like that if you really feel the need to impress someone."

"I'm sorry, Paul, I forgot that you can only read Dan Brown and Alex Jacobson novels."

"Bite me!"

With Paul pretending to be insulted but smiling and happy, I quickly arranged to meet Izzy for lunch outside her classroom, downed my coffee and scuttled off. Izzy even took my mug to save me the trouble of going via the kitchen. I was glad my classroom was free and I could be alone and compose myself.

I could not concentrate on marking or even face-checking for messages on my phone, so I took advantage of my desire to pace and nervous energy to finally tackle the various piles on top of my desk, in my drawers and on the window ledges around me. Most of it was so old, it could simply be chucked in the recycling bin, which the cleaners simply put in the same black bin-liner as the normal bin when they came each morning. But by the end of break my classroom looked Head of Department or even SLT observation ready and I felt a bit lighter and free of baggage, too. I gave it five minutes after the bell went for all the stragglers to have dragged themselves to lessons and then left my hideaway to venture into the now empty corridors to fill my water-bottle.

I was calm enough to check for messages. There were texts, WhatsApps, missed calls and a voicemail. Much as I feared. I knew that Robbins was the most likely voicemail, but I went through messages and WhatsApp first. The messages were Julia checking in with me. No unexpected visits, just asking if I was okay, offering to come round, checking for updates and wishing me well. Izzy had also sent me a message telling me she loved me, which I read twice. Or three times. And confirming we'd meet for lunch and reassuring me that things would be fine.

The WhatsApps were from Lexi. Checking on me, wishing me well and telling me she had had a great evening with lots of gossip if I wanted to meet for a drink. It was followed by a random selection of emojis starting with kiss, lipstick, heart and moving to a selection of uniform emojis, then random vegetables and finishing with a zebra followed by a rhino emoji. I assumed that she was having a slow day at work and decided it would be best not to reply unless I wanted to risk getting sucked in.

The missed call was from DS Robbins. I was glad that he had called back promptly, but feared that the quick reply meant that he had run it past his inspector and had quickly been told to drop it. I knew I had to listen to the voicemail, but was terrified that if he told me that he could not proceed against Whetstone, I would start to cry and be seen by the students. I looked at my watch and saw that I still had nearly half an hour until my next lesson, so I forced myself to play the message.

His tone sounded friendly and reassuring. He told me that he had briefly spoken to the inspector, but they wanted to hear the recording in full. He dictated his email address and repeated it and asked me to send it to him and any other details like a filled-in transcript. I still had my email to Julia with the video and our typed-up dialogue attached in my sent messages, so I deleted the message to her and forwarded the rest to Robbins, reminding him to not share it and asking him to keep me updated quickly. I dithered momentarily, unsure whether to trust Robbins and considering checking with Izzy or Julia, but we had agreed that we would trust him. In the end, I decided to send it because the email address was his name and definitely not an open email. I was still worried that we had committed to trusting the police and gone against what Whetstone had told us to do. All I had left to do now was force myself to calm down, focus on my teaching and try to look forward to lunch without dreading whether Fay would now be interrogating me about why Izzy and I were suddenly afraid of the police. I texted Julia and Izzy just to keep them informed and even though I knew Izzy was teaching, both sent me a fingers-crossed emoji straightaway. Izzy even sent a 'x, lunch, x' after it.

Battered by the Rollercoaster

I sat down at my desk convinced I would be unable to concentrate on lesson plans, but as I collapsed into my chair, I realised that I finally understood what it meant to be 'past caring' — mentally I felt like I had been riding the world's longest rollercoaster, but the ride had just gone on too long to be thrilling or frightening any more. Now it was just something I did not seem able to get off. Frankly, if it had to end by spinning off the tracks, taking me to some inevitably implausible and terrifying end, at least it would be over. If Robbins was using me to add a drug bust to his CV and then abandoning me to Whetstone rather than deal with the comeback, or if he was still trying to help but Whetstone still managed to hurt me, then so be it. I was too tired to run and inured to stress. I took a sip from my water-bottle and got on with my work.

I was amazed how much I had achieved when the bell for change of lessons made me jump with surprise. My Year 11s were so unnerved by the cheerful way I greeted them for the lesson that we all found ourselves enjoying *Much Ado About Nothing* more than we had all year. I imagined my story as a Shakespearean comedy and considered setting them a task of fitting all the crazy scenarios into a comedy drama as a language/literature crossover piece, but decided to stick to my original homework task instead.

I was stress-free and happy as I made my way to Izzy's classroom, only to be met by her and Fay coming to collect me. I paused in my step and nearly cursed aloud as I remembered that I still had to deal with Fay's suspicions from break time. Izzy gave me a look over her shoulder which I interpreted as a combination of "sorry" and "we just have to do this, she is my friend, so help!". I smiled back and gathered my now familiar "pull yourself together, just one more thing" mentality.

We walked to lunch together and Fay steered us to the edge of a table, ensuring that Izzy and I were right at the end and she would be a buffer between us and anyone else who sat down. Normally, everyone just filled in lines on the staff tables, so our physical position made it clear we, or at least Fay, wanted privacy and no one came to sit beside us whilst we ate.

I let Izzy do the talking. Fay interrupted mainly to direct questions at me. She quickly reacted with shock and hostility.

"What, so you kept all this from her? And put her in danger, too?"

I shrugged and started to speak, but Izzy stepped in.

"No. I mean yes, but we have gone over that. It's hard to know how you or I would have reacted if we were in the same position. I mean, this kind of thing doesn't just happen every day."

"No — neither of us would have been in this position. That is why it does not happen every day. Normal people don't go to these places and then get involved with motorbikes and drug dealers and gangs."

I could not suppress a tiny grin at the idea of Fay listing motorbike ahead of drug dealer in terms of danger, but aside from a quick glare which disappeared quickly as Izzy continued, I got away with it. I decided that she had chosen to see it as nervous laughter, which was partly true, and I left Izzy to talk whenever I could. Worried as I was about including Fay in my — now our — secret, it was a relief to me to hear the way Izzy described it. Her version made everything sound a bit more reasonable and she made allowances for me at every stage. I was clearly forgiven. And, right now, that mattered to me almost more than getting out of this without losing my job, being arrested or worse. I had forced myself to shut down all thoughts of what 'worse' could be, but being beaten up, robbed, extorted, sold into prostitution or murdered, had all crossed my mind over the months this had endured.

Izzy managed to summarise everything quite succinctly and Fay actually seemed to accept things. Izzy clearly knew how to manage Fay and I wondered whether she did the same to me. Certainly, I changed whenever I was with her, but I assumed that that was a conscious thing I was doing. I mentally decided to have a chat with Julia about how she saw my relationship with Izzy. Fay was asking me a question.

"Don't you think that you should have told her so she could decide whether she wanted to get involved in your mess?"

"It was precisely because I didn't want her involved in the mess that I didn't tell her until I thought it was over. Fay, I know you don't like me, but you do know I care about Izzy. I didn't want to hurt her."

"Yes. But you can't just not tell her and hope for the best. You'd better be honest with her next time."

"There isn't going to be a next time. What — do you think I get involved in this kind of thing every day? Just for fun?"

I was aware that I was starting to raise my voice, not in anger but exasperation, and Izzy shushed me.

"Sorry — but, you know. I took a wild holiday and made a couple of silly decisions, but really, I was unlucky. I couldn't have known this would happen."

"Yes. This was unlucky, but I don't even know you that well except through Izzy, and 'unlucky' things seem to happen to you all the time. You're like an adventure addict, adrenaline junkie, and things just happen to you."

"Maybe. Maybe I do attract a bit of trouble, but this was one helluva wake-up call. Nowadays, I do anything to avoid trouble and I go out so rarely I'm practically agoraphobic."

Izzy laughed and whispered, "Hardly", and Fay softened and even laughed a little, too, before she replied.

"Yeah. I can see that. You have changed. Grown up, almost. I didn't want Izzy to get back together with you, but I could see you were changed. I still think you should have warned her and not got her involved, but I believe you didn't want to. She is too forgiving of you, and if you care about her, you will not take advantage. And I do care about her, so I will not let you."

"Okay. Fair."

It felt like I was applying for her permission to date Izzy, but Fay was important to Izzy and getting her approval, again, was important.

"And you won't tell anyone?" I asked.

"No — but you do need to work with the other police."

"Oh, yes. Izzy, I forgot to tell you — I sent the transcript to Robbins."

Izzy updated Fay and we continued to talk as we took our trays back and headed to the staffroom for coffee. Somehow, by the end, we had agreed to go to the cinema, the three of us, on Friday. An arts cinema in Greenwich. I forced myself to view this act of penance as an opportunity to become more cultured and reassured myself that *Un Couple Parfait* could prove to be a thoroughly entertaining film.

Undercover

DS Robbins did not get in touch until after school the next day. Izzy had plans, so Julia and Natalie offered to come back to the flat to keep me company. I was glad of the company and did not want to be alone, but felt like an awkward liability who needed babysitting. Julia assured me they did not mind and that it would be nice to see me, but I was very glad when I came home from work to find Julia alone. We hugged automatically, but I found myself clinging on, needing her comfort, and she withdrew, looked at me and then hugged me back. I felt a tear start to run down my right cheek and stifled a lump in my throat before it could become a proper sob. Julia held me tighter, then withdrew and stared at me.

"Oh, Jo. What has happened now? Is it Izzy? Robbins? Whetstone? What?"

"No — nothing. I'm being silly. I don't know why I am crying. Well, not crying."

Julia hugged me again and I pushed her away. It was so long since we had been alone together and the relief of having her to myself and her comfort seemed to break down my show of strength.

"Come on, I'll make tea. You sit down or shower or whatever and then we'll catch up. Natalie is behind on a commission so will either come later or perhaps not at all. Do you want me to tell her just to stay put?"

"Yes. Well — you know how much I like her. It's just — you know. We haven't spent time together by ourselves for ages."

I felt clingy and weak and felt my eyes water and lip tremble. Julia understood.

"I know. We've been so busy, you and I, with relationships, undercover ops, intrigue, we forgot to pay any attention to ourselves. I'll cancel her. It will be good to catch up."

"I'll just get out of my work stuff and then sort out some snacks for us."

I was surprised by how pleased I was to see her. I had been so fixated on Izzy and everything, I had forgotten how close Julia and I had become and how much I valued her advice and support. I wasn't jealous of her and Natalie, especially since I had Izzy, but she understood me better even than Izzy and Lexi. I realised that the relentless cycle of fear, excitement, lust, busyness, work had distracted me from how much I missed her gentle presence and moreish baking. I even missed the things I used to find annoying — such as her scented diffusers, protective crystals, mindful breathing. I was glad of her presence in case Whetstone returned, especially now I had contacted Robbins again, but I was just glad to see her. Alone. Without Natalie or Izzy. My friend who had been with me at my worst point, who had supported me and criticised me fairly and when needed. I was glad to have this evening and irritated when the phone rang.

It was caller ID withheld, but I knew it was Robbins. I was prepared for the worst, but knew I had to answer and find out. We both said cursory hellos and then he got straight to the point.

"Look. I've played the tape to my DI and showed him your text filling in the bits. But it's mixed news. It's clear that he's involved and that he shouldn't have come to yours and is not behaving professionally, but some of the key bits are what you filled in. I believe you are telling the truth, but once he gets involved with his union and maybe has some back-up from any friends and tries to rake up or manufacture some dirt on you, he could get off with a slap on the wrist and some mandatory training. And if he has friends involved, he could get one of them to find reason to give you a traffic violation or minor anti-social charge or something. We could block it, but I can't promise you'd be hassle-free as things stand. There is something we could do. I don't have time to come over today, but I could on Friday."

"I can't just keep on waiting. Please just tell me on the phone."

I had sagged back down onto the sofa and Julia had her arm round me, holding me partly to comfort me and partly straining to hear what Robbins was saying. I put him on speaker.

"Well. The problem was that we needed better audio. And ideally show a pattern of behaviour."

"You mean, wait for him to come back to my flat and threaten me again."

"Yes. Sorry. I mean, you did so well, helping us catch Jonno, my DI trusts you to pull this off."

"That's great, that he trusts me. He's taking a big risk, isn't he?"

I was angry and so was Julia, but she still part-mouthed, part-whispered, "We need him. Now more than ever. I'm furious, too, but we have to keep him on our side."

"I'm sorry, Jo. You should be able to trust the police. I know that you think that I have put you in danger and you resent me for it. But I promise that I want to help, and so does my DI. Whetstone is old-school and it is difficult to clean up corrupt officers like him. But we will do everything in our power to get him."

He sounded genuine and, anyway, I had no choice but to trust him.

"Okay. Thank you. So what is your plan?"

"It's hard over the phone — are you sure you don't want to wait?"

"No — please — at least an outline."

"It's complicated. I won't lie to you. With the Jonno op, we had a fixed time and place and could be there in person and do a proper job. We don't know what time Whetstone will show up. We are not even a hundred percent it will be your flat. There is a risk of him going to Ms Aguda's flat."

"Who's Ms Aguda?"

Julia answered for me. "It's Natalie. That's her surname."

I realised that although Natalie had been part of my life for so long, I had never even asked her surname. Now Julia had spoken, I vaguely remember seeing it on a leaflet for one of her shows. I mouthed my apology to Julia, who dismissed it with a pat on my knee and a shrug. Robbins took my ignorance in his stride.

"Yes — your friend. He could go there and we could set that flat up as a secondary target, but we can't a hundred percent rule out him meeting you somewhere else. It is hard for us to track, but also hard for him to know where to find you. So I don't think that would happen. But my DI and I have considered the possibility that he might hang around her to meet you outside your flat in the car park or something when you get home. We think him going to your school is an even lower risk."

I could feel anger and fear rising within me and Julia rubbed my leg and helped to calm me down before I spoke.

"So what — you put me under surveillance?"

"Unfortunately, not, Jo. We can't do that. But…"

"But what? Sorry, Jo, it's too expensive to protect you, so let's just gamble on it not happening?"

"It's not just the cost, Jo. The more officers involved, the less chance it has of working. I just want you to know that there are risks. I want to protect you and I will do everything I can. But you don't need me to lie to you. You are smart and you have shown how brave you can be. You just need to do one more thing."

"It's always one more thing. And then the next and so on. Each time the risks are higher."

"Again, sorry. I don't have much time now. Do you want an outline and then time to think about it? It will be your call, but I cannot stress enough how much I believe that this is your best option."

So he outlined the plan to me. I would call the police via 101 and leave a message to talk to DS Robbins. Robbins was on the case notes for Jonno, so Whetstone already knew he was my link. This would be logged with an incident number and Whetstone would be able to find it if he was tracking me. Robbins would log the call and put notes on Jonno's file, too. He would ensure that he then had good officers in the area for the next twenty-four hours — himself, DC Bishop, PS Brennan and other officers who had been on the Jonno job. He would set up proper, discreet recording equipment in my flat, basic stuff in Natalie's flat or just let her rely on the equipment she already had from when we recorded Jonno last time. I would be loaned some high-quality personal recording equipment and a discreet personal camera which I would have to remember to switch on at potential danger times, such as getting out of my car at home or walking in the area near my flat. If that didn't work, he would call Whetstone in for questioning the next day and then step-up surveillance. He said that he would not question Whetstone properly, but he would mention my concerns and pretend to dismiss them, but

Whetstone was based at a different police station, so he could not just bump into him otherwise.

It was a plan. But it was tenuous at best. No risk to Robbins or anyone else. Lots of undefined risks. Robbins's attempts at reassurance fell very flat.

"I very much doubt he would do anything physical. He doesn't want to leave proof, so he is relying on threat and hassle. My guess is that he will just talk and try to be more intimidating and make you think he will do something, but he won't. If he tries anything, it will be to stop and search you or try and frame you for something minor that won't be properly investigated."

"But it could be enough to cost me my career."

"It won't come to that. Jonno is just one of hundreds, thousands even of petty drug dealers, who was emboldened by his links to Whetstone. Whetstone can just find another stooge to exploit. He is not going to risk doing anything major to you. You're not an easy target, Jo. You have a good group of people around you to back you up, a proper job, money to get a solicitor and bundles of fight to keep going no matter how many times you get knocked down. I can't give you promises, but I am as sure as I can be that this will work. I have to go, but take your time, think about it. But remember, this is the best plan we have and we don't really have a plan B. You just not co-operating with us over Jonno will just make them more confident."

I knew he was right and although I would have to consult Izzy and Natalie and, of course, Lexi, too, I knew already that I would end up just agreeing to his plan. I was exhausted. Again. I wondered whether I had as much fight left in me as he believed. I couldn't face the telephone again, so I texted Izzy that Robbins had a new plan, and Lexi, asking her not to reply, but giving a quick outline. Julia offered to talk things through, but I let her call Natalie. I realised we had not had supper and although I did not feel hungry, I thought I should make something for Julia and take my mind off things. She followed me into the kitchen whilst still on the phone to Natalie and mouthed "Rajah" and I nodded and used my iPad to order our usual, which I had not had for months. I suddenly felt famished and tried to distract myself through the half an hour wait for delivery a bit of planning. Izzy called me during a break in her tennis game, saying that she could not talk properly but she could cancel tennis and her evening out if I needed her to. I knew she had not met up with her friends from her old school for ages and, although I missed her, I knew we would end up just going round in circles.

"It's okay. I want you to enjoy yourself. I just needed to touch base. Shitty situation and shitty plan from Robbins, but I just have to go along with it. I'll tell you tomorrow. I just needed to hear your voice and that you'll support me."

"Of course I will. It feels good to feel needed and I will support you all I can."

I let her go back to her friends, feeling a little stronger and more loved. She texted a heart and Lexi texted a fingers-crossed emoji and a kiss and a 'here for you if you need me'.

The doorbell rang as I was carrying drinks through to the dining table. I nearly dropped a glass, instinctively thinking it was Whetstone. Julia gave a start, too, but I could practically smell our curry through the door. I called out through the door to confirm and opened it as he shouted "Rajah", and the welcome smell of curry was enough to start to help me feel better. Julia and I began to tuck in and after quickly agreeing that we had to trust Robbins and go along with his plan, I emailed him to confirm and then we tucked into our comfort food and concentrated on being together and relaxing.

Undercover Again

I got to work early, having agreed to meet Izzy in my classroom early enough so that none of my tutor group would be there. I had wanted to share a rare breakfast with Julia, but she told me that I needed to show Izzy that she was a priority. Besides, having slept on it and talked to Natalie, she said that they would be happy to move back into the flat for the next few days so that "we can finish this thing together". Izzy must have arrived at school just before me and I caught up with her in the corridor on the way to my room. She was wearing black patent loafers and light brown cords that accentuated her curves to anyone looking as closely as I was, but were respectable enough to the casual observer. She had a loose, white pattern blouse and a short pinky-orange cashmere cardigan on top. She had clearly had time to straighten her hair in a neat bob which framed her face beautifully as she turned to me and brushed her fringe back behind her ears. I felt scruffy in my wear-at-least-once-a-week black trousers and blue jumper, but she complimented me anyway.

"I love that outfit on you."

"You look great. I like your hair."

Even though there was no one else in the corridor, she looked around, self-consciously, so we headed straight to my room. I switched on my computer and logged in automatically — the lottery of whether updates would take longer than the whole of registration, leading to passive aggressive reminders from the admin team or, for multiple offenders like my former self, directly condescending and brusque ones from the deputy head, about not taking the register made us all get in early enough to begin the daily start-up of the classroom computer.

I told Izzy what little I knew and that, reluctant as I was, I had no choice and would just have to do whatever DS Robbins suggested.

"Gosh. Now I understand a bit of what you have been going through. I want to be there for you and I will come and stay with you until this is, well, over. Will it ever be over? But I can't say I'm not scared and I think I see why you acted as you did — it is so hard to think and know what to do."

I wanted to hug her or at least step towards her. She was sitting on a pupil desk and I was on my desk, but the classrooms had glass windows, so I grabbed the desk with my hand to help control my impulse to go to her. She smiled as she looked at my hand.

"I know — I want to hold you, too. But we mustn't. I should have stayed with you last night."

"It's okay. Julia helped."

I saw her stiffen, just for a moment.

"I missed you, but I was all right."

She recovered herself and softened.

"I understand. You've been through a lot. Did Natalie help, too?"

"No, she had to work. But they have offered to stay at the flat, too. I won't let them if you don't want them to. But I think I would feel better having four of us there. And I would worry less about putting you in danger. And it means that Whetstone will have to turn up to my flat because they won't be there if he goes to Julia's. Easier for the police surveillance."

"Oh, I didn't think they would be there."

"They don't have to be. Izzy — I don't want to do anything to jeopardise us, but they are my friends and have been dragged into this by me. I want you to get to know them and be friends, too, and we will have safety in numbers."

She hesitated and chewed her lip.

"Okay. I get it. But won't it put Whetstone off if he has to deal with four people instead of just you or us?"

"No — I don't think so. You saw what he was like. He clearly has contempt for women. And he might even say more things if he thinks I am so scared I called for back-up. He won't know Natalie, but Jonno must have told him about her. Julia and I moved in together because of Jonno's threats, so it seems only natural that we stay together because of Whetstone."

She nodded and I gave her a moment to think before speaking, distracting myself by logging on to my computer. I checked my emails and saw one from DS Robbins. He would come by briefly after school with a DC Gupta, whom he trusted and had worked with before, to sort out surveillance at my flat and brief me, and then I should phone 101 to report Whetstone after that. He also asked to confirm whether Julia and Natalie would need any equipment at their flat. I replied that they would stay at mine and confirmed that I could be home by four thirty p.m.

It was both frightening and somehow liberating to send the email. Time and time again I had been wrongly convinced that this would be the last bit, but one way or another I had to be reaching the end of the line. Izzy knew how I felt. Our fear of being intimate in school made it tortuous to be so close. She stood up and touched me on the shoulder and tried to offer reassurance.

"I'll be with you and it will be okay, won't it?"

"It has to be. But, despite everything, I think it will."

"Ever the optimist, hey? Never one to accept defeat."

"Well, I guess we're proof that persistence pays off."

"Yes. I shouldn't underestimate you."

We were interrupted by Freddie Hodges, one of my tutees, swinging the door open loudly and following his cricket bag into the room. He looked surprised and at a loss to see me and another teacher in the room.

"Morning, Miss Briggs, Miss Finch — sorry. Can I come in?"

"Of course, Freddie. Miss Finch was just leaving. How are you and why have you brought that enormous kit bag into my room instead of leaving it in your sports locker?"

"I, erm, forgot my locker key."

"Well, given that you seem to forget one thing every day, Freddie, I suppose that it's good to know that you'll have all your homework books and equipment for your lessons today."

"About that, I may have also forgotten to do the homework you set. But I got in early to do it now. I was wondering how you'd feel about giving me an extension — you being my favourite teacher."

"Hmmm. Make a start now. You have time, but if you don't finish, I'll take it tomorrow."

I liked Freddie and was almost glad that he was too preoccupied about my homework to suspect anything about Izzy. Students could be uncannily perceptive and seemed to know far more about all the teachers than we knew about each other. The last thing I needed right now was to be the sudden focus of gossip on top of everything else. Having him in the classroom was a welcome distraction, too, forcing me to stay calm and neutral as I emailed Robbins to confirm details and then quickly moved on to marking and planning before the rest of my tutor group started to arrive. By the time he emailed back to say he would be sending DC Gupta to prepare my flat, I was mid-register and took it in my stride like a pro.

Covert Ops

Izzy had to go back to her flat to pick up more clothes and check on the place, so I was alone when the doorbell rang. I asked who it was before opening the door and was answered with, "DC Anita Gupta."

I was not sure what I was expecting, but I did not expect a police officer to look like that. DC Gupta was tall, with shoulder-length glossy black hair, brown eyes and smooth, caramelly skin that was wholly without make-up and was naturally radiant. She was wearing a crisp, tailored pink shirt tucked into a tight black skirt, worn the same length as most of my students, but without causing me the usually reflex urge to tell her to unroll and lengthen it. I was suddenly very glad that Izzy had gone back to her flat instead of home with me.

"Jo, Jo Briggs, nice to meet you DC Gupta."

"Oh, call me Anita. It's okay to call you Jo?"

"Of course! Do come in. Let me get you a drink."

"Thanks. A cup of tea would be great, if it's no trouble?"

"None at all."

"Do you mind if I have a quick look round to see where to set things up? I can do it by myself whilst you make tea. If that's okay?"

I frantically tried to remember if Izzy or I had left anything lying around in the bedroom and thought about doing a quick sprint round the flat to check for any dirty underwear left on the floor beside the laundry basket and things like that. Actually, my flat looked pretty okay and I did not want to appear crazy. I wondered how much she knew about the Jonno situation and what she thought of me. I feigned casualness as I told her to feel free to look around and get on with things. My heart was beating unnaturally fast and I realised that she was the first woman I was attracted to other than Izzy for a long time. And Izzy could turn up at any moment. As the kettle boiled, I was mentally trying to estimate how long Izzy would be at her flat and considered texting her to ask her to pick up some groceries. I knew I was being ridiculous and, for all I knew, Anita could have a boyfriend. Most importantly, I loved Izzy and there was no way I was going to jeopardise that. But I missed flirting. The thrill of the chase. I decided to settle for a cold water, strong tea and a hastily eaten chocolate bar, swallowed quickly as I screwed the wrapper in my hand as Anita came into the kitchen.

"Lovely place you've got here. You live here by yourself? And a friend?"

Was she just making polite conversation?

"Yes. No. It's complicated. You know I don't want to be alone at the moment."

"Yes — Ben, I mean DS Robbins, has filled me in with essentials, but I can see why you don't want to stay here on your own."

I could almost feel my different urges fighting inside me. She was beautiful and I have never dated a policewoman before. But Izzy was the one. I had been stupid once before and everything had been a disaster since then, albeit with some very enjoyable interludes. I could never betray her. And I did not want to get caught flirting with Anita. Frankly, I was scared that Izzy would arrive now and just know that I had been tempted and leave. Self-preservation kicked in.

"No — anyway, there's your tea. I'll get you a biscuit. I'm sure you're busy."

I could see the mix of bemusement and amusement on her face and her eyes sparkled with laughter underneath her raised eyebrows. I still had no idea whether she batted for our team, or was straight. She clearly knew how attractive she was and I wondered whether she was just playing with me. But above all, I wondered exactly when Izzy was going to walk in and see us together. I decided that now would be a good time to clean the kitchen and told Anita that I would stay here and help when she needed it. Of course, she then decided to put some equipment in the kitchen, "because that is where you were when he came last time".

She seemed to know a lot of details for someone who had just been briefed quickly. She also seemed to make my kitchen even narrower than it normally was as she bustled to and fro, passing me repeatedly. I made the decision that she was straight and just entertaining herself with some casual flirting of her own or, perhaps, bi-curious. After my first break-up with Izzy, I had been more than one straight girl's experiment and I quite enjoyed being used in that way. But she was not worth it. Izzy was.

By the time Izzy arrived, I was still in the kitchen and Anita had finished there, the living room, the hall inside my flat and was in the corridor outside when she bumped into Izzy. Izzy said hello through the open door and I came straight out of the kitchen to greet her. Izzy showed none of her usual self-consciousness as she kissed me, marking her territory a little as she had clearly noticed Anita's good looks. I was happy to be claimed and kissed her back. Izzy's deliberate message quickly broke the sudden tension that had appeared on her arrival and Anita was clearly more amused than disappointed by her display of affection.

"Good to meet you — you must be the girlfriend. I'm surveillance. Anita."

Thereafter, she was friendly but crisp and business-like as she quickly showed us how everything worked, and left after reminding us to call 101 and report Whetstone.

"She was pretty."

Izzy's voice was more high-pitched than usual and I knew she was trying to be casual. I did not want an argument and, although I had done nothing wrong, I felt guilty and I knew Izzy suspected me of something.

"Not as pretty as you."

"So you compared us, then?"

"No. Look, I don't want an argument. Yes, I noticed. So did you, clearly. But I love you. I just stayed in the kitchen and was polite. You can trust me. Even if she had ripped off all her clothes and thrown herself at me, begging me to make love to her, I'd have had a quick look and politely declined because I already have the woman I want."

Izzy smiled, reassured.

"Thrown herself at you naked, begging for it! I mean, seriously, you think yourself.! And, by the way. You don't have me. We may be dating, but you don't own me. But I suppose I can allow you a quick look."

She moved towards me to gently slap me and I pulled her close and we kissed. Slowly, on the mouth, as our bodies came together and her leg slid between mine. I pushed her back towards the wall, but she pushed me backwards, leaning past me to pull the lid off the pasta pot as it boiled over.

"Later. Maybe. I'll finish this and you call the police."

"Yes, miss. I love it when you're so masterful."

"Just when I think you've grown up, back to square one."

She smiled and I felt happy and full of love, enough to carry me through the first few minutes of my 101 call. I gave the details, making sure to give Whetstone's name and Jonno's and the crime reference from the Jonno case to ensure that if he was monitoring the case, it would be added to the notes. I made sure to say that I did not think it was an emergency, I just wanted someone to come and look into it, and left details of a specific time I would be home. By the time I finished my call, Izzy's and my embrace had become a memory and the mood had changed. We gradually relaxed over supper and spent the evening much as Julia and I used to — working companionably together, chilling out with a bit of TV on the sofa together; but, unlike with Julia, we snuggled up together, holding hands. And somehow, sitting holding Izzy's hand and viewing a rerun of a programme I was barely watching, became exactly what I wanted to do and so much more comfortable than making love against the kitchen wall would have been.

Ambush

Izzy and I were so happy that I barely gave a thought to whether or when Whetstone might show up. Izzy had not spent a whole year worrying about Jonno and Whetstone, so was still able to summon up some nerves and tension. She insisted on another run-through of our equipment, which had some motion activity cameras in the flat, a panic button to keep in my pocket which alerted the police and a small Dictaphone-style voice recorder to also keep on me at all times. I decided that carrying all these, along with my phone, justified me wearing trouser-like black jeans to school.

The jeans and Izzy made me feel so relaxed that Whetstone was the last thing on my mind for most of the day. Only sudden reminders, such as supportive texts from Julia and Lexi, and nearly dropping the Dictaphone down the staff loo when I had been forced to wait a little too long during one lesson, were the only major incidents in my day.

Izzy and Fay had a standing arrangement to meet for coffee on Thursday, which she offered to cancel if I needed her.

"I'll see her tomorrow when we all go to the cinema, anyway," she said.

I could not hide my disappointment at the reminder. My life was too full of surveillance and romance to have room for French cinema, or Japanese or Danish for that matter. I had forgotten the name of the film and really did not care, but knew I owed this to Izzy.

"I know it's not your thing, but, you know, new you and all. You might find you like it, now you are becoming a grown-up."

I knew she was being playful, but although we were alone in the kitchen, there were teachers outside the open hatch through to the rest of the staffroom. We both felt self-conscious.

"Fay's booked tickets, so we do have to go."

"It's okay. She's important to you. So she's important to me. And, let's be honest, I'll be happy to talk to her as she is far more interesting than any Almodóvar film."

"The film we are seeing is French, but well done for knowing the name of a director other than Mr Disney. Five points. I'll cancel coffee as penance."

"Patronising much! I'll be fine, enjoy your coffee! I've got my panic button if anything happens. If and when he does show, you'll probably be back anyway. And you'll have to make it up to me."

"You're on. Thanks."

And so I ended up going home alone, with only a pile of books, too large for my school bag, brought home in a ripped and faded Waitrose bag. Dragging both bags outside my car, trying not to drop my recently-purchased incredibly cool designer coffee mug was so distracting that I only noticed Whetstone as I struggled to close my car door with my foot and accidentally swung my trusty Waitrose bag into him as he loomed behind me, almost touching me. My involuntary yelp and jump of fear were clearly the reaction he had been expecting. My hands were too full to reach easily into my pocket to press 'record' on my Dictaphone thing or to reach for my panic button. He was not in uniform, but wearing jeans and a bomber-style jacket. I felt cold and shivery and tried to suppress a tremble as I fought to regain my composure.

Luckily for me, the force of the impact of my bag of books into Whetstone's leg was enough for it to finally give up any pretence of being a bag for life. As the old rips spread, books started to slide out, one at a time, beginning a gentle slap, slap as they hit the floor, gathering pace and capped by the clanging of my mug following them, then bouncing and rolling underneath my car. For a brief moment, the only thing I cared about was whether my £20 coffee mug would survive the fall and I chased after it, circling the car to see where it would roll.

"Allow me — I'll get it for you."

I swung round to see a young man in shorts and a running top jogging over to me. I had seen him before in my building and we had smiled politely as we passed on the stairs, but had never spoken. He leaned under the car to grab the cup as I stammered out my thanks. I could see that it was Whetstone's turn to feel shaken and he clearly did not know how to react.

"I'm Steve. And you are…?"

"I'm Jo."

"Bad day?"

"You don't know the half of it!"

"Let me help."

He gathered my books with me as Whetstone took a step back, unable to mask his irritation. Steve looked at him with contempt and at me with a mix of pity and concern. Steve had an athletic physique and easy smile and the contrast between him and Whetstone was enormous.

"Are you okay?"

I did not know what to say. I wanted to tell him I was in danger, but I needed to get Whetstone on tape. Before I could form a response, Steve spoke again.

"At least let me carry these up for you. You've got your hands full and I simply cannot leave you to struggle alone."

His words were directed with almost physical presence in Whetstone's direction. I accepted his offer, knowing it would provoke Whetstone, possibly into doing something dangerous, but still forced myself to allow Whetstone to follow us up. With my hands free, I was able to switch on my recorder and ready my panic button. I desperately wanted to press it, but knew I had no choice but to allow Whetstone into my flat to be caught on camera. I wondered where Robbins was and how long it would take for the police to respond if I had to press the button.

We were at my flat too quickly. Whetstone's anger and my unease were too strong for either of us to hide and I could see Steve hesitating to leave me alone with him. As he left, he looked directly into my eyes and spoke.

"Are you sure you are okay? I can come in and wait for a bit. You seem shaken up."

"She's fine. I'm a police officer. I can look after her."

Steve was briefly shocked by Whetstone's admission, but then he looked even more concerned.

"I guess policemen come in all shapes and sizes. But I didn't ask you, I asked your girlfriend."

The idea that he could even consider that I would be Whetstone's girlfriend was revolting, but I realised that it was only natural for him to view me as an abused and helpless girlfriend. His words stung deeply enough for me to muster a bit more anger and courage.

"Thanks — I really appreciate your help. But I'll be okay. He's not my boyfriend. He's a friend of a friend and I have to sort something out because of my friend. Thanks."

"Okay. I'm going for a run, but, if you don't mind, I think I'd like to knock on your door on the way back."

"Thank you."

I almost gushed at him. Whetstone looked furious, but I could not hide my relief at Steve's words. Whetstone knowing Steve would be back to check on me and had seen him meant that he would almost certainly not risk hitting me or hurting me, but that he would still not know I was working with Robbins.

"Okay."

He hovered as I opened the door and he made a point of handing my stuff to Whetstone as I went in first and watching carefully how he would react. Whetstone feigned manners and asked where I wanted them and I told him to put them in the living room. Steve left reluctantly and I took advantage of the few seconds it took Whetstone to drop my books on the floor to check the cameras and recorders were all on.

"Think you were being smart, did you?"

He advanced on me as he spoke so he would have been breathing directly into my face if he was not almost a head taller. I stepped back so I was almost against the wall, but made sure not to cover the camera and kept him where he would be most audible and in sight. I hated him more than ever at the moment and did not want to give him the satisfaction of seeing how scared I was, but I allowed myself to show it, knowing that my weakness would make him bolder and more likely to incriminate himself. It had worked with Jonno.

"What did I tell you about going back to the police?"

"Not to. I didn't go back."

"Yes, you did — I checked the calls. You can't go back to the police. I can call up your records any time."

I knew I already had something usable against him and desperately wanted to settle for that and press my panic button, but I went on.

"Okay. I called them. I'm sorry. But what do you expect? I can call the police again if you threaten or hurt me."

"Only if you are able to call, love. Don't push me or I will hurt you now, even if Mr Knight in Shining Lycra comes back."

"If you hurt me, he'll be a witness. And then the good police will arrest you."

I could see that he knew what I was saying was true, and although there was still a chance that he would lose control and hit me anyway, I felt as reassured as I could in the circumstances.

"I am the law. Don't you forget it! Maybe I won't hurt you myself. I'll just call in a favour from a con who owes me one. Maybe I or one of my friends will just find some evidence on you on a routine stop and search. Even personal use could cost you your teaching job in that fancy school you work. Oh, I've checked it out. Possibly I might find you with enough drugs to supply your students. You could be famous — front page of the papers. Or you might want to shut up, stop trying to threaten me or think you can win and start doing as you're told. Like a good little girl. Now, DO YOU UNDERSTAND?"

"Yes."

"Answer me properly!"

"Yes."

"Right. Number one: no more going back to the police about me. Last warning. Next time you get hurt. Answer!"

"Yes."

"Number two: you've got to undo the damage you've done. So you will call them now whilst I am here listening. Quickly, before Lycra twat returns. You'll tell them that you made the whole thing up. You'll say you made all the stuff about Jonno up to get back at him for hassling you for being a lesbian. And you then decided to make stuff up about me because you thought I knew him because you panicked and started getting paranoid. If you stick to that and cry a lot about being hormonal, you probably won't even get charged with wasting police time. I leave that bit up to you when they come round. Either way, once you've made the call with me checking you do it right, you won't be taken seriously whatever you say next."

I knew I had enough now, so I pressed the panic button. I had no idea whether it had worked, so I pressed it a few times in hope. Now I had to stall.

"I can't. I won't. I'll lose my job."

He stepped up again and bent down so that when he spoke, bits of spittle landed on me as I stood trapped against the wall.

"There is no more 'I can't' or 'I won't'. You do what I say and the more hysterical and desperate you sound, the better for me and the more likely they are not to charge you for wasting their time. And you're making the call now. Don't mess with me."

As he finished speaking, he turned round and dialled 101 on my landline and handed it to me. I reminded myself that everything was being recorded, so even though my call might make me look crazy, I had proof I was being coerced.

I took the phone and asked for the police and began my story, trying to look at my watch, praying for Robbins or Steve or Izzy to return. Part of me wanted to protect Izzy and keep her safe. She was most likely to be the first back, but Whetstone would just force her to do what he wanted, too. So, with a trembling voice and fighting back real tears, I spoke into the phone, trying to say as little as possible with Whetstone leaning over me, listening to everything. Fortunately, the woman on the other end did everything slowly. Finding my records and wasting valuable minutes reading the file and repeating everything to me. I wished I had checked how far Steve would be running and I wondered when and if Robbins was coming as she kept reading things back and checking them.

Suddenly, there was a knock on the door. Whetstone immediately stood in front of me, one finger on his lips and his fist raised. The knock came again. Then someone shouted.

"Hello — anyone in there?"

It was not Steve's voice, but it sounded vaguely familiar and I struggled to place it. Fortunately, it was loud enough for the woman on the phone to hear, too.

"Is someone at your door? You can answer it if you like."

Whetstone shook his head to tell me not to.

"It's okay. Probably just Jehovah's Witnesses."

I longed to open the door, but did not know how to get past Whetstone to do it.

"Hey — I just heard you. Open up. It's the police."

More banging and this time the receptionist heard it, too.

"Did he say he was from the police? You'd better answer it. Are you okay? I'm recording everything."

Whetstone was clearly rattled now and sweating, but he took a deep breath and he opened the door.

"Hold on, son. Stop banging. I'm police and already here dealing with this lady."

As he opened the door, I recognised the man behind the voice. PS Brennan, who had been there on the Jonno arrest. He saw that I was okay, and Whetstone was clearly taken aback by the fact that we knew each other and allowed him to walk past, taking in the stripes on his arm as he did.

"Just following up your call from the other day. DS Robbins will be here soon, but he was a bit stuck in traffic so he sent me because I was round the corner. Not sure what is happening here. You say you're police, too. What's your name and why are you here?"

"I could ask you the same."

"I'm Acting PS Brennan, Tim if you prefer. And, as I just said, I'm responding to a call from the other day."

"So am I."

"And who are you?"

Whetstone hesitated. He knew his name was on the report, so he was clearly reluctant to say anything.

"Look, lad, clearly this only needs one of us. If you're keen to be in charge, then I've got a stack of paperwork waiting for me back at the station. This doesn't need a humble PC if there's an acting sarge already on the case."

"Just wait a moment, please."

His tone was firm but polite. He looked at me and asked, "How we doing? Robbins will be here very soon, but are we okay? With everything."

I was sure that I had enough evidence now. Whetstone's threat about asking someone else to hurt me made me hesitate, as did my fear that the recording equipment may have stopped working. I was still holding the phone and the operator was trying to attract my attention. Brennan would not move from the door, where he was blocking Whetstone's exit. I realised that, if I had nothing else, I had Whetstone's presence in the flat as I made the call as some evidence.

"Yes."

I spoke to the operator first. "The police are here. It's all right. But can you keep that recording as evidence."

"We always keep the evidence, madam. Do you want me to speak to the officer to confirm you are safe?"

Brennan hesitated to move, but by this time we could hear footsteps running up the stairs and Robbins appeared, slightly out of breath. Doris opened her door at the same time and spoke first.

"My goodness, it's been like St Pancreas this evening. What on earth is going on? I can't keep track of how many men have come and gone this evening."

"It's all right, ma'am. Police business. Nothing to worry about. Go inside and leave us to do our job."

Robbins flashed his badge and Brennan stepped aside to let him in. I felt fine and told the operator that I really was okay now and Robbins realised what was going on and took the phone, gave his details and hung up for me. Whetstone was several inches taller than Robbins and considerably wider, but he backed away from Robbins and grinned nervously as he opened his mouth to offer some explanation. Robbins dismissed him with a raised hand and spoke to me.

"How we doing? Did you get anything?"

"Yes — I, or you, need to check it was all recorded, but if it was, it has to be more than enough to arrest him."

I pointed to the cameras which he checked were on and I pulled the Dictaphone out of my pocket and rewound it a bit and pressed 'play'. Whetstone's voice was loud and clear. And the cameras would have recorded him, too. Whetstone went pale and looked around, searching for an exit and realising that there was nowhere. I realised that this must, surely, be the end. It was over. I needed Izzy and suddenly I was overwhelmed by huge, body-shuddering sobs of fear and relief intermingled. I was too exhausted to care how ridiculous I looked as I started to weep. Fortunately, Izzy appeared at that moment, pausing at the door to take in all the disparate parts of our extraordinary tableau before squeezing through to me.

"I'm sorry I wasn't here. What happened? Did it work? Why are you crying?"

Izzy's touch was enough to soothe me a little and Robbins had given me a handkerchief to wipe my tears, but I still found myself breathless and trying to heave back fresh sobs, so he spoke for me.

"It's over. Jo did brilliantly. We haven't listened to the tapes properly, but from the quick bit she played, I'd say we have him — what's the phrase they use on TV? — 'banged to rights'. PC Whetstone — do you want to come quietly?"

The sight of Whetstone's lip curling with impotent fury as his massive frame shrunk and he silently nodded, was enough to push the sobs and shivers out of me.

"Shall I do the honours, sir?"

As Brennan spoke, he whipped some handcuffs out from underneath his jacket and Robbins nodded to him. Whetstone turned round, eyes downwards, avoiding meeting anyone's eyes. His face was pale. I watched on and Brennan looked at me, winked and mouthed, "Well done!"

"I'll need a statement, but I think it can wait. If you don't mind helping me gather all the recording equipment you used so I can listen to it now, we'll leave you alone. I think you need to calm down now."

"Thank you — yes. I don't think I could face giving a statement right now."

"I'll show you everything," said Izzy.

I handed him my recording pen and, for a few seconds, stood staring blankly into space and then realised how badly I needed a drink and pointlessly went to search the cupboards for a brandy or port, knowing my choice was actually warm white wine or tea. I offered everyone else, but they all declined and I just automatically made one for me and one for Izzy and they were all leaving just as Steve reappeared at the door, red-faced and sweaty after his run.

"Oh, my God! Are you okay? I knew I shouldn't have left you."

"Who's he?"

Izzy looked at me with a flash of suspicion and jealously, which subsided as Robbins took control.

"Yes, sir? I'm DS Robbins and may I ask who you are?"

He looked around and saw Whetstone in handcuffs being led by the arm by DS Brennan, which made him relax, but he was still lost for words. I had enough time to regain some composure.

"It's okay. He lives in my building. He helped me. Whetstone ambushed me by my car and Steve walked us back upstairs and tried to protect me."

I saw Robbins easily relax at this, too, and Steve stood taller as my would-be protector.

"Yes — I saw him trying to bully her and I wanted to interrupt, but she said she was okay. I came back to check on her because I was worried about her. He said he was a policeman."

"Yes — but hopefully not for long. We're proper policemen. Jo was helping us with a job. We may need you as a witness."

"Happy to help. Glad that she is okay. I'll get you my card from upstairs if you need to call me."

"Thanks."

I smiled my thanks and waved and he jogged off to get his details. Robbins and Brennan were finished and Izzy and I were happy to see them following a handcuffed Whetstone out of the door and along the stairs away from us. We closed the door behind them, picked up our teas and collapsed onto the sofa together, in each other's arms, too weary to speak but unspokenly sharing our relief together. Our shared moment was brief as my phone pinged. I felt too tired to even lift my bum off the sofa enough to prise the phone out, but I realised it could be Julia and I forced myself to read it.

It was from her: 'any news?'. Izzy and I looked at each other. For a moment I could not even face telling the story to Julia, but we both knew I owed her that. I called her and told her it was over and she started to jabber questions into the phone, with Natalie interrupting and asking her to repeat things in the background. Then they insisted on coming over. Already our exhaustion had become relief and as the weight of fear, suspense and dread came off our shoulders, we were suddenly swamped with euphoria and a sense of freedom and victory. I texted Lexi to join us, too, and we text-co-ordinated a takeaway order. Tonight, was our night. The world could do what it wanted tomorrow.